CONFEDERATE GOLD

A Modern-day Romp
through the
Civil War History
of
Richmond, Virginia

CONFEDERATE GOLD

A Novel

PENN MILLER

MCP Books
2301 Lucien Way #415
Maitland, FL 32751
407.339.4217
www.millcitypress.net

Edited by MCP Books

Printed in the United States of America

ISBN-13: 978-1-54561-552-2

Visit

www.confederategoldnovel.com

for photographs of sites featured by

chapter, printable maps, and more.

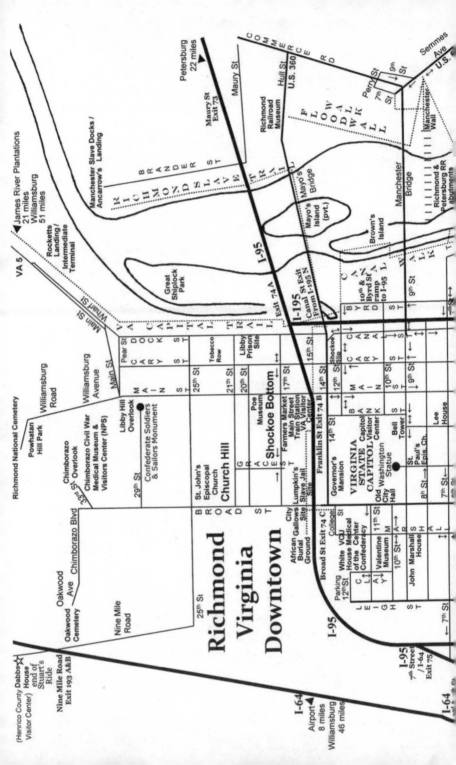

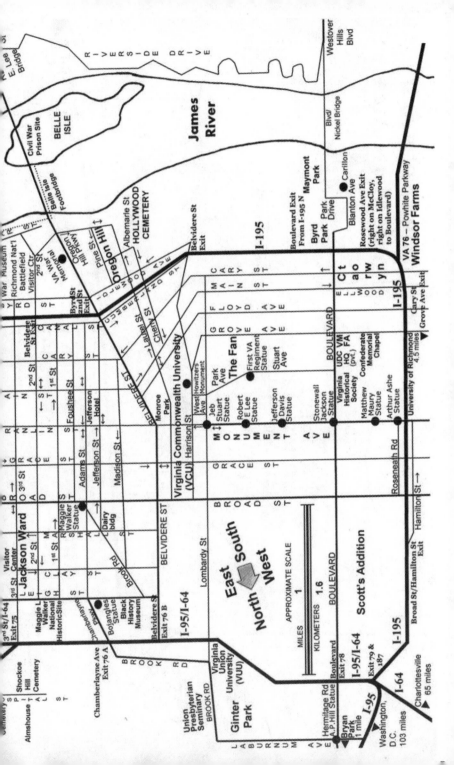

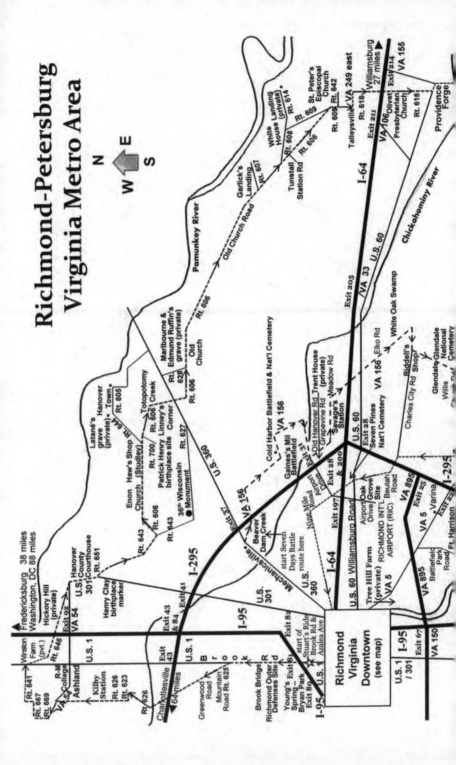

Richmond–Petersburg
Virginia Metro Area

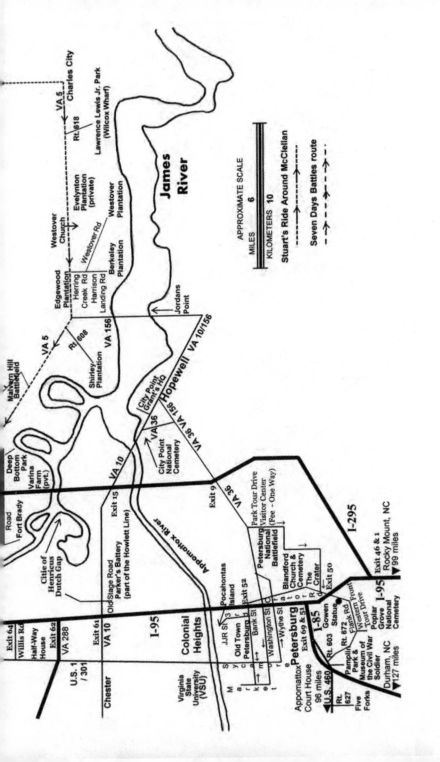

For while an angered man may again be happy, and a resentful man again be pleased, a state that has perished cannot be restored, nor can the dead be brought back to life.

—Sun Tzu
c. 544–496 BC
The Art of War

CHAPTER 1

A pickup truck shot out of the entrance of Harrison Landing Road, passing a sign nailed to the trunk of a loblolly pine. The homemade placard, lettered in red paint on plywood, pointed the way back to this weekend's reenactment: CIVIL WAR ↑.

Driving the pickup, Raleigh Fuqua, the captain of his company, chauffeured three members of the 14th Virginia Infantry in his Dodge Ram. Gordon Barrett rode shotgun. Raleigh couldn't think less of Gordon, but with real wars going on, it was hard to fill the ranks for past wars. In the backseat, Pat McCandlish, an engineer by day, sat with Gordon's fifteen-year-old nephew Hezekiah Shreve, the color bearer of the unit.

Raleigh careened around a fork in the gravel road, barreling down the drive to Westover, the James River plantation of William Byrd II, the founder of Richmond.

Gordon braced himself against the dashboard. "Slow down, Raleigh, before you kill us all."

Raleigh clutched the steering wheel. "We don't have much time. We need to get back for the dance tonight. I just wanted to check out where McClellan's men were bombarded by Stuart." He rumbled along the tree-lined lane another mile, kicking up dust.

Pat moved forward in his seat and grabbed Gordon's headrest. "Turn here."

Raleigh reeled left onto a bypath and followed it until ending at the edge of a soybean field. The men piled out except for Hezekiah, keeping in his seat and listening to music on his iPod.

Pat walked toward an adjacent grove of beech trees and yelled over his shoulder, "I have to go see a man about a horse."

From the bed of the truck, Gordon lifted out his metal detector and turned it on.

"We agreed you weren't going to use that." Raleigh scanned the perimeter to make sure no one saw them. "This is private land. You don't have permission to hunt here." Raleigh's irritated voice rose. "I'm sure the whole area has been picked clean. You're not going to find anything. Put it back in the truck before you get us all arrested."

Gordon stepped away from Raleigh, and the detector beeped.

Raleigh scoffed. "False signal, I'm sure."

Gordon waved the detector back and forth across the ground and received a resonating ding, ding, ding.

Raleigh's black mustache twisted. "It's probably a pull tab."

Pat cut his call of nature short and crashed out of the woods. He moved toward Gordon, fumbling to button the pants of his Confederate uniform. "Sounds like a good target."

Gordon worked the search coil in crossing sweeps to pinpoint the object. To mark the spot, he dug the heel of his right brogan into the ground, then turned off the detector and set it down.

Gordon looked at Pat. "What do you think it is?"

"Don't know, but it seems to be big or a lot of it."

Raleigh sneered. "Yeah, a lot of trash."

Gordon boomed, "Hezekiah, bring me my shovel." Hezekiah pulled out his earbuds.

Gordon hollered again. "Bring me my shovel. It's in the back of the cab."

The gangly teenager jumped out of the truck and fetched the little relic shovel.

Raleigh grabbed for the shovel as Hezekiah approached. "Let me do it."

Gordon snagged the spade before Raleigh could and eased it into the sandy Tidewater soil, careful not to damage what he was looking for. With the shovel halfway into the ground, he announced, "Got something."

Gordon tried another spot a few inches away, netting the same result. After several scoops, he'd removed enough earth to see the top of an iron box. He threw the shovel aside, and in unison, all four men dropped to their knees, feverishly clawing out the dirt with their hands. In a few minutes, they had dug around a strongbox with a padlock hanging from it. They lifted it out of the hole by its metal handles.

"Heavy as hell." Raleigh strained his small frame.

Gordon gently clasped the padlock and let go. "We should try to save the lock."

Raleigh snatched the shovel lying on the ground and with a lightning downward thrust broke off the lock.

"So much for saving it," Gordon said as he released the latch and slowly lifted the lid, revealing rows of paper cylinders.

They each grabbed one of the cylinders and opened them like rolls of Ritz Crackers to unveil gold coins.

Pat plucked one of the coins from his roll. "Wow, it's a Liberty Head, 1858."

Raleigh pulled out a coin. "This one's 1860." He flipped it over to read the tail side. "United States of America, Twenty D," he proclaimed. "I'll be damned, twenty-dollar gold pieces."

Gordon closely examined a coin, holding the edges between his forefinger and thumb to prevent from damaging it. "Coronet double eagle, almost an ounce of gold." He racked his brain trying to determine the origin of the precious medallions. "It's the same kind of coinage taken from the Confederate treasury and put on the second to last train out of Richmond when it fell in April of 1865." He hesitated. "It can't be from the treasure train. All that gold was dispersed from Greensboro to Georgia."

Hezekiah checked the dates on his coins, flipping through a roll like a mini-record bin, and reading out each date louder than the last one. "1859, 1861, 1857, 1860." Hezekiah crescendoed. "None of them is after 1861."

Hearts raced, heads pounded, and limbs quaked from the excitement of the find. Above all, sweat poured as they tried to remain calm in their wool uniforms under the June sun.

Gordon, a guy who seldom stopped talking, found it hard to speak when it dawned on him. "It must be part of the British loan to the Confederacy supposed to be buried near Berkeley Plantation, and Berkeley is right over there." Gordon pointed in the direction they had come.

"It doesn't matter where it came from." Raleigh reached for more rolls. "It's ours now."

Gordon swiftly slammed the lid down on the box. "Get your hands off and give me back those coins. You didn't even want me to pull out my detector."

Raleigh protested. "I didn't know you were going to find Confederate gold. I'm sure we can work something out."

"Go screw yourself, Raleigh."

Raleigh snapped back. "Did you forget who drove you here? You going to walk back to Richmond with that chest of gold?"

Pat stepped in between Raleigh and Gordon. "Take it easy."

Raleigh gaped down at the chest. "There's probably enough gold here for all of us to retire. We can do whatever we want."

Gordon held a roll of gold tightly in one hand and kept a foot on the lid of the coffer. "I don't think you'll be retiring anytime soon, Raleigh, but I can buy that cannon I've always wanted. Hell, I can buy a whole battery of cannons."

Tears welled up in Hezekiah's adolescent eyes. "You're just a bunch of hypocrites, aren't you? All I ever hear you all talking about is saving Civil War battlefields, saving the hallowed ground. Now we have some money to save them, so why don't we?"

Pat put his hand on Hezekiah's shoulder. "The boy has a point."

Raleigh raised his voice. "This is different. We just won the lottery. This is a once in a lifetime deal."

Hezekiah, normally intimidated by Raleigh, challenged him. "I thought one of the reasons we're reenacting is to raise money to save battlefields to honor the men who fought. You keep saying all the battlefields that aren't already gone will be gone in ten years if somebody doesn't do something. Well, now we're somebody who has a chance to do something."

Gordon shook his head in embarrassment. "Hezekiah is right. We could prevent another 'Manasshole.' We can leave a legacy. I don't know how much gold is here, but we've got a chance to save some ground."

Raleigh's face tensed up. "Gentlemen, that's a nice, lofty idea, but I don't think we should be too hasty. We don't even know how much this gold is worth. There may be plenty enough to buy some battlefield land and set part of the gold aside for ourselves."

Pat peeled back his kepi and scratched his head. "We might as well try to donate it to a charity. We're not going to be able to keep this gold."

One of Raleigh's eyes started ticcing. "What do you mean we're not going to be able to keep the gold?"

"Once we remove these coins, we've probably broken a half-dozen laws, and when the word gets out, the federal, state, and local governments are all going to want their cut, and the landowner and the descendants of the previous landowners, plus all their ex-wives, will want a piece of it."

Raleigh looked around in paranoia. "We can decide what we're going to do later. Let's just get it out of here before somebody sees us."

Gordon pushed back his shoulder-length brown hair underneath his slouch hat, then stroked his orange beard with one hand and drummed his fingers on his sizable stomach with the other. "We'll take it back to my place and count it."

Raleigh rubbed his eye, trying to make his tic go away. "Fine. Fill in the hole."

CHAPTER 2

Across the wide and marshy Herring Creek, the Virginia Division of the Sons of Confederate Veterans (SCV) were hosting a reception, kicking off its annual convention on the lush lawn of Evelynton Plantation.

Evelynton, originally part of Westover Plantation and named after William Byrd II's elder daughter, was intended as her dowry. But the Protestant Byrd thwarted Evelyn's Catholic suitor and she died brokenhearted. One hundred and ten years later in 1847, the land sold at auction to Edmund Ruffin, Jr., the son of the radical Southern secessionist. Ruffin's old man got what he wanted, so when the Yankees showed up at Junior's front door in 1862, they burned down the house and outbuildings, girdled the trees, and salted the fields. Seventy-five years after that unpleasant incident, the secessionist's great-grandson built a Georgian Revival manor where the old house had stood, overlooking the tidal creek.

The SCV was having its party under a huge white tent beside the new "big house." At the edge of the tent stood a spotting scope, set up for the pleasure of the conventioneers to view the lands of Westover and Berkeley Plantations on the other side of the water. They could gaze over to where General McClellan withdrew the Federal Army after the Seven Days Battles. From this vantage point, Confederate General Jeb Stuart took potshots at the Union encampment with a single howitzer until chased off the ridge by the Yankees.

Carter Flood, a long-time member of the Sons, was heading to the bar in his ill-fitting brown suit, smoking a cigarette, when he noticed no one at the scope. He walked over to the field glass for a look-see. Holding the cigarette in his lips, he focused on the open area across the creek and saw a group of men digging up something. At that distance, he couldn't see what they had discovered, but he knew what they had.

His jaw dropped and the cigarette fell out of his mouth. "My God, they found it," Carter said to himself in a heavy smoker's voice. "Great-Granddaddy wasn't telling a tale." Astonished, he watched the men through the lens discussing their find.

Wendell, Carter's brother, walked up on him and asked, "What are you looking at?"

Startled, Carter jerked his head away from the scope. "You won't believe this. They found it."

"They found what?"

"The British loan treasure. Take a look."

Wendell, a stocky carbon copy of his brother, didn't have to bend down far to look through the glass. "I just see some guys loading up a chest into a truck. How do you know it's the treasure?"

"What else could it be? And it's ours. The government took Great-Granddaddy's land, but we're taking back that gold. Let's go have a little chat with them." Carter tugged at Wendell's arm.

Wendell slowly moved away from the scope. "Don't we need to tell the commander we're leaving?"

"To hell with the commander. I'm tired of hanging out with this bunch of whiners. It's time to stop talking about the war and take some action. It's time for the shooting to start again. That gold will finance our New Confederacy."

The two men made their way down the circular driveway to the parking lot. Blocked in, it took some time to find the owner of the vehicle obstructing their gray utility truck. As soon as they were able to get onto Highway 5, they raced west up the winding byway, cutting through the farms and forests, paralleling the James River. They quickly made it to the turnoff for Herring Creek Road, leading to Berkeley and Westover.

Carter slowed down a little. "I don't think they're still back in there, and we didn't pass them on the way here. They must have gone on up the road." Carter gunned his truck around the curve.

Making wild time on the snaky road, in a dozen minutes they were at the junction of Richmond's beltway. Wendell looked ahead and spotted a bluish-gray truck going under the interstate bridges. "I think that's them."

Their mark pulled away, and Carter drove faster to catch up. The two trucks flew toward the village of Varina. Their pace slowed as traffic congested at the hamlet's stoplights. Carter and Wendell found themselves several cars back from a cadet gray Dodge Ram. A couple of more miles down the road, they were right on the Ram's bumper.

Carter read the license plate aloud, "NCNATIV, Virginia tags." He let off the gas, providing a little braking distance. "We'll just follow them to wherever they're going."

The trucks took the southbound ramp of the Pocahontas Parkway to cross the James River. The Ram merged over to the Smart Tag lanes.

"Can you cover this?" Carter asked Wendell. They watched their prey breeze back into the asphalt world as they scrambled to pull together the toll in white and brown money. After making the payment, Carter accelerated out of the toll plaza, but only up to the speed limit, knowing a trap lay in wait.

"Shouldn't you slow down?" Gordon asked Raleigh as they picked up more speed coming off the downside of the bridge.

As soon as Raleigh replied, "Shut up and let me drive," the throbbing blue lights of a state trooper's cruiser appeared behind them. "Oh, crap. Everybody put on your seatbelts." Raleigh pulled his truck over, and the trooper pulled in behind him. "Damn it. I can't afford to have my insurance go up."

Gordon gasped. "Let's just hope he doesn't open the chest."

The utility truck crept past the Ram and the cruiser, but not without the reenactors noticing the Confederate battle flag painted on and taking up the truck's entire high-panel side, faded with time and obscured by a layer of dirt.

A tall black state trooper stepped onto the roadway. The officer glanced down at the Heritage Not Hate bumper sticker. He approached the driver's side window and looked in, but he didn't do a double take when he saw that all the men in the truck were wearing Confederate uniforms. He looked down at Raleigh and in a bass voice said, "The war is over, boys, and the 'bottom rail on top dis time.' May I see your license and registration, please?"

Raleigh knew the voice instantly. "Damn, Powhatan, it's you. I didn't recognize you in the Smokey hat and sunglasses."

The trooper broke out in a smile and seized the license and registration from Raleigh's hand. "You can call me Officer Dubel. Why were you boys in such a hurry?"

"We're just trying to get back for the dance tonight. You going?"

"No, I'm on duty. But I'll be shooting at you this weekend with the rest of the US Colored Troops."

"Did you forget, Powhatan? I mean Officer Dubel. It's 1862 tomorrow. The Colored Troops weren't formed until 1863."

"Yeah, but I'll be shooting at your ass anyway, just for demonstration purposes. You all bivouacking at Berkeley?"

"Uh-huh."

Powhatan looked back in the bed of the truck. "What do you have back here, some sort of old ammunition chest?"

Raleigh's eyes darted. "I picked it up at a junkyard. I'm going to make a provision box out of it."

"Looks like you got a lot of cleaning and fixing up to do on that one."

"So, Officer, can I have my license and registration back?"

"Not so fast. You were doing 74 in a 55, plus you fit the profile of groups of grown white men traveling together, wearing Confederate uniforms."

"Come on, Powhatan. Give me a break."

Powhatan handed the license and registration back. "You do need to slow it down, Mr. Fuqua. I don't want you to die until I get a chance to kill you myself tomorrow."

"Yes, sir. Thank you, sir."

Raleigh pulled away with them all relieved from their release. He got up to the speed limit and stayed there, all the way to Gordon's South Side apartment. They carried the chest up to Gordon's third-floor flat and set it in the middle of the living room floor on the brown carpet.

"All right, Gordon, you found it," Raleigh said. "You count it."

They all sat on the floor except Raleigh. Gordon took an open roll and counted fifty coins.

Raleigh stood over Gordon's shoulder. "Now how many rolls?"

Gordon carefully laid each roll out on the dusty carpet. "One hundred rolls."

Hezekiah did the math. "One hundred rolls times fifty. That's 5,000 coins, times $20 a piece, that's $100,000," Hezekiah said with a smile that wouldn't come off his rosy-cheeked face.

Gordon took a deep breath. "That's face value, but gold is at record prices these days. Double eagles this old, depending on their rarity and condition, are probably worth, I'm guessing, at least $1,500 a piece."

Hezekiah's eyes lit up and he ciphered. "That's $7.5 million."

They were all dumbstruck by the sum. Then Gordon added, "But we haven't counted the historical value. If we could tie these coins to the Confederate treasury, the story behind them could make them ten times more valuable."

Hezekiah's grin and eyes reached their maximum size. "Seventy-five million dollars."

"What is that? Eighteen or nineteen million apiece," Raleigh answered his own question.

Gordon flinched. "There is no 'apiece,' Raleigh. I'm sure Pat's right. We're not going to be able to keep these coins. We might as well donate them for buying battlefields."

Raleigh's thin lips crooked. "Right, battlefields."

Pat pulled his lanky body up from the floor. "There's a lot of things to sort out here. We'll need to get an appraisal, and we'll need to figure out how to get the most battlefield for our buck. And most importantly, we're going to need a good lawyer to figure out the best way to cash these coins in without landing in jail."

Gordon pulled at his beard. "Sterling can help us with all that."

"We can talk to him tonight at the ball," Pat said as he surveyed the gold on the floor.

Gordon smiled. "Wait till the guys at the Round Table hear about this."

Raleigh's tic started back up, and he barked, "Don't say anything to anybody until we get this straight."

"It's okay, Raleigh," Pat said. "We'll keep it to ourselves, but what do we do with the gold in the meantime?"

Gordon volunteered. "It'll be fine here."

"I guess you're right." Pat looked around at the décor of Künstler and Troiani prints, Civil War flags, books, and toy soldiers. "No one in their right mind would want to break in here."

CHAPTER 3

G ayle ungracefully hoisted herself into the passenger side of the Ram, wearing a dress supported by a hoop skirt and all the other bulky undergarments that went along with it. Raleigh, already in the driver's seat and impatient for his wife to get in, rat-a-tat-tatted, "Let's go, let's go." He wanted to make sure they secured a good parking spot for the dance. Gayle couldn't move any quicker under the weight of her clothes, and his commands only made her more annoyed with him than she usually was.

As soon as Gayle fastened her seatbelt, Raleigh tore out of the driveway, leaving behind their "little Tara," a two-story brick house with skinny, square columns across the front and a North Carolina 1861 flag flapping on a pole in the yard. Once out of the neighborhood, they turned east on Midlothian Turnpike, the main sprawling commercial strip in Chesterfield County, the suburban county south of the City of Richmond. From the turnpike, they caught the ramp for the downtown toll road.

Raleigh was dying to tell Gayle about the gold, but he knew he shouldn't. He saw the gold opening up a world of possibilities. He was just sorry it had been found by Gordon, a Northern apologist. Raleigh knew he had played a key role in the discovery and couldn't stop thinking if his fair share should really go to battlefield preservation.

They crossed the James River and tacked toward Monument Avenue. Whenever Raleigh and Gayle ventured into downtown Richmond, they always took Monument Avenue, a road ridiculed as the Lost Causeway. Despite the sobriquet, the street was still one of America's grand boulevards, lined with American Renaissance architecture and punctuated by traffic circles containing Confederate memorials.

The first monument the Fuquas came upon during their second-place victory lap wasn't to a Confederate, but to a hero from a different age placed there with a unanimous vote by the black-majority Richmond City Council in 1996.

As they sat at the stoplight, Gayle stared at the statue. "Poor Arthur Ashe, the only winner on Losers' Lane."

Even though Raleigh was preoccupied with the gold, he managed to fire off his standard Arthur Ashe statue rant. "Why didn't they put another Confederate general here? This would have been a great spot for a North Carolina–born commander, not Braxton Bragg, but maybe Armistead or Pettigrew."

Raleigh had moved from the Tar Heel State with his parents when he was eight years old. As children, his parents were taught the three Rs: reading, writing, and the road to Richmond. Raleigh still saw himself as a citizen of North Carolina, "the valley of humility between the two mountains of conceit," the Southern state that lost the most men during the Civil War.

Raleigh clinched his teeth. "For God's sake, you don't put a tennis player where the second line of the Confederate earthworks ran for the defense of Richmond."

Gayle sighed. "There's nothing wrong with Arthur Ashe, but why didn't they put him overlooking the Byrd Park tennis courts, where they wouldn't let him play?"

The light changed, and they rolled on, engulfed by the towering oaks planted in the broad, grassy median. They approached the first monument to a Confederate, Matthew Fontaine Maury, better known as the Father of Modern Oceanography rather than his exploits as a Rebel. Maury slumped in a chair below a titanic globe and allegorical figures.

The car behind them honked its horn. Raleigh, reflexively ready to flip off the driver, looked in the rearview mirror to see Gordon and Hezekiah waving. Raleigh smiled his unnatural smile and raised his right hand in acknowledgment. Raleigh and Gayle made it through the next yellow light at the Boulevard, but the red light caught Gordon and Hezekiah. In the middle of the intersection sat the Stonewall Jackson monument. Stonewall, accidentally shot by his own men at Chancellorsville, was portrayed here on a pedestal on a horse facing north, eternally on reconnaissance for the South. Pigeons rested on both of his shoulders like epaulettes. Gordon and Hezekiah promptly saluted.

Gordon, at the wheel of his old yellowish-brown Delta 88 convertible with the top down, reached inside his shell jacket for his breast pocket where some reenactors kept their Bible. He retrieved a bandless cigar and used his infantryman's side knife to cut off the cap against the steering wheel. The cap disappeared between his legs, and he stuck the unlit stogie in his mouth. All talked out about the gold, he decided to rattle off his Monument Avenue lament. Hezekiah had heard the requiem at least a dozen times, but he knew it was pointless to remind Uncle he was repeating himself.

"Northerners make fun of the South. They say we're obsessed with the Civil War and still fighting it. Yankees see the Civil War as an aberration in America's great history. They tend to concentrate on their beginnings with their Pilgrims and Revolutionary War heroes. But the Civil War to Southerners is the wellspring. Everything led up to it, and everything since has flowed from it."

Gordon fired up the cigar using a wooden match. "The war had a much greater effect on the South than it did on the North. Most of the war was fought here, most of the dead are buried here, and for those left, their society changed. Our sacrifice of blood and treasure was proportionally much larger than the North's, and you're going to hear about it whether you want to or not because Southerners love to talk. We can't hold it in like stoic New Englanders. It's called oral tradition."

Hezekiah bent his neck forward. "The light's green."

Gordon pressed on the accelerator as his belly pressed against the bottom of the steering wheel. Once they made it through the intersection, the oaks in the median were replaced by sugar maples and the road surface changed from asphalt to paving blocks. The car began to vibrate.

Gordon puffed and the smoke revolved around his head. "First, look at the property loss. The South was left in economic ruin that took decades to recover from. Cities went up in flames, and the countryside was stripped, while the North was left relatively untouched.

"And of course, they took away the South's major source of labor and wealth, emancipating four million people. But who could put a price on human bondage?" Gordon posed his rhetorical question to the passing maples and answered. "The South could. Before the war in today's money, the average cost of a slave was around $18,500, but a healthy young male would cost you much more, about $30,000. A woman and child together would go for only about half that."

Gordon and Hezekiah passed the Jefferson Davis Monument, encased by a half circle of thirteen columns, eleven columns for the seceding states and two columns for the states sending the Confederacy representatives and troops, Kentucky and Missouri. The one and only president of the Confederacy was molded into an oratory pose, stepping up with his arm flung forward.

Hezekiah shouted out, "Deo vindice."

"Yeah." Gordon rolled his eyes gently and murmured, "Deo vindice?"

Directly behind the Davis statue rose a sixty-foot column with the Confederate motto *Deo vindice* wrapped around its apex. It was Latin for "God will vindicate" and Confederate for

"The South was right." "Miss Confederacy" capped the column, pointing to heaven.

They rambled by the revival-styled mansions, built mostly during the good economic times between the Panic of 1893 and the Stock Market Crash of 1929. By the 1920s, Monument Avenue was a full-fledged bourgeois suburb. Today, the neighborhood housed a more diverse demographic, from college students to multimillionaires.

Gordon's roll of tobacco began to smolder. "Then there's the loss of life and limb. When the Civil War ended, one in three Southern white men were either dead or wounded. That means you had a lot of mothers and widows in the parlor and a bunch of guys without an arm or a leg out on the porch spending way too much time spewing venom at the North and the federal government, and telling war stories till the day they died."

Gordon brandished his stogie like a sword, coming close to hitting Hezekiah in the eye. "A war with those kinds of costs will affect the attitudes of a region for generations, especially since the South not only lost the war, it lost badly. And for white Southerners to admit they were wrong for starting the war in the first place was totally out of the question. Then how do you reconcile such a catastrophe in judgment? You turn defeat into victory, into something fabled, into a holy war, the South's jihad. To save face, you portray yourself as a victim of Northern aggression and claim the moral high ground of honor and bravery. You transform your foot soldiers into noblemen and your generals into gods. You say the war wasn't about protecting the South's investment in slaves. It was about self-defense and obtaining liberty. But self-delusion is small compensation."

Gordon maneuvered around a traffic circle and looked up sixty-one feet to his left at the man on the highest pedestal on Monument Avenue. They saluted the statue of General Robert E. Lee riding his horse, "Traveller". Before there were houses on the grand boulevard, there was the statue of Lee, rising out of the ashes of war and the humiliation of a punitive Reconstruction on the white populace. Installed in 1890, it was the first monument placed on the avenue, and one of the many memorials to Civil War heroes erected across the nation by the political and financial power of aging veterans and ladies' organizations. With Lee's hand firmly on the reins and his mount's head bowed, the statue screamed white supremacy was back, and it was, for the next seventy-five years. In the South after Reconstruction, Jim Crow laws enforced racial segregation and the repression of African Americans until the passage of the Civil Rights Act of 1964 and the Voting Rights Act of 1965.

Gordon's cigar went out. "The Civil War is still important to the South because they lost. When you win, you just take it all for granted. In the end, if you leave a people dispossessed, they're going to hang on to their past and imagined glories because that's all they have. The Irish are still talking about the Normans invading in 1169, the Serbs are still talking about their defeat by the Ottoman Turks in 1389, and white Southerners will be talking about their Confederacy for a long time to come. And who wouldn't remember a war where horses played an integral part and an individual's character made the difference time and time again."

They saluted the giant bronze action figure of Jeb Stuart on a bristling mount. As Monument Avenue turned into Franklin Street, they spotted a soldier on a real horse.

"Hey, there's Pat," Hezekiah said. Pulling alongside him, they waved and tooted.

Pat's horse, Shiloh, was unspooked by the disturbance, and Pat waved back. Pat kept his horse at his farm in Varina, and for tonight's event, he'd brought Shiloh to town.

Gordon hollered, "See you at the ball," and pulled away. They glided deeper and deeper into the older sections of the city, sweeping through Virginia Commonwealth University (VCU). What the urban school lacked in green space, it made up for in eclectic architecture. At the eastern end of the campus was Monroe Park. Once used as a training camp for Confederate troops, the park was now a hangout for the homeless.

They crossed over Belvidere Street, where the modern high-rises mixed with the older architecture, then turned onto Fifth Street. On the left was the Second Presbyterian Church, where Stonewall Jackson had worshipped. Gordon knew the significance of each Richmond landmark as it related to the Civil War and was always trying to relay the town's war history to Hezekiah or anyone else who would listen. He had come to love Virginia's capital city. Charlottesville had Jefferson's Monticello, Williamsburg had Rockefeller's rebuilt colonial town, but Richmond had the story of the American Civil War.

Gordon had followed his older sister to the city. They were part of the Appalachian diaspora. They came from Lee County, the most western county in Virginia, a six-hour drive away from Richmond, where beauty was bountiful and jobs were scarce. He still carried a hint of the accent of the pre-Revolutionary War settlers of the Eastern mountains, a region derided as the South's South. Most of his native dialect, a web of Scots-Irish, English, and German, had been wrung out of him with public ridicule when he came to Richmond. But Gordon still thought it was these people in the lowlands who talked funny, not him.

With inspiration from their father, a Presbyterian minister, Gordon's sister had become a theologian, teaching in Richmond at Union Presbyterian Seminary. Gordon's only predestination up to this point was to become a ne'er-do-well preacher's kid. He tried taking classes at Reynolds Community College but didn't last long. He worked one crummy job after another and was turning thirty next month as a sales associate for Best Buy. Life seemed only to be leading to the next reenactment, but now he had the gold.

CHAPTER 4

At the bottom of Fifth Street, Gordon pulled in behind Raleigh and Gayle. Gayle tumbled out of the truck in her awkward dress, while Raleigh checked his mustache in the rearview mirror. Gordon and Hezekiah got out of the Delta and walked up to Raleigh's truck as Raleigh opened his door. Gordon tilted his head toward the walkway. "Looks like trouble."

Greeting the reenactors from across the street were silent black protestors, lining the walk along the refurbished Haxall Flour Mill Canal and holding up handmade signs.

Raleigh focused on one of the demonstrator's posters: SLAVERY WAS OUR HOLOCAUST. "Why do they always have to throw that up in our face?" He stepped out of his truck, pulled his sword from the backseat, and strapped it on. "Why can't they just get over it and leave us in peace? They messed up our Confederate Christmas, and now this."

Gordon shrugged. "We're going to wait for Pat to catch up. You want to wait with us, and we'll walk the gauntlet together?"

"I'm not afraid of those people. Let's go, Gayle."

Gayle took Raleigh's arm, and they promenaded past the raging stares of the protestors, going under the banner displaying "Welcome to Dixie Days, June 18–27." They sashayed on down the sidewalk to their destination, the gun foundry. Though the foundry didn't look like much more than an oversized brick barn with a smokestack, it had been part of the Confederacy's most valuable industrial asset, Tredegar Iron Works. During the war, the iron works produced almost 1,100 cannons and the armor plating covering the USS *Merrimack*, converting the frigate into the ironclad CSS *Virginia*.

For tonight's occasion, the wooden doors of the gun foundry were open, and Gayle and Raleigh entered. The building once wheezed, fumed, and hissed with manufacturing activity but was now part of the American Civil War Center at Historic Tredegar, filled with exhibits and artifacts.

Gayle and Raleigh strolled through the displays and out the other side of the foundry, leading into an inner courtyard of the nineteenth-century military-industrial complex. Candles burned brightly in the twilight, flags of all of the Confederate states hung high above the patio, and underneath, amid bunting and roses, couples danced the Virginia reel.

Pat arrived a few minutes later. He met up with Gordon and Hezekiah, and tied up Shiloh. The three of them went dateless through the door.

Gordon was always prospecting. "Hezekiah, just stick with me and we'll get some women."

When they reached the party, a girl in a ball dress with a boyish haircut shouted from across the courtyard. "Hey, Hezekiah, you going to dance with me tonight?" Hezekiah's face turned red, matching his carrot top.

Gordon grinned. "See, I already got you one. Go on over and see her. I'll find you before we meet with Sterling."

Hezekiah went over to see Kim Dansey. Kim and Hezekiah were the same age, and their parents had taken them to Civil War reenacting events since they were babies. They had grown up wearing clothes too hot for summer days and drinking Vernor's ginger ale.

"Hezekiah, this is my friend, Katie Ambler. Katie, this is Hezekiah Shreve."

Katie's eyebrows creased. "Hezekiah?"

"It's biblical. I'm named after the rebelling King of Judea who tried to gain independence from the invading Assyrians."

Kim changed the subject. "How do your parents like Edinburgh?"

"They email me every day. They're having a good time."

"I can't believe they went to Scotland this summer to teach and left you with your uncle Gordon."

"They asked me if I wanted to go with them or stay here with Uncle. I figured I'd have more fun with Uncle."

"Wasn't your mother worried about leaving you?"

"No, she's more worried about Uncle."

On the stone tiles of the courtyard, Mary Beth Crenshaw danced with General McClellan's aide-de-camp, the Comte de Paris.

"I am merely an observer in your country," the Count said in his bad French accent, "but I know when I see a beautiful woman I could love forever."

"Oh, Count, you are such a flatterer."

He pressed his white cotton dancing gloves firmly against the tight-fitting kid covering her hands. "I only speak truth."

"Oh, Count, we're only dancing."

"Yes, but we could be doing so much more."

Mary Beth looked up into the eyes of the gentleman of questionable royal heritage. "Count, I cannot accept your advances because my heart belongs to another man."

His eyebrows rose below his wide forehead. "This other man must be careful, or I will steal your heart away when he is not looking."

Gordon and Pat made their way over to the bar, set up in front of a Brooke rifled cannon cast at the iron works.

"How about a Fox on the Rocks?" Gordon recommended.

"Sounds good."

They got their drinks and perused the crowd. Gordon whispered, "Hey, there's the guy who plays Jackson at the State Capitol on Lee-Jackson Day. And there's General Lee, and General Lee, and there's another General Lee over there. Uh-oh, and there's Mary Beth. Better hide."

"Mr. McCandlish."

Gordon turned and mouthed to Pat, "Too late."

"Mr. McCandlish, I've been looking all over for you. Have you been hiding from me?" Mary Beth felt the chemistry, but Pat just felt queasy. "Mr. McCandlish, you must dance with me."

She grabbed Pat's hand and dragged him out onto the dance floor. As they waltzed, Pat noticed a gal in an emerald-green evening dress with short, spiky black hair. Half the crowd consisted of non-reenactors, wearing formal attire. Some reenactors bristled at the mixing of apparel, but it was a fund-raising event for the Museum of the Confederacy, and the spectators in modern civilian clothing paid a premium for admission.

Mary Beth attempted to look into the eyes of her dance partner. "Mr. McCandlish, when are you going to take me for a ride on that horse of yours?"

Pat still had his eyes on the woman in green.

"Mr. McCandlish, are you listening to me?"

Pat's attention was forced back to Mary Beth. "Yes, of course. What were you saying?"

"Do you ever think of marriage, Mr. McCandlish?"

"Someday, I guess. I just have to meet the right girl."

"You know, Daddy has a house on the river in Tappahannock. He lets me use it anytime I want. Won't you come to the river with me next weekend? Maybe I could help you find that right girl."

The music stopped and Gordon broke in. "Miss Crenshaw, I'm sorry to interrupt, but I need to take Pat away to discuss some business with Mr. Overstreet."

Gayle and Raleigh were also coming off the dance floor, and Gayle took Mary Beth by the arm. "Come along, Mary Beth. I'll talk to you. They don't want to talk to us anyway."

A passerby unknowingly stepped on the bottom of Mary Beth's dress, ripping away some ruffle, and kept on walking.

Mary Beth shot a dirty look at the offender and huffed. "These skirts weren't made to be worn in crowds."

Gayle patted the back of her hair bun. "They weren't made for a lot of things."

The women laughed together as Pat, Raleigh, and Gordon approached a big man watching a waterwheel turn. He wore a tuxedo and horn-rimmed glasses with his hair closely cropped, revealing a flat, broad face, punctuated by a nose almost as long as the cigar he smoked. Sterling Overstreet, the Virginia director of the Trust for the Preservation of Civil War Battlefields, nodded and smiled as they closed in.

Gordon offered his hand. "Sterling, how are you doing tonight?"

Sterling pressed the flesh. "Splendid. Good to see you." Then he shook the hands of Pat and Raleigh.

Raleigh wouldn't let go of Sterling's hand. Half the size of Sterling, Raleigh looked like the dog that caught the car. "Sterling, we need a few minutes of your time."

"Certainly, what can I do for you?"

"We need to talk to you—not here, in your office."

"Make an appointment with my secretary, and I can see you sometime next week."

Raleigh squeezed Sterling's hand harder. "No, we need to talk to you now."

"Boys, the party is just starting. We don't want to leave."

Raleigh still wouldn't let go. "It won't take that long."

"All right then. If you insist, let's go up to my office." Sterling stopped a passing waiter. "Would you please bring a bottle of Virginia Gentleman up to the company store with four glasses."

"Make that five," Gordon said. "I'll get Hezekiah."

The summer sun had gone down, and the lamppost lights reflected off the James River. The men exited the party out the back of the courtyard through crumbling brick archways. The ruins, though reminiscent of the Richmond Evacuation Fire of 1865, were the remnants of Tredegar's Central Foundry after the flood damage from Hurricane Agnes in 1972.

They proceeded up a metal stairway, avoiding eye contact with the Abraham and Tad Lincoln statue at the top. The contingent ambled to the rear of the property to a building with a stepped gable roof, backed up against the towpath of the dry James River and Kanawha Canal. Embedded in the bank beside the structure that had served as Tredegar's company store was a set of old railroad-tie stairs that they walked up to reach the second floor.

Sterling opened the door with his key, turned on the lights, and let them in. It was all one room with small windows in the front and larger ones in the back. Pinned on the walls were maps of Civil War battlefields the trust was struggling to obtain. Sterling herded the reenactors over to the far side of the room to his desk and on the way pulled a couple of extra chairs over from his secretary's space to provide seating for all. Once Sterling had everyone settled, he circled around his desk and plopped down in his high-backed leather chair. The light flashed on his bald spot and his degree from the University of Virginia on the wall behind him. "So what's so important?"

Gordon put down a twenty-dollar gold piece in front of Sterling.

Sterling picked up the coin and examined it. "Double eagle, 1861. So you went out and bought yourself a double eagle?"

Gordon straightened up in his chair. "We went out and found some double eagles."

"You found some double eagles? How many?"

"About $75 million worth."

Sterling sneered. "Oh, come on, boys, I don't have time for this."

Gordon looked Sterling in the eye. "We found 5,000 coins. They may be worth $75 million if we can prove they're linked to the Confederacy."

"Five thousand coins? Confederate gold?" Sterling looked at the coin, then back at the men. "You boys shouldn't be jerking me around. Everybody knows the Confederacy was broke in the end."

Gordon leaned forward with his bulky body. "Yeah, they were broke in the end, but there was money in the beginning."

"You're serious?" Sterling dropped the coin on his desk. "What makes you think they're linked to the Confederacy?"

Gordon spoke in a measured tone. "Where we found them, what we found them in, and the dates on the coins."

"Where did you find them?"

Raleigh flared up. "The less you know the better."

Sterling grabbed the arms of his chair, still showing skepticism and concealing his excitement. "Let me make sure I'm hearing you correctly. You found 5,000 double eagles?"

Gordon beamed. "All dated before 1862."

"I'd have to see them to believe it." Sterling shook his head and paused. "So are you here just to brag?"

"We wanted to turn the gold into dirt and grass."

Sterling's eyebrows shot up. "You want to donate it to the Trust to save battlefields?"

Pat bit his lower lip. "Yeah, but with the treasure-finding laws, we're afraid most of it would just get taxed and split up with third-party claims. We wanted to know from you if there was some way to protect it, so most of it could go to battlefield preservation."

"Well, as long as you didn't trespass, but if you did, you definitely will have some landowner problems. And if you looted a historic site, you're probably going to have problems with the Archaeological Resources Protection Act. We're talking substantial fines and prison time."

Raleigh snapped. "Who said we looted anything? Don't worry about where we found it. Do you want to help us or not?"

"I'm going to have to see the coins, and I'm going to have to know where you found them before I can put the Trust to work for you."

Gordon looked at his pards, then at Sterling. "We can show you the coins. We found them near Berkeley Plantation. We think it's the Confederate British loan treasure."

"The missing British loan to the Confederacy? The British loan treasure was a hoax."

"It may have been a hoax, but the treasure we found is real."

"You are serious. The British loan treasure. This could be a very delicate matter." Sterling looked down at his calendar. "Why don't you come back and see me, say, noon on Wednesday?" He looked up. "In the meantime, I'll make some discreet phone calls. I should know more on how to assist you by then, and we can discuss this further. In fact, why don't we meet at the Jefferson Hotel for lunch, then you can take me to your gold."

Raleigh thrashed in his seat. "Don't tell anyone directly about these coins."

"I said I would make some discreet inquiries on your behalf."

A knock came from the door, startling everyone.

"Who is it?" Sterling shouted, not wanting to be disturbed.

"I have your bourbon, sir."

"Come in."

A wiry, young, brown-skinned waiter, wearing black-framed glasses, brought in the Virginia Gentleman.

"Just set it on my desk. Thank you. That is all."

The waiter paused to receive his tip, but none was forthcoming, so he left.

Sterling poured the bourbon. "What about the boy?"

"Give him a drink," Gordon said. "He's a full pard."

They stood up and raised their glasses.

"To the gold," Sterling said.

"To the gold," the others chimed.

CHAPTER 5

I n the East End of Richmond just below the fall line on the
south side of the James River, a hundred miles from the
ocean, the fresh waters of the mountains and the piedmont rolled
down, commingling with the flat tidal waters of the coastal plain
at the Manchester docks. The docks developed into a major port
for slave ships in the first half of the nineteenth century.

In 1778, Virginia outlawed the importation of enslaved
Africans, more as a way to protest British policies and increase
the price of their current slaves rather than as a moral objec-
tion. Nonetheless, Virginia's slave population continued to grow
through encouraged breeding and miscegenation. The state went
on to deplete its soil with a monoculture of tobacco and no longer
needed a growing slave population. High demand for slave labor
persisted in the cotton fields and cane plantations of the Deep
South. Virginia had more slaves to sell than any other state, and
by the 1840s, large quantities of human "goods" were shipped
out of Richmond, and selling people became Richmond's biggest
business. Built on bondage before the outbreak of the Civil War,
Richmond was the East Coast's leading exporter of slaves, traf-
ficking hundreds of human beings "down the river" each month.

Nothing was left of the Manchester docks except for a
granite-block seawall built after the Civil War. Two men and
a woman stood on the wall. It was one o'clock in the morning,
and the smells of the water and honeysuckle mixed in the gib-
bous moonlight.

Hark Carrington was one of the two men. He had changed out of his white waiter's jacket into a black paramilitary uniform crowned with a Che beret, but he still wore his black-framed glasses. "They have $75 million worth of gold coins that may have come from Confederate coffers. They'll meet with Sterling Overstreet on Wednesday at the Jefferson Hotel and take him to the gold. We can seize the coins when they lead him to it."

"You've done well, Hark," Fattah Absalom said. "Let's keep an eye on these Confederate sympathizers. We may be able to take the gold from them before they even meet with Overstreet."

Fattah gazed the short distance over to the river's north bank, thick with overhanging trees. He was a graying but fit middle-aged man with a careworn face, covered partially by a trimmed beard. He sported a dashiki and a black leather kofia. Fattah had gone to Harvard on scholarship in the 1970s and on to Harvard Law School as Jerry Bryan. When he graduated, he came back to his native Richmond but found few opportunities in the racially divided backwater. He moved to Chicago. That's when he became Fattah Absalom and took Frederick Douglass's advice to "Agitate! Agitate! Agitate!" He managed to agitate himself out of the Illinois Bar and a couple of marriages. He was weary of trying to work the system and decided to come home to roost. He had been trying to raise interest and money for his dream of a black separatist nation in America but had made little headway.

Fattah, knowing the historical weight of these waters, stared into the deep, opaque channel that carried the slavers and their human cargo. He raised his head and started speaking as if he had a large congregation as his audience.

"In the 1830s and '40s there was a senator from South Carolina. His name was John C. Calhoun. In the Senate, Mr. Calhoun became the head cheerleader for slavery. He defended slavery as a 'positive good,' calling slavery a 'peculiar institution,' making it sound quaint, giving it almost a colorful legitimacy. But there was nothing positive or peculiar about the economics of forced labor enforced by violence, making it cheaper to enslave a person than to hire a person. A college is an institution. Slavery is an evil practice that has gone on since the beginning of civilization and is still going on today."

Hark soaked up Fattah's words of rage. The discourse fueled the young man's fire of resentment.

Like a bellows, Fattah drew more air in, then pumped it back out. "Our people have spent almost four hundred years building this country up, and what have we received in return? Plantations have been replaced by prisons. And look at that cursed monument." He pointed across the James and up to Church Hill at the Confederate Soldiers and Sailors Monument, a pillar poking out above the tree canopy. "That monument and all the others in this town still dominate over us. Monuments to people who fought to prolong our suffering. Monuments to people who saw us as an inferior race. People who thought we could only be happy in their service. This worship of our oppressors has gone on too long. These statues must be toppled."

In the darkness, Fattah looked to his left at his lady friend, Leela Almond, then to his right at Hark. "Our people are on the brink of becoming an insignificant minority. Are we going to be pushed aside by the white man like the American Indians, now that we have outgrown our usefulness?"

"No," Leela and Hark answered in soft desperation.

"We will never be given reparations for slavery and the economic exclusion that followed. So we must take what we can. That gold is rightfully ours, and we will use it to buy land to establish a free and independent black nation. We will build a New Jerusalem in America. And if we are not allowed to establish our nation, then we will have to fight for our sovereignty in self-defense. Gabriel's Insurrection failed, but ours will not.

Gabriel was inspired by a white man's dream of freedom." Fattah pointed back up to Church Hill. "In St. John's Church on that hill, Patrick Henry said, 'Is life so dear, or peace so sweet, as to be purchased at the price of chains and slavery?'"

"No. No," Leela and Hark said, almost shouting.

Fattah finished Henry's quote, "'Forbid it, Almighty God—I know not what course others may take; but as for me, give me liberty, or give me death!'"

"Death or liberty, death or liberty," Leela and Hark chanted like backup singers.

CHAPTER 6

The Church Hill neighborhood was the namesake of St. John's Episcopal Church. Built around the colonial church in the nineteenth century, the area was Richmond's premier historic district. This collection of charming homes could help Richmond compete with the tourist trade of Charleston and Savannah, but for now, it was just another historic resource underutilized by the city.

From Church Hill, the view of the curve in the James River reminded William Byrd II of the River Thames from Richmond Hill in England, even though the water flowed in the opposite direction. In 1737, Byrd was under political pressure to give up his warehouse monopoly at the James River fall line, so he commissioned William Mayo to lay out a town grid to sell lots and called it Richmond.

Turning the corner at Twenty-fourth and East Grace Streets, bordering St. John's Church, Carter and Wendell Flood walked at a fast clip over the uneven brick sidewalk, illuminated by the yellow glow of gas lampposts. Breathing heavy from their out-of-shape bodies, they stopped halfway up the block and waited at a chained iron gate set into a high brick wall, securing the churchyard.

From down the street came Garnett Pollard, built like a bulldog, dressed in camouflage, combat boots, and a black army beret. The beret's flash displayed a Confederate battle flag insignia and below it a smaller insignia of a blue cockade, symbolizing advocacy for succession before the Civil War.

Garnett didn't acknowledge the Flood brothers, but instead pulled a small bolt cutter from a side pocket of his pants, effortlessly severed the chain on the gate, and held it open for them. The men slipped up a narrow set of concrete stairs to the churchyard and sidled around the white wooden-framed colonial church. They stayed out of the glare of the spotlights lighting the church and its steeple topped with a wooden cross. Each avoided stepping on the gravesites, some with unreadable headstones worn by time, in the oldest cemetery in the city. Under a hackberry tree, they gathered around the grave of George Wythe, Virginia's first signer of the Declaration of Independence.

Garnett handed Carter an envelope. "Here's the run on the NCNATIV plates. The truck belongs to a Raleigh and Gayle Fuqua."

Carter rasped, "We'll pay the Fuquas a little visit," as he gripped the envelope tightly.

Wendell looked at the envelope, then at Garnett. "When we find them, I can take them out with my .308 from a thousand yards."

Garnett smirked. "The way you shoot, Wendell, you may want to consider just going up to their front door and knocking."

"Are you making fun of the way I shoot?"

"Oh, drop it, Wendell." Carter turned to Garnett. "Have you talked to the Compatriot elders about the gold for financing the New Confederacy?"

"I'm going up to West Virginia to meet with them this weekend and won't be back until Tuesday. I'll let you know how it went when I get back."

Carter blinked in the half-light. "We need the backing of the elders."

"Get me the gold first, then I'll get you the backing. We'll launch a successful Second American Revolution, and the abolitionists won't win this time."

Carter glanced to his left and to his right. "Maybe next time we could meet someplace a little more convenient, where we don't have to break and enter."

"I like meeting here," Garnett said, focusing on the church. "Washington was here, Jefferson was here, and Patrick Henry, too, in 1775. This is where Henry sparked the Revolutionary War, convincing Virginia to provide troops when he said, 'For my own part, I consider it as nothing less than a question of freedom or slavery . . . . The battle, sir, is not to the strong alone; it is to the vigilant, the active, the brave. . . . The war is inevitable—and let it come! I repeat it, sir, let it come!'"

"Liberty or death," Carter said, accenting the conviction.

"Liberty or death," they all repeated, gazing across the tree-tops and rooftops from the hill's highest point.

The Lucky Strike smokestack rose in the distance, and their voices drifted down to the street where a lady in black listened.

CHAPTER 7

"Reveille" cut through the early morning air. Gordon grabbed his head and recoiled into a fetal position. His knees struck Hezekiah sleeping beside him in the dog tent.

Hezekiah screamed out in pain. "Put the bugler in the guardhouse."

A late night at the dance had ended with driving back to the reenactment bivouac at Berkeley Plantation to spend the weekend.

They heard the sergeant outside the tent. "Turn out. All up."

Hezekiah pushed his blanket away. Having slept in his full uniform, he scooched out to the dewy edge of the tent, needing only to put on his boots.

Gordon clung to his blanket for a few more minutes, his head hurting from drinking and his body hurting from sleeping on the ground. He managed to fall into the roll call line as the sergeant called off their names and the men answered in turn.

A farb's phone rang and he answered. "Hi, honey. Yeah, I'm standing in the roll call line right now and—"

The sergeant confiscated the phone and sternly reprimanded the fresh fish. "The captain does not allow cell phones in camp. We're fighting in the Civil War, not the cellular war."

The roll call continued without electronic interruption. Afterward, the men started their breakfast fires to cook bacon. Gordon passed on the fried fat fest and would have shown up for sick call if he hadn't drawn guard duty. He headed over to the tree line to relieve Pat, who had stood watch at the edge of the camp through the night.

When he found him, he inquired, "Any Nationals?"

"You can see their pickets from here." Pat pointed to the hill. "They don't seem to be a threat right now, but keep an eye on them. I'm going to go get some breakfast."

Gordon only had to watch two thousand Union reenactors compared to the 73,000 non-reenactors General Lee had to keep an eye on after the Seven Days Battles in 1862. The Union Army had retreated to Berkeley for protection provided by Federal gunboats in the James River. Gordon surveyed the historic landscape.

Berkeley Plantation, twenty-two miles downriver from Richmond at Harrison's Landing, was the birthplace of the ninth US president, William Henry Harrison. On July 8, 1862, the sixteenth US president, Abraham Lincoln, visited the plantation, conferring with General McClellan and confirming McClellan was not the right man to lead the Army of the Potomac. Around the same time, the bugle call "Taps" was arranged and played here for the first time, a sad foreshadowing of how much longer the war would last.

As soon as Pat was out of sight, Gordon walked over to a tree, laid down his rifle, and sat down using the tree trunk as a backrest. He pulled out a thermos and a newspaper hidden from the authenticity police from underneath his shell jacket. He poured some coffee into a tin cup. He shouldn't have had the brew. The Union blockading of Southern ports during the Civil War forced the Confederates to turn to coffee substitutes. But Gordon wasn't substituting his java for acorns, chinquapins, persimmons, or anything else for anybody. He settled in with the latest edition of the *Civil War News* until he heard some rustling leaves in the woods beside him. He put down his newspaper and reached for his gun with his free hand. A violent sneeze came out of the thicket, catching Gordon off balance and causing him to slosh his coffee. Stumbling out of the woods to greet Gordon was a slight, sullen teenage boy in a gray sack coat with long, curly black hair growing out from underneath his battered, mashed-down derby. It was Raleigh and Gayle's son Jimmy, eating a big bag of Doritos.

"Jeez, Jimmy. You scared the hell out of me. Your allergies bothering you?"

Jimmy gripped a corn chip, and with the back of his hand, brushed away the hair hanging in his face, rubbed his nose, and wiped one of his watery eyes. "Yeah, they're pretty bad this year." Jimmy offered the snack bag to Gordon. "You want some? They're a lot better than hardtack."

"Why not?" Gordon reached for the junk food. "Have a seat. What's going on?"

"Not much."

"I didn't see you at the dance last night."

"I just stayed here."

"Where did you pitch your tent?"

Jimmy pointed to a spot between the Rebel and Yankee lines.

"Why are you sleeping in no man's land by yourself?"

"Dad doesn't want me in camp because he says I'm not authentic enough."

"Oh man, sometimes your father is too hard core."

"I really don't want to be in the Southern camp anyway with Mom and Dad fighting all the time. Dad tells me I need to grow up and asks me why I can't be more like Hezekiah. He says I embarrass him." Jimmy shook his head and pointed at his chest. "I embarrass him? Gordon, no offense to you and Hezekiah, but is this all I have to look forward to when I grow up? Wearing a Confederate uniform?"

"I don't know. I haven't grown up yet."

In the early afternoon, the units had broken up from drill. The soldiers had a little free time before reporting back for the Battle of Gaines's Mill. Pat waited nervously in line for the Porta-Potty, keeping an eye out for Mary Beth. He was second in line when he saw her coming across the field in her bell-shaped skirt, holding a parasol.

"Oh, God," he said with a quiet dread.

The stall vacated and a young woman with short, spiky black hair in front of him noticed his unease. "You look like you need to go worse than I do. Why don't you go ahead?"

"Are you sure?" Pat looked over his shoulder as Mary Beth approached. She hadn't spotted him yet.

"Sure, go ahead."

"Would you mind holding this for me?" Pat handed his Enfield to the willowy lady in blue jeans. He dashed in and relieved himself, then peered through the side plastic vent to see if Mary Beth had passed. He couldn't see her, but he could hear her.

"You haven't seen a man who's tall and skinny, blond hair, clean-shaven, a really handsome fellow?" Mary Beth said to the woman holding Pat's gun.

"No, haven't seen anybody like that. All these reenactors look the same to me."

Mary Beth twisted a curled end of her bottle-blond hair. "Now that's a nice Enfield. My boyfriend has one just like that. Are you holding that for your boyfriend?"

"Just a new acquaintance."

Hot, stuffy, and stenchy in the toilet, Pat started sweating. He wondered how much longer he could stay in the plastic cocoon. The potty at the far end of the row became available.

"You may want to go down there," the lady said to Mary Beth. "I think this one's going to be a while." In a minute, Pat heard a soft voice through the polyethylene door. "It's safe now."

Pat came out sheepishly.

"Here's your gun back. So was that your girlfriend?"

"No, she's not my girlfriend."

"That's not what she thinks."

"I know. Thanks for helping me out of a jam. I'm Pat McCandlish." He offered his hand but quickly withdrew it.

"Hi, I'm Ann Calico. I guess you'll want to leave before she comes out."

"She'll be in there awhile with that skirt."

"Then wait for me. I'll only be a minute." Ann ducked into the toilet.

When she came out, Pat stammered, "Can I buy you a root beer at Dr. Fogworth's to pay you back?"

"Sure."

"Their tent is right down the hill." They started walking toward it, and Pat oscillated, looking at the lady he had just met and peering over his shoulder for the one he had left behind. "Didn't I see you at the dance last night, wearing a green dress?"

"Yes, I was there."

Pat noticed her green eyes. "So were you there with your boyfriend?"

"No, I was there with a girlfriend. What do you do when you're not in uniform?"

"I'm a structural engineer," Pat said flatly, then struggled to figure out what to say next. "What do you do?"

"When I'm not giving safe harbor to reenactors?"

"Yeah." Pat turned a little red.

"I'm a fourth-grade teacher at Fox Elementary."

They arrived at the stand for Dr. J. Fogworth's Indian Tonics and Elixirs. Behind the counter, an overweight black woman poured pop from wooden kegs into glass bottles, then added a cork to seal them.

"Root beer okay?" Pat asked. "They have cream soda too."

"I'll take a cream soda."

"What size would you like?"

"A small is all I need."

"One small cream soda and one small root beer," Pat ordered, then turned back to Ann. "So you must be interested in reenactors? I mean reenacting."

"I thought I might get some ideas for teaching Virginia history to my students."

"Are you from Virginia?"

"No, I'm from Kansas."

"Ah, a Jayhawker."

"Are you a basketball fan?"

Pat shook his head. "Closet abolitionist."

Ann smiled.

Pat grinned back. "What brings you to the Old Dominion?"

"I went to school at the University of Richmond and decided to get a job here. Are you between battles?"

"I am and I'm going to be late for my next one if I don't go, but you should come and watch us fight at two thirty. We win this one, and I don't even have to die." Pat paid for the soda and handed Ann a bottle. "Thanks again for helping me out. It was great to meet you." He paused and blurted out, "There's a reception at the Virginia Historical Society Monday night." Pat's voice started to shake. "It's for a Civil War photography exhibit. Would you like to come? Maybe you could get some more ideas for your students."

"That sounds nice."

Pat, surprised by her response, asked again just to make sure, "So you would like to come?"

"Definitely."

"Where do you live?"

"I'm in the Fan on West Avenue. I could walk to the historical society from my place to join you."

"No, I can give you a ride. It starts at seven. I could pick you up around six forty-five."

"Okay."

"Would you write down your address and phone number for me?" Pat pulled out a small journal and pencil from the breast pocket of his shell jacket.

As the sun dropped in the sky, Gayle stirred stew in a big black kettle shaped like her skirt. The pot hung over an open fire, and she was working the pottage with a wooden oar when Captain Fuqua rode in on his horse at the end of the day. He dismounted, took one look at Gayle, and bellowed, "Woman, the soldiers are ready to eat. Hurry up with their supper."

She shoved the oar into the stew and stepped away from the caldron. "Why don't you feed them yourself?"

Raleigh, caught off guard by her reply, lowered his voice and leaned toward her to prevent his men from hearing him. "Gayle, you're not doing your first person impression properly. Let's try it again. You address me as *Sir*."

Gayle swiftly pulled the oar out of the pot, raised it above her head, and hurled it at the captain. She missed him but spattered his uniform with the soup.

Shock went over Raleigh's face. "You have soiled the uniform of an officer of the Army of the Confederate States of America."

"That's right, and you're going to have to take it to the dry cleaners yourself."

"Is something bothering you, Gayle?"

"Yeah, something is bothering me. I spent all morning at the Kids' Tent teaching little children how to roll rifle cartridges. I spent all afternoon standing over this damn pot, sucking in wood smoke, while you and your buddies are out riding your horses and shooting off your guns. And the only attention I get from you is to tell me to hurry up with supper."

"I was just reenacting."

"Well, why don't you reenact something a little more worthwhile like our marriage?"

"I do not care to discuss this in front of my men."

"Why not? They already know you're an asshole."

Raleigh's company, standing in a semicircle watching the domestic disturbance, snickered at Gayle's comment, then nervously dispersed.

Raleigh grabbed Gayle's wrist. "Look, we've been through all this with the counselor."

She jerked away. "I know, and it isn't working out. I took the counselor's advice and tried to become more involved with your interests. But you never got more involved with mine. I just can't take it anymore. Grown men dressing up, playing army. I'm tired of the nineteenth century. I want to live in the present."

"We're not playing army. We're celebrating our heritage."

"Maybe we should be mourning our heritage." She sat down on a stump and sobbed.

That night after the camp tours ended and the gates closed to the public, the soldiers gathered around the campfire. With the sun down and a drop in the humidity, it was almost comfortable in their wool until they eased close to the flames. The reenactors were pulled to the light despite the heat.

Gordon took a swig of busthead, passed the jug, puffed a cigar, and waved his arms like a choir director. "Everybody sing."

"I wish I was in the land of bottoms,
Good times there are not forgotten."

Everyone joined in the rowdy rendition of "Dixie" with X-rated lyrics. They finished up with a rousing cheer around the fire circle, followed by a tattoo drumbeat in the distance signaling for the final roll call of the day.

"Oh, suck my arse," Gordon screamed back into the darkness at the drummer. "I'm not going to bed right now." He turned back to the fire. "Gentlemen, I know you all wonder why I don the Confederate uniform. Is it because of my love of history, or is it because I wish to honor my Southern ancestry? Both of those things are part of it, but I put on the uniform mostly because I got tired of wearing women's clothing."

After the laughter died down, Pat stared into the fire and captured the audience with a lowered voice. "Or maybe we wear the uniform because we're not that crazy about the life we have or the world we live in. Every time I get on the interstate and have to battle for a pole position, or go shopping at Wal-Mart and have to battle to get my cart down the aisle, I know why I reenact. I just want to escape the modern swirl. Golf, deer hunting, or even Virginia Tech football doesn't seem to do it for me."

Raleigh jumped in to take the leadership role. "When I was a kid, I never played cowboys and Indians, I always played Civil War. I always wanted to be a Civil War soldier. Now, as an adult, I know there is a higher purpose, because I have come to understand what our ancestors went through. My mission today is to preserve and honor the memory of our forebears who fought so bravely for a just and noble cause. I want to make sure their story is told. And to do that, we have to educate the public and fight for battlefield preservation."

"Here, here," echoed around the circle with the exception of Pat, Gordon, and Hezekiah, rolling their eyes at each other over their captain's bluster.

Raleigh stayed on his high horse. "And that's what we're all about. Many of our families and friends don't understand our passion and commitment to living history. We've all read about the war, but you're never really going to learn about it until you live it. And it's not enough just to look like a Civil War soldier, you also have to think like one. And once you get out on that battlefield, it becomes real. You get so caught up in the moment, nothing else matters."

A graybeard from another unit, who had walked up to the fire and had been listening intently, spoke up with his eyes downcast underneath his forage cap. "I know when I was in Vietnam and out on patrol, I didn't know if I would see the end of the day. So every moment felt large, and I'd soak it all in because I knew this might be my last. It was a constant adrenaline flow, and it made me feel alive."

The stranger looked up into the campfire faces. "When one of my buddies died, I hated it, but then I loved it, because I was still living. I was still in the fight, and I didn't want it to stop. I'm at peace with myself now, but I still like to pretend I'm at war. It's like what Lee said at Fredericksburg, 'It is well that war is so terrible. We should grow too fond of it.'"

Everyone fell silent. All they heard was the crackle of the fire.

CHAPTER 8

The next day at lunchtime, Sutler's row buzzed with shoppers down by the river. Two lines of white canvas tents faced each other, set up on the terraced lawn beyond the formal gardens of the great Georgian plantation house. Merchants sold clothes, guns, and whatever else it took to supply today's Civil War soldier, civilian, or enthusiast.

Two little boys in period garb chased each other through the grassy street, shooting off their cap rifles. Women in their wide-load skirts bustled along the mall of tents. And Gordon and Hezekiah made their way down the row to the beat of a band playing "Rosin the Beau" underneath one of the canopies.

Gordon poked Hezekiah in the side. "Check out Scarlett O'Hara. Oh, and look at the blond in black."

A hand on Gordon's shoulder abruptly stopped the viewing exercise. It belonged to a New York Zouave wearing his signature baggy red pants. The man with big jowls looked more like a Shriner in his fez than someone imitating an American Civil War soldier imitating mid-nineteenth-century French military fashion. He cocked his eye at Gordon. "Shouldn't you be moving along, soldier?"

Gordon fired back. "We're not hurting nobody. Why don't you mind your own business and do everybody a favor and get out of those pajamas and put on a real soldier's uniform."

"This is a real soldier's uniform."

"Maybe for Walt Whitman." Gordon grabbed Hezekiah by the arm. "No need to fraternize with the mollies, Hezekiah. All they want to do is spoon you. That's why I hate these big events. They let anybody in."

The Zouave thumped his chest with his fist. "I'd rather be a private in the 5th New York than a general in any other outfit."

"Yeah, yeah, yeah. So how you been doing, Hiram?" Gordon reached out and vigorously shook the Zouave's hand.

Hiram George was the product of a mixed marriage. His mother was from Richmond and his father, like the fanatic abolitionist John Brown, was from Connecticut. His parents met in college, and after marrying lived in New York City for forty years. When Hiram's father died, Hiram's mother moved back to Richmond, fleeing the congestion and bad weather of the Northeast, and reacquainting herself with old friends and making new ones.

Hiram had generated a pile of money in the high-tech industry in California, selling his stock options before the crash in 2000. He decided to swear off trophy wives and retire early. He moved to Richmond to watch after his aging mother and to live out his fantasy of becoming a Southern gentleman. Hiram had lived in Richmond going on eleven years, but no matter how long he lived here, he would always be a Yankee to his neighbors. During his time in Richmond, he developed a new career. He used his business and organizational skills to move masses of men on reenactment battlefields and was one of the main organizers of this event. In his new passionate pursuit, he became well connected and well fed.

Gordon, one of the first people Hiram met when he moved to Richmond, introduced him to reenacting. They became friends while Gordon was doing some painting work on Hiram's house in Windsor Farms, Richmond's most exclusive neighborhood. Hiram found the young man refreshingly friendly, unlike his neighbors, even though they advertised themselves as famous for their hospitality. As a group, Hiram found the Richmond white establishment snooty, self-righteous, and in possession of a kind of smugness that made a society susceptible to slipping into a protracted conflict. Looking back, Hiram saw Gordon and himself hitting it off because neither one of them was "from around here."

Hiram glanced up the line of purveyors. "So what are you in the market for?"

Gordon bobbed. "Some horizontal refreshment."

"If you were looking to go down the line, I saw a stray cat a little ways down the lane." Hiram laughed heartily. "So are you ready to lose again today?"

"Maybe not."

"Maybe not?" Hiram looked at Gordon, puzzled. "It's not like you have room to maneuver. It's a straightforward script. You charge, we shoot, you die."

"We'll see." Gordon smiled and continued the banter with Hiram while Hezekiah wandered over to a sutler's tent full of paintings.

One painting caught Hezekiah's eye. It was *The Last Meeting of Lee and Jackson*, but instead of portrayed on their steeds in the Chancellorsville's moonlight, they were mounted at a well-lighted McDonald's drive-thru.

The sutler greeted Hezekiah. "Young man, you have an excellent eye. This painting is on the saber's edge of Civil War art. Why buy something trivial when you can buy something like this?"

Hezekiah shrugged. "I guess?"

The sutler persisted. "We all get tired of print after print of Pickett's Charge, the Iron Brigade, or Nathan Bedford Forrest. This painting will survive the test of time."

Hezekiah shrugged again. "I guess?"

Another teenage infantryman came up beside Hezekiah and whispered in his ear, "That painting sucks."

Hezekiah jumped back. "Kim?" He then leaned back in and whispered. "Kim, why are you dressed up like a soldier?"

"Because I'm tired of wearing those big skirts."

"Are you going to be in the battle?"

"Yeah, going to sneak in. Where's your uncle Gordon?"

Hezekiah looked over his shoulder. "He was over there talking to Hiram. I don't know where he is now."

Gordon had said good-bye to Hiram and was drawn over to a photographer, barking like a carnival caller in front of his odd-looking darkroom wagon known as a What-is-it.

"Get your image struck before you die. I'll mail it to your loved ones if you don't get the chance. Ambrotypes, tintypes, and *cartes de visites*. All with Mathew Brady quality."

Down the way from the photographer's wagon, Gordon heard music he had never heard at a reenactment before. He followed the sound to the end of the row and found two black minstrels playing. One had a banjo, the other a quaqua, a skin-covered gourd used as a drum.

These original blues reached across the historical timeline and mesmerized Gordon. Behind the musicians, he spotted a beautiful dark-skinned woman dressed as a fancy female. She smiled and approached Gordon.

"Welcome, sir. How long have you been in the field?"

Gordon panted. "Too long."

"I would like to thank you for your valor. Would you like to free me?"

"Emancipate you?"

"Yes, but it's going to cost you."

Gordon reached into his pockets to play along, but all he felt was one of his newfound double eagles he couldn't resist carrying around with him. He kept fishing in his pockets for other money, and the coin accidentally dropped onto the ground, along with his business card. The fancy girl scooped up the coin and the banjo player stepped on the card without missing a lick.

Gordon grabbed the coin away. "You can't have that."

"Then you can't have me, Johnny. Get out of here."

CHAPTER 9

Hezekiah clung to a branch twenty feet up in a bald cypress by the river in the early evening and heard huzzahs over on "Malvern Hill." It wasn't the real Malvern Hill, a gem of the Richmond National Battlefield Park, but a designated hilltop at Berkeley Plantation serving as General Lee's objective for today's reenactment.

"What's all the cheering about?" Raleigh hollered up, standing by the trunk of the tree.

"It may be Little Mac reviewing the troops," Hezekiah yelled down, looking through field glasses.

"You mean 'Little Coward,'" Raleigh shouted skyward. "They shouldn't be giving that bastard huzzahs. He needs to go on back to his gunboat to move out of harm's way so the men can fight."

Hezekiah took a closer look through the glasses. "Wait a minute, they're not cheering McClellan. I think they're cheering Henry Hunt."

"What are they cheering him for?" Raleigh asked.

Hezekiah watched as a group of Federal soldiers stood around the artillery commander on horseback. The horse collapsed. Another big huzzah went up.

"He's practicing having his horse shot out from under him."

"They shouldn't be treating an animal like that. Come on down. It's about time to get into formation."

With their assigned parts to play, the reenactors on both sides positioned themselves for battle. The Confederate infantry lined up in the woods at the bottom of the hill. The Federal artillery and infantry massed at the top of the hill. Battle flags lay flat against their staffs. There was no cool of the evening, just thick Virginia summer air. It had been a long day in wool.

The hydraulic lift on a bucket truck rose on the edge of the field. Inside the loft, a cameraman prepared to film the action, while Hiram squeezed in beside him and spoke into a walk-ie-talkie, directing the order of battle. A deputy sheriff rode up the sideline in a golf cart with a rebel flag flying from the back, motioning spectators to move behind the crime-scene tape. General Lee rode by on Traveller, waving like a beauty queen on the back of a Buick, and the crowd applauded with adulation. A small plane flew overhead, dragging a banner advertising high-speed Internet service, while the artillerists wondered if they could shoot it down.

A voice came over loudspeakers placed in trees along the border. "Welcome, ladies and gentlemen, to the Battle of Malvern Hill, the last of the Seven Days Battles. Today's battle is sponsored in part by the caring people at Charles City Landfill Corporation, taking pride in taking out your garbage."

An antsy spectator looked at his watch. "It's seven thirty. Let's get this fight started."

One of the thirty-seven Federal cannons perched on the crest of the hill opened the ball by ejaculating a giant smoke ring and rattling eardrums. General Lee's left grand battery returned fire, but with only sixteen artillery pieces, the Confederates were out-gunned more than two to one. Lee's not-so-grand right battery rolled up one cannon at a time, causing the Federals on Malvern Hill to split their fire. The Federals threw their heavy metal, plug-ging both Confederate positions.

While the mismatched artillery duel went on, the Federal green-uniformed Berdan's sharpshooters cautiously moved for-ward to get within range of the Confederate artillery crews, using wheat shocks as cover in the freshly cut field. To chase off the skirmishers, Confederate General Lewis Armistead ordered the 14th Virginia Infantry, portrayed by Raleigh's regiment, along with the 38th and 53rd Virginia Infantry, to advance.

The three reenacting regiments moved with deft quickness, even the tubby, bearded guys, known as the TBGs, all stimulated by the adrenaline flow of being in the moment. Shooting and screaming, Armistead's men made the sharpshooters scatter back through the smoke-filled battlefield. The Confederate regiments came under heavy fire from Malvern Hill, forcing them to advance farther to obtain shelter in a shallow gully.

"This is the part I hate," Jimmy grumbled to Gordon beside him. "We just have to lie on our stomachs in this ditch for the rest of the show."

"Not this time," Gordon said.

Pat looked over at Gordon, wondering what Gordon knew that he didn't.

Raleigh unnecessarily screamed at Hezekiah, who was lying directly beside him. "Make sure you hold our colors high so the Yanks can put holes in it."

Hezekiah straightened his wooden staff so the imaginary bullets could penetrate their company banner.

As the battle progressed, Lee reconnoitered with Longstreet, looking for a way to flank the Federals, when he received two messages. One from General Magruder, on the right, reported Armistead making a significant advancement up the hill, repelling the enemy. The second one, from General Whiting on the left, reported the Yankees retreating. In reality, Armistead's advance men remained pinned down and the Yanks weren't retreating. They were just moving in fresh cannons.

With bad intelligence, Lee thought he had McClellan on the run. He issued orders for Magruder to attack so the enemy wouldn't get away.

"Prince John" Magruder earned his nickname from his flamboyance and high living, but was taken down a notch a couple of days before when Lee reprimanded him at Savage's Station for not being aggressive in pursuing the enemy. Magruder knew this wasn't going to be a show of strength like the one he had given at Yorktown three months earlier, faking out the Federals into believing they were outnumbered. This was the real dance, and Magruder was going to have to accept the gage, following his boss's orders no matter what the ground looked like. His judgment most likely was clouded from lack of sleep and food, and from his morphine-based medication for indigestion. The reenactor playing Magruder tried to emulate the general's state of mind with an overdose of cough syrup.

The problem was Magruder knew he had to attack but couldn't because his men were in the back of the line. They were late for their deployment because Magruder had spent most of the day marching them down the wrong road. The men in the front of the line were General Benjamin Huger's, and Huger was located two miles behind his men and had no intention of attacking. Magruder asked Huger's men to attack, and they obliged. They hadn't seen action during the first six days of the Seven Days Battles and were anxious to get in on the fight on the seventh day.

The men came out of the woods, roaring rebel yells, intending to run 400 yards up a coverless slope to the top of a 150-foot hill as all forms of munitions rained down on them from the summit. The slaughter of the Confederates began in earnest with no chance of them penetrating the Federal line.

After hearing the battle initiated by the drugged-up Magruder, Confederate General D. H. Hill on Lee's left believed it to be Armistead's men advancing, signaling him to move out. Hill ordered his entire division to attack based on an outmoded three-and-a-half-hour-old dispatch from Lee. Instead of attacking *en masse*, Hill's five brigades took turns making forlorn-hope charges up the hill against the Federal line.

The Federal reenactors' cannons on top of Malvern Hill continued belching blue smoke, accompanied by echoing booms. The charging Confederate reenactors responded with their choreographed imitation of "autumn leaves falling in the wind," some applying fake blood after hitting the ground. Many who took hits did their best to look immediately like a stiff and bloated corpse with a one-knee-up Antietam death pose, without giving rigor mortis time to set in. Some cried out in pain or for their mothers or water or all three. Others attempted to reproduce the "singular crawling effect" described by Colonel William W. Averell of the 3rd Pennsylvania Cavalry the morning after the actual battle as he watched the logjam of wounded men trying to move around the battlefield. But a few just propped themselves up and watched the action while smoking unsanctioned cigarettes or filming with unauthorized smartphones.

The ground was littered with the bodies of Confederate reenactors, falling between one hundred and two hundred yards from their objective. Night was coming on and the firing lulled. The fog of war and the smell of the gunpowder diminished. The battle appeared to be over when the Confederate who had made it closest to the Federal line, the sixth and last-to-die color bearer of the 3rd Alabama, resurrected, and with a rebel yell, moved defiantly forward carrying a flagless staff.

Gordon popped up from the ravine. "That's our cue. Come on, boys, let's salvage this battle."

"What are you doing? Get down," Raleigh commanded.

The dead, wounded, and pinned down men of Magruder, Huger, and Hill followed suit by rising up and joining the charge. The skulkers in the rear, who had avoided throwing themselves on the ground to prevent dirtying their freshly dry-cleaned uniforms, were close behind.

Giving in to peer pressure, Raleigh could no longer resist breaking from the battle's plotline. He placed his hat on his sword and pointed the way forward for his men who had already left him behind.

From the crown of Malvern Hill, as the big guns cooled, the Federal infantry recommenced firing. But the butternuts came on, all refusing to die even when shot point-blank. They hadn't driven hours in their cars just to fall on the ground.

Hiram observed the scene from on top of the crane. "Damn them to hell. What are they doing? This isn't in the script."

Henry Hunt pretended to have his horse shot out from under him again. The reenactor portraying Fitz John Porter, the Federal V Corp Commander, screamed, "Not now, you idiot."

Horse and Hunt recovered. "We need reinforcement."

Porter's forehead twitched, completely offended by the affair. "Meagher's Irish Brigade won't make a difference. These men aren't playing by the rules. They've screwed up a perfectly good reenactment."

In the dusk, the Confederates broke through the Federal line. The Southern spectators reveled in the turn of events.

Fitz John Porter pointed to the first man to cross the line. "I'll be reporting you to the Committee on the Conduct of Reenacting. It's this kind of behavior that makes us never want to go south of Fredericksburg to reenact."

The man ignored him and went for the flag of the 1st Rhode Island Light Artillery. A wrestling match ensued over the colors as more Confederates poured over the line.

During the battle, General McClellan stayed as far away from the fight as possible to be considered still on the field. But General Lee had been in the center of the tempest, directing his troops from his headquarters in the saddle. When Lee's impersonator saw his troops breech the Federal line, a smile ran across his face, for today the Battle of Malvern Hill was won, even

though it was Lee's lopsided loss on July 1, 1862. Out of character for the general, the reenactor waved his hat and whooped,
causing Traveller to rear up. The general brought his arm back
down from over his head, covered his chest with his hat, and fell
off his horse. He lay on the ground as the celebrating Army of
Northern Virginia strutted around the batteries of the Army of
the Potomac, amid spotty hand-to-hand combat.

CHAPTER 10

"I can't believe Marion is dead. We'll never have a better General Lee," Raleigh kept saying while folded over like a piece of white bread as the passenger in Jimmy's little orange Hyundai Excel as they drove home from the reenactment. Gayle had left early and taken Raleigh's Ram, pulling the horse trailer with his horse in it. They kept the horse at Gayle's sister's place, and that's where Gayle had gone to stay for a while.

Jimmy pulled his subcompact into the driveway of "little Tara" around eleven that night. All of the lights in their house were on.

"Damn it, Jimmy, you piss me off so much when you leave the lights on."

"I didn't leave the lights on. I'm not five years old anymore."

Raleigh threw his hands up. "If you didn't, who did?" Then slowly, Raleigh let his hands down. "Oh, your mom must have come by before she went to your aunt Linda's and left them on."

They got out of the car and stumbled wearily up the front walk.

"I can't wait to get out of this uniform and take a shower," Raleigh said as he reached to put his key in the lock, but the door was already slightly open. "She left the door unlocked too?" Pushing the door the rest of the way open, he discovered the inside was in shambles. "Damn it, she didn't have to tear the house apart. This is uncalled for."

Raleigh's face turned crimson with anger. He reached for the home phone and pressed the speed-dial button for his sister-in-law. When he placed his ear to the phone, he didn't hear a dialing sequence but instead was greeted by a man's voice.

"We want the gold for the New Confederacy," the voice came roughly over the line.

Raleigh's head jerked. "Gordon, if this is you, I'm not in the mood."

"We are the Compatriots. We want the gold for the New Confederacy. We saw where you found the gold, so I wouldn't call the police if I were you, unless you want to go to jail. You've got two hours to bring it to us, or we're coming back to your house to get it."

Raleigh turned from angry to scared, looking around his ransacked house. "Bring it where?"

"Do you know where Marlbourne is?"

"Yes."

"If you value your life and your family, meet us at the gates of Marlbourne with the gold in two hours."

Raleigh was silent and the caller hung up. He slowly placed the phone back in its carriage.

"Who was that on the phone, Dad?"

"I don't know." Raleigh looked around in desperation. He held his forefinger perpendicular to his lips, grabbed Jimmy by the arm, and motioned with his head to follow him. They walked back outside, and Raleigh opened the passenger door for Jimmy. "I'll drive. Give me your keys."

"Where are we going? We just got home."

"I don't know, but we can't stay here."

"What's going on?"

"Just get in the car."

Jimmy stayed silent until they were out of the driveway. "What's going on, Dad?"

"I shouldn't tell you, but you're going to find out anyway." Raleigh looked all around as he stepped on the gas. "That was a guy on the phone who wanted our gold."

"What gold?"

"Gordon, Pat, Hezekiah, and I found $75 million worth of old gold coins near Berkeley on Friday."

"You found what?"

"Gold coins. It's so much gold we think it's connected to the Confederate treasury. But someone must have seen us dig it up, and they want it for themselves."

"Where's it now?"

"It's at Gordon's. We've got to call him, but we'd better call your mom first and tell her not to come back to the house."

Jimmy pulled out his cell phone, forbidden by his father at the reenactment.

Raleigh shook his head. "No cell phones. These people may be listening in. They may be watching us. We've got to go some-place crowded with a landline."

Raleigh drove west on Midlothian Turnpike past the car deal-erships and the strip malls. After a mile and a half, he was satis-fied they weren't being followed. He turned onto Koger Center Boulevard and pulled into a hotel parking lot. They walked in the side entrance as music from a band playing at the adjacent Visions Dance Club flowed into the hallway.

A woman tending the dance hall door, sucking on an unlit cigarette, tossed Raleigh a saucy look. "The cover is eight bucks."

The bouncer intervened. "Sorry, gentlemen, this isn't a gay bar."

Raleigh puffed out his chest. "We're not gay. We're Confederate soldiers." Raleigh retrieved a US dollar among his Confederate currency in his wallet and handed it to the lady. "We just need change for a payphone."

The big beefy man looked Raleigh up and down, then winked at him. "Clara Barton and I can't help you, since we don't have any payphones, but you can use the house phone over there if it's a local call."

Raleigh stepped over to the white phone and dialed his sister-in-law's number.

"Hello," a half-awake voice said.

"Hello, Linda. This is Raleigh. Can I speak to Gayle?"

"She's asleep and I was too. I gave her one of my sleeping pills. I think you've talked to her enough already."

"Linda, it's important you tell her not to come back to the house."

"Oh, don't worry. I don't think she's ever coming back to your house."

"I'm serious, Linda. It would be dangerous for her to come back."

"What do you mean it's dangerous? Is the roof falling in? I told you, you needed to get that fixed, but you're so cheap, Raleigh."

"It's not that. There's people who want to hurt us."

"Hurt you? Are you involved with drugs?"

"No."

"Then what is going on?"

"I can't say. Just make sure Gayle doesn't go back to the house anytime soon. Tell her I'll call again as soon as I can and that I love her."

"Where are you now?"

"I don't want to say."

"You don't want to say? You must be in deep, Raleigh. It sounds to me like you're at a party. Are you running around on Gayle already, and who's taking care of Jimmy?"

"I'm not running around on Gayle, and Jimmy is with me." Raleigh, not used to being on the receiving end of a grilling, couldn't take it, and his sarcasm bubbled up. "You've always been so understanding, Linda."

"Don't be a prick your whole life, Raleigh."

Raleigh heard a loud click in his ear and began to tremble but managed to dial Gordon.

The phone rang a few times, and Raleigh urged an answer. "Come on, Gordon, pick up, pick up."

"Your humble and obedient servant, Gordon Barrett."

"Gordon, this is Raleigh," he said almost inaudibly.

"Raleigh? I thought you'd be in bed by now."

"Look, Gordon, somebody saw us find the gold."

"What?"

"Somebody saw us find the gold, and they want it for themselves. Some guy called me and told me the Compatriots want the gold for a New Confederacy."

"The Compatriots? A New Confederacy?"

"They said if I don't deliver the gold to them in two hours, they're coming back to my house to get it."

"Whoa, whoa, whoa. When did all this happen?"

"When Jimmy and I came home tonight, we found the house tossed. I thought Gayle had done it, and when I picked up the phone to call her, this guy was already on the line, demanding the gold."

"What else did he say?"

"That I shouldn't go to the cops unless I wanted to go to jail. Look, Gordon, if they found my house, they're going to find your apartment. We'd better get the gold out of there."

Gordon gathered his thoughts. "Let me call Pat, and we'll decide where to move it."

"Okay, but let's move it tonight. I don't think we can wait till tomorrow."

"Where are you now?"

"We're at Visions."

"Let me call Pat first, then I'll call you back."

Gordon hung up, got Pat on the line, and filled him in.

Pat volunteered. "We could hide the gold out here at the farm. We could bury it in one of my fields, and I can put Raleigh and

Jimmy up until things subside. It would probably be safer for you and Hezekiah to stay out here, too, for a few days."

"That's a good idea. I'll call Raleigh back and tell him to meet me at my apartment to help me load up the gold, and we'll be over at your place as soon as we can."

After burying the gold in Pat's cornfield, Gordon and Hezekiah went back to the apartment to pack some extra clothes. The door was ajar. With caution, Gordon pushed it open. His Civil War prints were on the brown carpet and had been stepped on. His extensive collection of Civil War books were pulled out of their shelves, and scrawled on the wall in black spray paint were the words, "The Gabrielites Will Have Your Gold. Death or Liberty."

They stared at the graffiti with their mouths hanging open.

"The Gabrielites? Who are the Gabrielites?" Hezekiah asked.

"Gabrielites, Gabriel?" Gordon mumbled, then got the message. "Oh man, in Virginia before Nat Turner, there was Gabriel. His motto was Death or Liberty." He shivered. "Let's go back to Pat's before whoever did this comes back."

"What about the clothes?"

"Forget them. Let's just get out of here."

Gordon's ringtone of "The Girl I Left Behind" went off in his pants pocket, and they both jumped. Hezekiah looked at Gordon. "It might be Pat or Raleigh."

Gordon nodded and answered the phone. "Your humble and obedient servant, Gordon Barrett."

"Mr. Barrett?"

Gordon recognized the bluesy voice. It was the black woman from Sutler's row. "Yes," he hesitantly confirmed.

"You need to bring us the gold."

Gordon didn't say anything.

"Mr. Barrett, bring the gold to the parking lot above Young's Spring in Bryan Park tomorrow evening at eight o'clock. The gold is rightfully ours for the establishment of our nation. Bring us the gold, and we'll not harm you or your friends. We'll be waiting for you."

Gordon and Hezekiah drove up the dirt road to Pat's farm. Pat, Raleigh, and Jimmy were sitting on the front porch with their Enfields when they saw the headlights coming through the thick fog. They sprung up to take aim, then realized it was Gordon and Hezekiah. Gordon parked the car and they got out.

"You weren't followed, were you?" Raleigh asked through the mist.

"No, but we've got other problems," Gordon returned.

"Other problems? What other problems?"

Gordon and Hezekiah walked through the gate and onto the porch. Gordon explained. "When we got back to my apartment, someone had sacked it."

"Damn, they found you too. We got the gold out just in time."

"No, someone else found us. Somebody spray-painted a message on my living room wall. It said, "The Gabrielites Will Have Your Gold. Death or Liberty."

Raleigh looked confused. "Gabrielites?"

"As in Gabriel's Rebellion. I think it's safe to say whoever broke into my apartment is not associated with the New Confederacy. Before we left, I got a call from a woman who wanted me to bring the gold for the establishment of their nation to Young's Spring tomorrow evening at eight."

"Young's Spring? Where's that? And what nation?"

"Young's Spring over in Bryan Park. It's where Gabriel, the enslaved blacksmith, met with his followers in 1800 to organize the largest slave revolt in US history."

Hezekiah interrupted. "But it never happened. A flooded creek blocked the road to Richmond, and Gabriel was captured and hung."

"That's right." Gordon looked at Hezekiah, surprised he knew the ending. "Gabriel wanted to end slavery in Virginia, and my guess is these new disciples of Gabriel want to establish a black state and they want our gold to make it happen."

Pat had been taking it all in. "The Compatriots saw us find the gold, but how did the Gabrielites find out about it?"

Gordon shamefully confessed. "I spoke to this really good-looking black woman at Berkeley yesterday on Sutler's row. I'm sure it was her on the phone tonight. I was flirting with her and one of the double eagles dropped out of my pocket."

Raleigh jumped down Gordon's throat. "What were you doing carrying around the double eagles?"

"It was only one of them."

Pat thought aloud. "But she only saw one coin. How would she know we have 5,000 of them? Sterling is the only one we've told about the gold."

Raleigh snorted. "I'm sure Sterling didn't tell them, and at this point, it doesn't matter how they found out. The real question is, How long is it going to take the Compatriots or the Gabrielites to track us here? And can we hold our position?"

"If we can't hold this position, there's no position we can hold," Pat said. He looked into the fog, knowing the lay of his land in front of him. Like a miniature Malvern Hill, Pat's farmhouse stood at the top of a gently sloping prominence. The sixty-yard dirt driveway led down to a creek with a small bridge to the main road. The property also could be accessed from the back via an old wagon road, providing an escape route.

The idea of building a defensive position energized Pat in the early morning hour. "Raleigh, would you be willing to bring your backhoe in here, dig a trench line, and throw up an earth-work around the house?"

"I can do it, and I can dam up the creek while I'm at it, and you can put together that pontoon bridge you've been wanting to try out."

Pat had been wanting to try out a lot of things. He made a living as an engineer, but his true love was building all things Civil War. He had built a watchtower and a bombproof behind his house. His latest home-improvement project was a circle of fraise around his residence, broken only by the front and back gates. The low fence of sharp wooden stakes, slanted outward at a 45-degree angle, protected his home against an infantry attack.

Pat pointed to the far side of his property. "We can clear some of those trees over there for abatis and run some tripwires."

Gordon shook his head. "Time out. We're talking about fighting people who are likely armed to the teeth with semi-au-tomatic weapons, and we're going to defend ourselves with Civil War fortifications?"

"We're not talking about making a frontal assault," Raleigh said. "We're just talking about holding an entrenched position, or at the least, constructing fortifications that would provide us with the ability for a delaying action so we can retreat. It's just a precaution until we get things straight with Sterling."

"It's fortifications we're probably never going to need," Pat reassured them. "The Compatriots and the Gabrielites are both probably a membership of one, just a couple of nutcases, all flap and no throttle. And there's no shortage of those in Richmond."

Jimmy looked at Raleigh. "Maybe we just need to call the police, Dad, and get it over with."

"Oh, it will be over then. We'll all be going to jail. Remember those guys that got caught pilfering the Petersburg National Battlefield a few years back? They sent them straight to prison."

"Let's all take a seat and calm down," Pat said. "This is all going to be over in a couple of days once Sterling helps us unload the gold. I'm sure we have nothing to worry about." Pat leaned back in his chair. "I think I'm going to try to get some sleep before I go to work."

Gordon's face contorted. "You're going to work? I'm calling in sick."

"I've got a project I have to wrap up. It's probably better if we just carry on as normal rather than hiding out. We won't arouse suspicion and will draw less attention to ourselves if we just go about our normal business."

Raleigh looked at Pat with a doubtful face. "I don't know. You're not the one who had their house trashed, phone tapped, and life threatened tonight."

"I think we'll be safe if we just take proper precautions."

Raleigh yielded. "You're probably right. We do need to carry on as usual and just be careful. Whoever is after our gold most likely is loony and won't really harm us."

"I'm still calling in sick. It makes me ill to think about what they did to my Mort Künstlers and Don Troianis."

"Do what you want to do," Raleigh said. "I have a big planting job tomorrow. I mean later this morning. I have to be up early anyway to pick out my Mexicans. The boys were supposed to work with my crew today, but I'm sure they'll be worthless."

"Thanks, Dad."

Raleigh looked at Jimmy and Hezekiah. "You can sleep in, but since you'll be here holding down the fort, you might as well make yourselves useful. When you wake up, you can start cutting down trees for abatis. And Gordon, you can make sure they don't goldbrick. I won't be back until late tonight, but I'll be between jobs on Tuesday and can bring in my backhoe then and start digging out a ditch between the fraise and the house.

Pat, can you give me a ride down to Terminal Avenue to meet my crew before you go to work?"

Pat smiled without showing his teeth. "You don't want to drive yourself down to that dodgy neighborhood in Jimmy's old Excel?"

"I wanted to leave the Hyundai here for Jimmy in case there's some kind of emergency. If you could just drop me off, I can get a ride back with my foreman." Raleigh looked at Jimmy. "But I don't want you driving that car unless it's an absolute emergency."

Jimmy rolled his eyes, but said respectfully, "Yes, Dad."

Pat stood up. "We can sort this out more when Raleigh and I get home this evening, or it might have to wait until Tuesday morning. I almost forgot. I've got a date after work."

Gordon, with his slouch hat askew, looked at Pat. "You know, you may not want to carry on with everything as usual. This might be a good time to break it off with Mary Beth."

"It's not Mary Beth."

"Oh?" Gordon's curiosity piqued. "Who is it?"

"Come on," Pat said. "I'll show you all where you can sleep."

CHAPTER 11

Jimmy woke at noon, putting on his reenacting clothes from the night before, and hobbled downstairs to the kitchen. Gordon hovered over the table, also wearing his Confederate clothing because that's all he had.

"You want some pancakes?" Gordon offered as he rattled his car keys in his hand.

Jimmy, his mass of hair matted and eyelids not completely unsealed, muttered, "Yeah."

Gordon pointed toward a bowl of batter. "You're going to have to make them yourself. I'm on my way out. I have to run some errands. I should be back around suppertime."

"I thought you were supposed to be watching us."

"You'll be fine. I just need you and Hezekiah to start working on the abatis. There's a couple of chainsaws in the tool shed. When Hezekiah wakes up, you two can cut a few trees down, so you can show your father you did something."

"What if those people looking for the gold show up?"

"Nobody is going to find us out here."

"Then why do we have to build fortifications?"

"That's just to make your father and Pat feel good. I have to go," Gordon said as the back screen door swung behind him.

Hezekiah woke up in his Confederate wear when he heard the screen door slam shut and came downstairs. "What's for breakfast?"

"Pancakes. Let's eat and get out of here."

"Didn't your father want us to stay here and do some work?"

"Gordon left. Let's go down to the river and cool off. We'll be back before everybody else."

"Let's go to Belle Isle."

"No, let's go to the Pony Pasture. There's always more women there."

"I like it at Belle Isle."

"Of course you do, you geek."

Hezekiah's good nature deflected the gibe.

Jimmy relented. "Fine, we'll go to Belle Isle."

Gordon parked his car downtown on Grace Street. Most of the businesses on Grace had been boarded up for years, and most of the people on the sidewalks were homeless. Like other downtowns in America, Richmond had moved to the suburbs, but some new businesses were emerging on Grace, while some businesses had held on through the blight. One of them was Sy's Coins. The shop's windows were frosted, and the owner had to buzz Gordon in.

Sy Meyer, the old congenial Jewish proprietor, recognized Gordon from a previous visit and welcomed him to his sparse shop. "Good afternoon, Mr. Barrett, I haven't seen you for a while. How may I help you today?"

"I'm scouting the price of a few coins," Gordon said coyly. "I have a possible deal, and I wanted to double check their value."

Gordon pulled out his 1861 double eagle. "How much would you give me for this?"

"Let me take a look." Sy took the coin and placed it under his desk lamp. He examined it with interest. "I'll give you $1,379."

Gordon countered. "I found it listed on the web for $1,970."

"That's right. Seventy percent of 1,970 is 1,379. No dealer is going to give you more than 70 percent of the list price. I have to make a living on the resale, Mr. Barrett."

"What if I had a whole lot more to sell you?"

"How many more?"

"Five thousand counting that one, and they're all 1861 or earlier."

"Five thousand antebellum double eagles? Did you rob Fort Knox?"

"No, I found them."

"Right." Sy scratched his nose.

"What if I told you the coins came from the Confederate treasury?"

"Then they'd be worth a lot more money, and I don't have that kind of cash to buy them. But I'm sure I could work out a premium price for you through another dealer. You'd have to bring the coins in."

"To this neighborhood?"

"Or I'll come to your bank or your house to examine them, wherever you wish. I'm sure we could come to some arrangement."

"Let me see if my other deal works out first."

"Well, if it doesn't, you know where to find me. Give me your phone number and address so we can stay in touch."

Gordon wrote down his phone number. "Here's my number, but I'm staying with a friend right now. I'll call you if I want to do business. Thanks for the appraisal, Sy."

"Anytime, Mr. Barrett. Take one of my cards."

Gordon walked out the door, shoving Sy's card into his wallet, under the eye of a surveillance camera.

Sy picked up his phone. "Lichas, this is Sy."

"Do you have my money?"

"I've got something better."

"I'm listening."

"I just had a customer in here who says he has 5,000 Civil War era $20 gold pieces. We're talking coins worth millions of dollars."

"How many millions?"

"They're worth at least $7.5 million, maybe $75 million if they have historical significance."

"That would definitely cover your obligation to me."

"If he has them, he has them illegally, and there's no reason you can't take them off his hands. His name is Gordon Barrett. He's driving an old yellow Delta 88 convertible and the license plate is BUTRNUT."

"If this doesn't pan out, Sy, I'll be by to collect in full."

Jimmy looked out his open car window at the double, elevated train tracks running over the James River. A rope hung down from the trestle's underbelly. Teenagers lined up to swing out and drop into the water. "You want to do the rope swing while we're down here?"

"Not in these wool pants," Hezekiah said, looking out over the placid river. "'Let us cross over the river and rest under the shade of the trees.'"

Jimmy smirked. "Lee?"

"Stonewall Jackson, right before he died."

"Sometimes, Hezekiah, I think you're the son my father never had."

Jimmy drove his Excel a little farther down Tredegar Street where the trestle ran on dry land, and he parked under its shade because his air conditioner was broken. They left the windows rolled down with little chance of anyone wanting to steal the old, small car.

Jimmy and Hezekiah took the sidewalk leading to the 1,000-foot-long Belle Isle pedestrian bridge. The footbridge's concrete arch spans and aluminum guardrails made it look like a roller coaster track suspended from underneath the Robert E. Lee Memorial Bridge. Once on the hanging footpath, the constant west wind, funneling down the river, hit the boys in the face. Shaded from the summer solstice sun by the Lee Bridge above, the boys looked downriver and upriver at the granite basin of bedrock and boulders created 325 million years ago, when Africa collided into North America, pushing up the Appalachian Mountains.

The basin was the river's fall line, where it passed from the piedmont to the coastal plain. The falls of the James impeded the fish runs up the river, making the fish easier to catch, so the American Indians established villages here. When the white man showed up, the falls marked the end of the line for their oceangoing ships. Cargo had to be unloaded, and the commercial center of Richmond was born. The falls provided power to turn waterwheels for industry, and in the nineteenth century, some of America's largest flour mills were built here. Sailing ships filled with flour left Richmond for South America and returned with coffee, and guano for fertilizer. Today, the falls provided the best urban white water in the country.

From the middle of the bridge, Jimmy pointed to the figures upstream on the south bank. "Hey, I think I see some chicas on the rocks at the Hollywood Rapid."

At the end of the footbridge, they stepped out from under the shade of the big bridge and onto Belle Isle, a fifty-six-acre island in the river. The island was a wilderness in the middle of the city, furnishing refuge for wildlife, both natural and human.

The boys passed an overgrown field, partially surrounded by a dirt mound border two-and-a-half feet high. It marked the deadline for the Belle Isle Civil War prison camp, a precursor to Andersonville. If Union prisoners crossed the deadline, Confederate guards shot them. As many as ten thousand men at a time were corralled on these six acres. Around three thousand died during their internment on this sandy flat from illness, starvation, and exposure.

Jimmy and Hezekiah weren't thinking about the horrible suffering as they circumvented the location of the compound.

Jimmy had to ask Hezekiah, "So, have you had a first-rate time with Kim yet?"

"She's just my friend."

"But you want to have a first-rate time with her, right?"

"I guess."

"You guess?" Jimmy moaned and shook his head.

A mountain biker passed the boys as they slipped into a shady lane that sliced cleanly through a jungle of trees, grapevines, and poison ivy at the base of the island's wooded ridge. They walked a couple hundred yards beside the river, then hopped down to the river rocks, back into the sunlight to view Hollywood Rapid. A couple of kayakers floated to the brim of the rapid, then shot through the chute. The river level was normal and the rapid was relatively calm, but still deadly. The Class 3+ rapid with a six-foot drop got its name from its proximity to Hollywood Cemetery, located on the hill across from the swift water.

Jimmy surveyed the river. Anglers sought smallmouth bass, while great blue herons sought whatever fish they could swallow. A few mothers watched their kids closely at the temporary swimming hole above the big rapid. "No chicas today. I told you we should have gone to the Pony Pasture."

"I like it here." Hezekiah stared into the swirling green-and-white hypnotic hydraulics.

"It does beat cutting down trees for abatis." Jimmy paused to look at the fast-moving water. "Talking about work I don't want to do, I'm not looking forward to Civil War Camp in August."

"We'll have fun. They've got some great people to work with down there at the National Museum of the Civil War Soldier."

"I don't know, four weeks in Dinwiddie County. I just don't think I was cut out to be a camp counselor. I keep telling Dad I'm not Civil War material." Jimmy pulled out his gray bandana, pushed his raggedy hair aside, and blew his nose, still battling Richmond's exorbitantly high mold count.

Because of the noise of the water rushing between the granite, they didn't hear the man come up behind them. "How are you fellows doing?"

They were startled and turned around to see an olive-skinned man who spoke with a strange drawl.

"Okay?" Hezekiah said.

"It's a lovely spot," the man said in an accent, part Southern and part Portuguese. Underneath a straw hat, he had dark hair and dark eyes with a long face and a broad mustache. He looked downriver at the city's skyline, then returned his eyes to the boys. "My name is Ballard McMullan. I'm visiting from Brazil." He extended his hand.

The boys did not reciprocate. "Brazil?" Jimmy asked, puzzled. "What are you doing in Richmond?"

"I have a wealthy client who I'm representing."

"You a lawyer?"

"No, I'm a private investigator."

"What are you investigating?"

"I'm looking for gold coins that my client wants to buy."

"Gold coins?" Jimmy played dumb.

"My client is a collector. They say when the Civil War ended all the gold coins in the Confederate treasury in Richmond were never accounted for. My client is interested in finding and buying that gold. Do you boys know anything about it?"

"Why would we know anything about that?" Jimmy questioned.

"Just asking. But if you do hear something, give me a call. My client will pay top dollar. I can be reached at the Jefferson Hotel. I'll be in town for a while." He handed Jimmy a business card and walked away.

"We're going to have to tell Uncle about this," Hezekiah said with uneasiness in his voice.

Jimmy groaned. "I know. And Dad's going to find out I left the farm, and I'm going to be in trouble again."

CHAPTER 12

P at pulled his horse trailer with his silver Ford F-150 out the long, dirt driveway of his farm. He had inherited the farm from his parents. Pat's father hadn't worked the land but had kept horses and leased out the fields. He had made a good living as a machinist for Philip Morris for thirty-five years, and Pat's mother had kept house. Pat was their only child, and they had sent him to Virginia Tech. His father had retired three years ago. Coming back from a celebratory trip to Myrtle Beach, Pat's parents died in a car crash on Interstate 95.

Pat turned onto Osborne Turnpike, heading out of Varina. This section of Henrico County, east of Richmond, was named after John Rolfe's Varina Farms, established several miles away on the James River. Rolfe named his plantation after Varinas, Spain, where his tobacco seed stock had originated. His agricultural experiments with *Nicotiana tabacum* yielded America's first commercially cultivated tobacco in 1612. A successful tobacco crop meant a successful English colony. A successful colony meant more people growing more tobacco. And more tobacco growing meant a demand for slaves to do the backbreaking work required.

After all these years, Varina had managed to stay rural, but time was catching up, and Pat's boyhood Varina was disappearing. A 3,000-home development was slated to be built on Tree Hill Farm, where Richmond Mayor Joseph Mayo on the morning of April 3, 1865, rode out in a carriage to surrender the burning Confederate capital to Union General Godfrey Weitzel.

Pat wistfully surveyed the land where the super subdivision would sprout beside Highway 5, the same area where the great American Indian chief Powhatan, father of Pocahontas, was born in the mid-sixteenth century. He slowed his truck down to take in the view of the farmland by the river he knew would vanish.

He quickly hit downtown and rode on Main Street through a canyon of office buildings. On the day Mayor Mayo took his surrender ride, this business quarter was in the hub of a firestorm started by Confederate troops before evacuating the city. The fires were set to warehouses containing goods that might aid the conquering Yankees entering Richmond, but the flames were soon out of control. Thirty-five city blocks burned, around eight hundred buildings, consuming the core of the commercial and industrial center. Most of the homes in the city survived the conflagration, but there was nothing left to support those who lived in them.

Pat drove out of downtown to the Fan, a neighborhood of late-nineteenth and early-twentieth century town houses, noted for its harmonious architecture heavily influenced by the City Beautiful movement. The Fan was over a hundred city blocks in size and included Monument Avenue. The name referred to the manner its streets radiated to the west, giving the district the shape of a half-opened fan.

He gently maneuvered onto the intimate and charming West Avenue, a three-block-long, one-lane, one-way street. The turrets of Queen Anne town houses rose above the trees, lining the street. Looming above the house towers, a block away on Franklin Street was the copper-tarnished, forty-foot steeple of St. James's Episcopal Church, the church where Jeb Stuart worshipped and his funeral service was held.

Pat looked for Ann's address. At the end of the first block, he hit a pair of cobblestone speed bumps, placed there to protect the kids playing along the narrow street. Shiloh, who had been riding patiently in the trailer, made a distress snort when he felt the bumps. Pat found the address in the second block, but there was no place to park. He took a left onto an even narrower street and found a space to pull in. He unloaded Shiloh, walked him around the corner, and tethered him to a tree planted between the sidewalk and the road beside Ann's town house apartment. He rang the doorbell, and Ann looked out her window, recognizing Pat in his Confederate uniform.

She opened the door, giddy with the intoxication brought on by the anticipation of a first date that might work out. "Hi, how are you doing tonight?" Ann asked, flashing her green effervescent eyes.

"I-I-I'm fine," Pat stuttered. "You look great."

"Thanks. You look good, too. Do you always wear that uniform?"

"No, just on special occasions. This is my clean extra one."

Ann locked the door. "How far away did you have to park?"

"I'm right here."

Ann turned around and halted when she saw Shiloh on the sidewalk. "A horse? Do you know whose horse that is?"

"It's mine."

"Yours? Where's your car?"

"I don't have a car. I have a horse. I mean, I have a truck. I hauled my horse in from my farm, so we could ride him down to the historical society, if that's okay with you?"

"Sure," Ann said, not sure at all. Ann backtracked, "You know, I don't think I'm really dressed to ride a horse," she sputtered, standing on the sidewalk in a short green skirt, looking around to see if any of her neighbors were out.

"You'll do fine. Let me get on first." Pat untied Shiloh and hopped on the horse, then reached down for Ann. "Just put your foot in the stirrup. The other foot. Now take my hand and on the count of three jump up and swing your leg over. One, two, three, and up you go."

Ann straddled the horse with her long legs, landing on the back of the saddle, fitting tightly against Pat.

"Now reach around me and grab the saddle horn with both hands and hold on." Pat peered over his shoulder at Ann. "You all right?"

Ann nodded with trepidation, and off they clopped, past the tiny sidewalk gardens of flowers, shrubs, and ivy.

Making their way over to Park Avenue, Ann started warming up to the ride as the cooler air of the evening blew past them. Shiloh carried them down the claustrophobic corridor of homes. The road split, and they took a left at the small, triangular-shaped Meadow Park, a product of the fanning streets. At the apex of the park stood a refreshing statue of a colonial soldier.

The streets widened, revealing the architecture. Riding past Fox Elementary School where Ann taught, a little black boy on the school playground behind a chain-link fence screamed, "Miss Calico, Miss Calico." It was Aaron Bocock, a bright boy with a bright smile, one of Ann's best students. "Miss Calico, you're riding a horse."

Ann held on to the saddle horn and replied with delight. "It's my friend's."

They traveled two more blocks until forced to stop at a red light, receiving hoots and catcalls from the patio at Buddy's Place, a neighborhood bar. The light changed, and they progressed a couple more blocks where the avenue ended in a T at the Boulevard, a four-lane street with a small median strip, filled with tall crepe myrtles about to bloom. But there was no stoplight at this busy intersection, and it would take some negotiation.

Ann looked to her left and pointed with one finger off the horn at the building across the street. "I've always wondered. Is that a mausoleum?"

"You might say that." Pat grinned. "It's the headquarters of the United Daughters of the Confederacy, the UDC. Mary Beth is the president."

"Mary Beth?"

"The woman you saved me from at the sinks."

The traffic cleared and they crossed, veering onto the sidewalk.

To the right of the UDC headquarters stood the Virginia Historical Society. The original part of the neoclassical temple had been completed in 1913 by the Confederate Memorial Association to honor the Confederate dead. They called it the Battle Abbey, after the abbey established by William the Conqueror, the man who brought feudalism to England in 1066 after the Battle of Hastings. The only difference was William won his battle, but the Confederates lost their war. After the memorial association ran into financial difficulties, the Virginia Historical Society absorbed them in 1946 and moved in.

Pat and Ann rode Shiloh up the front steps of the historical society to a small lawn. The grassy patch contained a statue of a bent-over, broken-down, emaciated horse without a rider, donated by Paul Mellon. The engraving on the front of the granite base read:

> In memory of the one and one half million
> horses and mules of the Confederate and Union
> armies who were killed, were wounded, or died
> from disease in the Civil War.

Pat dismounted, then helped Ann down. He pushed his picket pin into the soft sod and tied Shiloh to it beside the horse statue as the sun set behind the historical society. Shiloh was satisfied to eat the grass as they walked around to the side entrance.

Greeting them as they walked through the door was a diminutive man with big tortoiseshell glasses on a cherubic face, dressed in a black suit and a burgundy bow tie. "Mr. McCandlish, how are you doing tonight? And who is this lovely creature you have with you?"

"This is Ann Calico. Ann, this is Julius Bohannon, the historical society's greatest treasure."

"You're too kind, young man." Julius reached out, clasping Ann's hand, and looked at her through his thick glasses. "Julius Bohannon at your service. I am one of the curators here at the Society." Julius leaned up to Ann's ear and whispered, "You'd better hold on to this one. I know I would." He glanced over at Pat. "He's looking so handsome in his uniform tonight, but my dear, you are truly the exquisite one." Julius then pulled back and lightly kissed Ann's hand.

Ann blushed and Pat smiled. "Julius, I left Shiloh out front."

"That is no problem whatsoever. It's refreshing to have a healthy animal out there instead of that poor beast that's with us all the time."

"So, how was your day, Julius?"

"How kind of you to ask, my dear boy. I was on the phone all day mediating with some dreadful people in Minnesota, trying to retrieve the flag of the 28th Virginia Infantry they stole from us at Gettysburg." Julius held the back of his right hand to his forehead. "Oh, it's just not worth talking about. Go get yourselves a drink and enjoy the exhibit."

The couple went over to the bar.

"So they know you here?" Ann said to Pat.

"Yeah, I come down and do research every now and then."

"What do you research?"

"Mostly how to build Civil War fortifications."

"That's interesting."

"You really think so? When I tell most people that, they usually turn and run."

"Let's get a drink," Ann said.

Pat got his usual Fox on the Rocks, and Ann got a glass of a Virginia chardonnay. They walked up the stairs to the exhibit of Civil War photographs, including those of Mathew Brady's assistants Alexander Gardner and Timothy O'Sullivan, who did most of Brady's work. Photography and America came of age at the same time. Because of this historical alignment, the American Civil War became the first major war photographed extensively. The result was the recording of an epic as never before.

Pat studied each wet plate photograph intently, looking for clues of how his ancestors lived, died, and built their fortifications. Many of the figures in the photographs were blurred like specters because of their movement. Others were crystalline.

Ann gazed at the images. "Some of these photographs look like they could have been taken yesterday. I can't believe how clear some of the faces are."

After viewing the photography exhibit, they wandered into the Mural Gallery. The gallery displayed *The Four Seasons of the Confederacy*, painted by French artist Charles Hoffbauer between 1913 and 1920. The fourteen-foot-high oil paintings on canvas, glued directly to the plaster walls, gave the room the feeling of a chapel wrapped in stained glass. But instead of messiahs, saints, and prophets appearing in mythological panels, it was Confederate generals and soldiers. Consuming most of the wall on the left was the *Spring* mural of Stonewall Jackson reviewing his infantry column, advancing in the Shenandoah Valley. Occupying the right wall was the *Autumn* mural of Jeb Stuart leading his cavalrymen on an uphill charge. Straight ahead, filling up Pat and Ann's field of vision, was the *Summer* mural, a lineup of Lee and his lieutenants in an ethereal glow of well-placed gallery footlights. In life, the thirteen Confederate generals were never in the same place at the same time. Nevertheless, in this Last Supper depiction, Lee was the Savior in the middle with his generals as disciples flanking him on both sides. Instead of everyone sitting at a table, they were in the field, standing or on horseback. The generals faced the *Winter* mural on the back wall, depicting the misery of war with artillerists positioning a cannon in the snow, and caisson drivers maneuvering around wrecked limbers and dead horses.

Pat reached out to hold Ann's hand as their bodies silhouetted against the generals.

CHAPTER 13

Pat reviewed the headline of Marion's obituary at the breakfast table, "Civil War Reenactor Dies on the Field of Battle." Gordon interrupted him. "How'd your date go last night?"

Pat looked up from his paper. "I think she likes my horse."

"But does she like you as a whole person? Did she hold tight to your saddle horn? Did you storm her breastworks?" Gordon pried as Jimmy and Hezekiah tee-heed, looking at Pat out of the corners of their eyes, and continued eating their eggs and toast.

Pat winked. "I'm going to meet her today in the garden at the Valentine Museum for lunch."

Gordon placed his palms on his cheeks and swooned. "Oh, the Valentine Museum. How romantic."

"Shut up, Gordon," Raleigh said, chewing a link sausage. "You're just jealous because you're not getting any."

"Oh, talk about somebody who's not getting any."

Raleigh came across the table attempting to throttle Gordon.

Pat leaped up and pushed his arms between them. "Would you two leave each other alone?"

Raleigh retreated into his chair, then turned to Jimmy and Hezekiah. "You boys didn't get too far cutting trees yesterday."

"Dad, I need to tell you something, but I don't want you to get mad."

"What is it?" Raleigh snarled.

"Yesterday, we met this man on Belle Isle."

"Belle Isle?" Raleigh blared. "What were you doing down there? I told you not to leave the farm. Gordon, did you know about this?"

Jimmy pulled the crumpled business card out of his pocket and passed it to his father. "He gave us this."

Raleigh studied the card and read part of it aloud. "Ballard McMullen, Investigative Services. Americana, São Paulo."

"Let me see that, Raleigh?" Gordon asked. Raleigh threw the card at him. Gordon picked it off the floor and glanced at it. He made the connection, hitting him like grapeshot. "Confederados."

"Confederados?" Raleigh asked. "Who the hell are Confederados?"

"You know, Confederados, Brazilians of American descent. When the Civil War was over, thousands of Southerners immigrated to Brazil where they could still hold slaves and grow their cotton and watermelons in peace, free from Yankee rule."

Raleigh turned back to Jimmy. "What did he say to you?"

"He said he had a wealthy client who wanted to buy gold coins from the Confederate treasury. He said his client would pay top dollar for the coins."

"Did you tell him anything?"

"We pretended like we didn't know anything."

"Do you think he thought you knew anything?"

"We're probably okay," Pat said, trying to take the heat off Jimmy. "It's just a private investigator asking anybody he thinks might know something about what he's after."

Raleigh looked at Pat. "But why would a private dick know to ask our boys about gold coins from the Confederate treasury? Somebody tipped him off about our find."

Gordon waved the business card in his hand. "Maybe we shouldn't look a gift horse in the mouth. Maybe this is the person who will give us the highest price for the gold."

Raleigh groused. "Or maybe this is just somebody else who wants to knock us over the head and steal our coins."

Pat tried to keep them on track. "We'll most likely hand the gold over to Sterling tomorrow, and he can auction it off, and it will be a done deal. If the Confederado is legitimate and is the highest bidder for the gold, Sterling will deal with him."

Raleigh eased up. "In the meantime, we can take care of our immediate problem, and that's to make sure we can defend ourselves against an attack."

Pat reached for a manila folder lying on the kitchen counter, pulled out a survey map of his property, placed it on the table, and started marking it up. "We can dam the creek here, and the earthwork should go here."

"I'll start on the dam first with my backhoe. Then I'll do the rampart," Raleigh said. "Now that I'm here to give the boys some proper supervision, I'll get them back on abatis detail, then have them run some tripwires. Maybe I'll have them build some cheval-de-frise."

"I can borrow some cannons," Gordon added. "Oh, and I've got to call my boss and tell him I'm feeling even sicker today. I think I'm going to be out sick for the whole week. If I'm lucky, maybe he'll fire me."

"I'm taking today and tomorrow off, too," Pat said. "The funeral's tomorrow and we're meeting Sterling. We have a lot of work to do to whip our fortifications into shape." The enthusiasm rose in Pat's voice. "I'm here this morning to help you all get started, and I'll be back right after my lunch date."

"All right," Raleigh said. "But watch your back and don't let anyone follow you home."

CHAPTER 14

P at and Ann entered the grounds of the Valentine Museum through a white-painted brick archway off North Tenth Street. The Valentine, established in 1892, showcased Richmond's history and was named after Mann S. Valentine, Jr., the institution's original benefactor who had made a fortune selling a beef-juice tonic. The museum also went by the name of the Valentine Richmond History Center to prevent confusion among tourists hoping to see cupid-related artifacts. Among curators, the Valentine was internationally known for its collection of eighteenth- and nineteenth-century costumes and textiles.

The couple went into the museum's café, purchased their food, and took it outside, walking past the sculpture studio of Edward Valentine. Edward, the brother of Mann, was a renowned nineteenth-century American sculptor. Edward's studio had been moved from three blocks away and rebuilt on the museum's grounds. The studio held the model for the "Recumbent Statue" of Robert E. Lee asleep on the battlefield, installed in the Lee Chapel at Washington and Lee University, where Lee was buried beneath. Pat cracked a smiled as he passed, remembering Gordon referring to the figure as *Lee on the Slab*.

Pat and Ann maneuvered through a garden of boxwoods and sculptures below the terrace of the 1812 Wickham-Valentine House, a white Federal-style mansion, donated by Mann to the museum. They found a table under the shade of an old magnolia

tree in bloom, beside a flowing triple-layered iron fountain encir-
cled by iron ducks waddling around its base.

As the pair enjoyed their meal, Mary Beth appeared on the
white-columned veranda of the house in a hooped dress and
did a double take when she spotted the couple. She came down
the walkway, swishing her handkerchief in her right hand, and
paraded up to their table.

Pat looked up, alarmed. "I didn't expect to see you here,
Mary Beth."

"Who were you expecting? Mary Boykin Chestnut? I didn't
expect to see you here either, especially with someone else." She
looked at Ann with scorn.

Pat bit the inside of his cheek and gently asked, "So, what
are you doing here?"

"I'm volunteering and authenticating some dress material for
my gown I was going to wear to the Confederate Cotillion next
month that you were taking me to. Remember, our annual fund-
raiser for the Children of the Confederacy?" She turned back to
Ann and snipped. "Aren't you going to introduce me?"

"This is Ann Calico," Pat said awkwardly. "Ann, this is Mary
Beth Crenshaw."

"Haven't we met before?" Mary Beth asked Ann, but didn't
wait for an answer. "I'm sure you won't mind if I sit down and
join you." Mary Beth plopped down between them, crowding
them with her pouffy skirt. "Are we going out this weekend, Pat?"

"I don't think so, Mary Beth."

Mary Beth turned to Ann. "Where are you from, Miss Calico?"

"Kansas," Ann answered apprehensively.

Mary Beth pushed her chair back abruptly and stood up in a
fury, attracting the attention of the other diners. Feeling bewildered and betrayed, she looked down at Pat. "Don't you see how
unnatural this is? You are choosing a Yankee over a Daughter of
the Confederacy, a Yankee who's not even from the North, but

from the uncultured frontier. Daddy is going to be very upset."
Mary Beth started weeping into her handkerchief and, with her
head bowed, withdrew to the big house.

CHAPTER 15

Fattah Absalom walked down Marshall Street in the hot morning sun, wearing a dark blue blazer and a light yellow open-collared shirt. He passed a brick fortress with giant milk bottles made of concrete blocks and covered in white plaster on three of its four corners, advertising the building's original use. The old Richmond Dairy had been converted into apartments.

Fattah fumed at the white man's idea of urban renewal. Taking every building, no matter what it had been, and turning it into apartments, replacing the old landlords with the new landlords. And in the process, most black people were priced out of the housing market. Fattah especially hated to see this going on in Jackson Ward.

Comprising forty city blocks, Jackson Ward was America's largest National Historic Landmark district associated with black history. It was also one of the most endangered historic neighborhoods in America. In the first half of the nineteenth century, it developed as a neighborhood of Italians, Germans, Jews, and freed slaves.

After the Civil War, political boundaries were drawn to contain most of the black residents into this section of the city. The remaining whites moved out, and more blacks moved in. Segregation forced blacks to develop their own businesses and institutions, and they did it here with tremendous success.

By the turn of the twentieth century, Jackson Ward, known as the Black Wall Street, had become one of the most influential black communities in the country. Civil rights activist Maggie

Walker had lived here, the first woman in the nation to found a bank. And oh how this place jumped in the 1930s and '40s. Clubs, theaters, and dance halls earned it another nickname—the Harlem of the South. The action had been centered on Second Street, dubbed the Deuce in its heyday, and the center of the Deuce was the Hippodrome Theater. Before integration, Billie Holliday, Cab Calloway, Nat King Cole, and many other black entertainers played this stop on the Chitlin' Circuit. The art-deco theater had been renovated and was now providing a fresh home for the blues and soul in Richmond.

But darker days preceded the recent revival. In the 1950s, an interstate highway was built through the middle of Jackson Ward. With the same insensitivity and disastrous results of an American Indian relocation program, over a thousand black families were evicted and moved, many into public housing projects. A long spiral of deterioration followed for the neighborhood. When integration came, blacks were allowed to spend their money in the better-stocked white-owned stores, and the black-owned businesses in the Ward shriveled up. African Americans now had access to live in other areas of the city, and many of those who hadn't been forced to move, moved out on their own. Jackson Ward became a ghetto of fine historic homes.

Some black people yearned for the way it was. They wanted African American families to move back into the Ward and again have a cohesive black community. But Fattah knew it would never happen. The damage had been done. The best blacks could hope for was gentrification, and that was already occurring. VCU was expanding from the west, and the Richmond Convention Center bordered the neighborhood's east side. Jackson Ward was ready to bloom again in a different way.

Fattah cut down gritty Brook Road to catch Clay Street. He moved hurriedly past houses with ornate cast-iron porches, part of Virginia's richest trove of decorative ironwork tucked away in the historic black district. Fattah slipped down another side street to access a cobblestone alley and entered Leela's backyard. Leela sat in her shady, hidden garden filled with trees and fountains, an oasis in the city. She rose, and they embraced and kissed.

Leela had restored the house and garden with her husband. The couple had sunk all of their money and energy into the property as pioneers to do their part in bringing back the old neighborhood. At least that's what Leela had thought they were doing until she found her husband cheating on her. He got the boot and she got the house. She stayed wounded for quite a while until she met Fattah. She couldn't help being attracted to him. He was more mature and smarter than her ex-husband, and he was sincere.

Leela and Fattah ambled out of the garden to Mama J's on First Street. They entered the soul food restaurant and were spotted by a voluptuous waitress with a mass of hair pulled back in a giant frizzy bun. The waitress swung her head toward the back of the dining room to point the way for them.

Leela and Fattah strolled past the bar and found Hark sitting at a table, dressed in light blue coveralls. They took a seat, and Fattah looked at his watch. "I don't have much time. I've got to get over to Union to teach my class."

"I knew you would be running late, so I went ahead and ordered for you both."

"Good, I'm starving," Leela said.

A waitress soon delivered fried catfish, candied yams, collard greens, and sweet cornbread muffins, with iced tea to drink.

Hark grabbed the hot sauce and started sprinkling it on his catfish.

Fattah looked over at Hark. "How long did you wait for the Confederate sympathizers to show up last night at Young's Spring?"

"About an hour."

Leela frowned. "They're not going to voluntarily give up that gold."

Fattah leaned in. "Any sign of them since you searched the fat one's apartment?"

Hark adjusted his glasses. "No, they abandoned the apartment, but we'll get a second chance at the Jefferson tomorrow when they meet Overstreet. I'll follow them to the gold from there."

"You'll get them," Leela said. "The fat one isn't very smart."

Fattah held his hands like the Dürer woodcut. "The future of the Nation of Gabriel depends upon the retrieval of that gold." Fattah reached inside his blazer and pulled out a crumpled brown paper bag, molded to its contents. "You're going to need this for backup." He passed the pistol to Hark.

Hark stuck the gun in one of the wide chest pockets of his coveralls, zipped it up, and patted the pocket. "We'll get the gold."

Once they finished their meal and stepped outside the restaurant, Fattah hugged and kissed Leela farewell and gestured good-bye to Hark. Fattah started walking at a fast clip toward Leigh Street on his way to Virginia Union University. Union was Richmond's historically black college, started after the Civil War in the former Lumpkin's Slave Jail. Fattah was an adjunct professor and taught a class called the "History of African Americans and the Law." Hark had been one of his students the year before.

Fattah enjoyed walking for his health, but when he made it to the corner where Leigh and Adams Streets and Chamberlayne Parkway came together, the oversized statue of Bojangles dancing affronted him. The statue infuriated Fattah as much as the statues of the Confederates. He saw it as a monument to the way white people wanted to see black people. There was Bill "Bojangles" Robinson, "the King of Tap Dancers," born in Jackson Ward, replicated in Reynolds Aluminum, stepping and fetching. He was the nonthreatening big black man who danced with the little white girl Shirley Temple. To Fattah, it symbolized the whites having the power and the blacks providing the entertainment. The statue may have been copasetic, as Bill Robinson would have said, with everyone else, but it wasn't copasetic with Fattah.

CHAPTER 16

In 1736, Patrick Henry, "the Voice of the American Revolution," was born in the broad and fertile Pamunkey River Valley, eighteen miles northeast of Richmond. In 1844, Edmund Ruffin, one of the more ardent voices for a Second American Revolution, moved to the valley and started making a name for himself as an innovative agriculturist. When others left the played-out Tidewater soil and moved on to the fresh fields of Kentucky and Tennessee, Ruffin discovered the land could be restored with lime deposits, abundant in eastern Virginia. This discovery and Ruffin's new farming methods of crop rotation and soil conservation helped revitalize the Tidewater economy and earned Ruffin the title Father of American Agronomy.

In 1855, Ruffin started his second career. He put down his plow and took up the cause of an independent Southern nation. Easily recognized as the old man with long white hair, he looked more like an American Indian chief than a Southern secessionist. He became famous for firing one of the first shots and one of the last shots of the Civil War. His first shot was fired from a cannon toward Fort Sumter on April 12, 1861. His last shot was fired from his rifle toward his brain on June 18, 1865. For this latter occasion, Ruffin wrapped himself in a Confederate flag and left a suicide note, referencing the "perfidious, malignant & vile Yankee race."

The Fire-Eater was buried at his plantation of Marlbourne, overlooking the Pamunkey River Valley, where he had conducted his agricultural experiments. The valley Ruffin had brought back to life was still fertile and lush but was now threatened by suburban sprawl.

In the valley a few miles down the road from the grave of the preeminent Southern nationalist was a compound littered with broken-down vehicles, junkyard finds, and home improvement materials that were never going to be used. In the center of the grassless yard was a dilapidated one-story, cinderblock house where Carter and Wendell Flood had grown up and still lived. Their father had been a tenant farmer for Mr. Elliott Crump, and their mother, a maid for the Crump household. They edged out blacks for these jobs because old man Crump preferred employing poor white people over poor black people.

When Carter and Wendell's parents died within a year of each other, both from lung cancer brought on by lifetimes of smoking cigarettes, Mr. Crump allowed Carter and Wendell to stay on in the house. The Flood brothers had been like sons to Mr. Crump, partly because he couldn't get along with his own children. Mr. Crump died ten years later, and his kids sold off the farm as quickly as possible to developers. But Mr. Crump had made a provision in his will for Carter and Wendell to inherit the cinderblock house with a half acre of land, much to the chagrin of his offspring.

Wendell had never moved out, and Carter had moved back after he divorced and lost his job with the phone company. They did electrical work when they ran out of money, flew their Confederate battle flag, and kept hunting dogs as their father had done on the dirt lot. But now, no longer surrounded by the old plantation fields, mansions of plywood and brick veneer hemmed them in.

Carter and Wendell's great-grandfather had been a young boy when his father left their farm in the Shenandoah Valley to fight in the Civil War. His father never came home, but General Sheridan did. Sheridan's troops burned their house, barn, and crops, killed the livestock, and destroyed the farm equipment. The Floods, as subsistence farmers, had no slaves for Sheridan to liberate.

The family was left destitute. Carter and Wendell's great-grandfather, the oldest of his five brothers and sisters, at twelve years of age, became the man of the house and spent his life building the farm back up. He kept his promise to his father to take care of his mother and siblings if something happened to him. As an old man during the Great Depression, the federal government came back again. This time the homestead was con- demned, so it could become part of Shenandoah National Park. The family refused to leave, so they were removed forcibly as the old man watched government agents set fire to his house a second time.

Carter and Wendell's grandfather, who was working the farm when the imminent domain was exercised, moved his family and the old man into the town of Luray and managed to lose the small amount of money the government had paid the family for the farm. Carter and Wendell's father came back from World War II wanting to be a farmer, but with no land to inherit, he became a sharecropper for Mr. Crump.

When Carter and Wendell were boys, they heard war stories, infused with bitterness and hatred for the Yankees and the gov- ernment, from their grandfather, who had heard them straight from his father who had endured the brunt of the blow. One story stood out. It wasn't the story of the destruction and seizure of the farm. It was the story of gold coins buried by the Confederates near Berkeley Plantation for safekeeping. After all these years of their hardpan life, they knew they were the rightful heirs to that gold.

A man pulled his Willys Jeep into the rutted depression beside the little cinderblock house, and the dogs started yelping. Carter and Wendell stepped out of the house into the blazing sun with cigarettes and beers in hand, wearing only cut-off blue jean shorts, flip-flops, and tattoos. They greeted Garnett Pollard as he climbed out of the Jeep. They all went inside, and the dogs calmed down.

"Have a seat. You want a beer?" Carter offered up his Virginia hospitality as he rubbed his hand across his head of unkempt, short, graying brown hair.

"I don't care for one right now." Garnett settled his muscular body into an old stuffed chair with a frayed floral pattern, deeply stained by Carter and Wendell over the years. Garnett's camouflage T-shirt and pants, along with his black beret, blended in so well with the filthy chair that only his bushy eyebrows were conspicuous in the dark den. He spoke over the hum of the air conditioner in the window. "Do you have the gold?"

"No," Carter said as he and Wendell flopped down on a disintegrating sofa facing Garnett. "Did you get the support of the Compatriot elders?"

"It's conditional," Garnett said, looking at Carter from underneath his big eyebrows. "Did you go by to see the Fuquas?"

"We did, but nobody was home and the gold wasn't there. What did the elders say?"

"If you supply the gold, the elders have given the go ahead for the war to start. With that kind of money, they believe full secession is possible."

"That's good news." Carter smiled, exposing his bad teeth. "I did cut into the Fuquas' phone line and told the man, what's his name, Raleigh, to deliver the gold to us at Marlbourne Sunday night, but he didn't show. And every time we drive by their house nobody's there. We're planning to drive back over this afternoon."

"Don't bother. I'm sure they're not coming back for a while. Besides, he might call the police, and you don't want to get picked up staking out the house."

"I don't think he's going to call the police. I think Fuqua is more greedy than scared."

Wendell fidgeted. "So what are we supposed to do now?"

"I think I have another lead for you. I saw an obituary in the paper for a Civil War reenactor. The funeral is tomorrow morning at ten o'clock at the Confederate Memorial Chapel. There's a good chance Fuqua will be there. If he is, you can follow him back to wherever he is hiding out, and I'm sure the gold will be there. Remember, without the gold, we have no second chance at secession."

"Don't worry. We'll get it," Carter said.

The hunting dogs started howling again. A minute later, the Compatriots heard a rap on the door and jumped. Wendell reached for his loaded Glock lying on the coffee table.

"Who's that?" Garnett asked in a hushed voice, not expecting anyone else to be knocking on the Flood brothers' door.

Carter looked out the window. "Oh, Christ, it's just that Yankee that lives next to us. I'll take care of him." Carter opened the door. "What do you want?"

"Hello, Mr. Flood, is it? I'm Russ Garibaldi, your neighbor." Russ, in his golf shirt, khakis, and Rockports, reached out to shake hands.

Still holding a beer and a cigarette, Carter didn't free up any of his paws to shake. "I know who you are. You're the Yankee from New Jersey."

Undeterred by the cold reception, the clean-shaven, youthful-looking Mr. Garibaldi pressed on as if giving a sales pitch to one of his clients for some bad bonds. "I need to talk to you about your dogs."

"They're beautiful dogs, aren't they?" Carter said as he stepped outside and closed the door behind him.

"They're keeping the whole neighborhood up at night."

"That's funny. They help me sleep. They make me feel safe." Carter took a drag off his cigarette.

"I represent the neighborhood association, and we would greatly appreciate it if you could keep your dogs from barking so much. They just don't blend in with the rest of the neighborhood, and quite frankly, we're concerned about property values going down because of the way you keep your place. Would you like some help cleaning it up?"

"Listen, you come-here, my brother and I were the neighborhood before you people showed up and built those big ugly-ass houses. And I would greatly appreciate it if you would just leave us alone." Carter ground his teeth, containing his ire, and had to ask, "So Yankee, when did your ancestors come to this country?"

Russ was surprised by the question but pleased to answer. "My grandfather came through Ellis Island in 1910," he said, swelling with pride.

"Well, my great-great-grandfather fought in the Civil War, my fourth great-grandfather fought in the Revolutionary War, and my twelfth great-grandfather was at Jamestown in 1607. So you see, Russ boy, we were here first."

Russ squinted. "Nonetheless, if you can't keep these dogs quiet, you leave me no choice but to call the county."

Carter got up in his face, repelling Russ with a variety of odors. "Call the county. My cousin is the animal control officer. I'll give you his number if you want. Look here, you damned carpetbagger, you'd better not step foot on my land again."

Russ backed away slowly, realizing there were bigger issues here than barking dogs.

CHAPTER 17

The Confederate Memorial Chapel stood tucked away behind the Virginia Museum of Fine Arts on the Boulevard. The chapel was one of only two surviving buildings on the site of the sprawling Old Soldiers' Home for Confederate veterans. The little white wooden Gothic house of worship, topped by a tarnished-green copper roof, served the residents of the home until their last Confederate soldier died in 1941.

Inside the chapel lay the body of Marion Galt in an open pine casket. In front of the coffin stood an arrangement of carnations in the form of the Battle Flag of the Army of Northern Virginia. Most everyone from the Richmond reenactment community plus many out-of-towners, all in Civil War period mourning dress, filled the curved hand-hewn oak pews. The dark interior flooded with sunlight, breaching the stained-glass windows, firing up their mosaics of cannons and rebel flags. More light rushed in from the back through the opened twin-arched wooden doors as the organist played "How Firm a Foundation," Robert E. Lee's favorite hymn.

Gordon noticed one of the ladies in black, sitting behind him. She looked familiar, but he couldn't place her. Then he remembered seeing her on Sutler's row at Berkeley. Her ringlets of pale blond hair fell down the sides of her face, complementing her blue eyes. They exchanged glances, and she averted her eyes down to pray.

When the organist completed the hymn, the chaplain rose and read 1 Corinthians 15, the chapter read at Stonewall Jackson's funeral featuring the "Death is swallowed up in victory" verse. When the reverend finished, he gazed upward to the bare wooden buttresses supporting the sanctuary's ceiling, then looked back down at the bereaved and spoke.

"This chapel is dedicated to the memory of the 350,000 Confederate soldiers who gave their lives for our country. Almost 1,700 Confederate veterans had their funerals in this chapel, and today we are here to grieve the loss of our comrade, to lay to rest this son of a son of a son of a Confederate soldier, Marion Arthur Galt. Marion Galt portrayed General Robert E. Lee on the battlefield and, like the great general, succumbed after a stroke. Reenactors who portray Robert E. Lee come and go, but Marion was the best. He looked like the general, he acted like the general, and, best of all, he had the integrity of the general. Like Lee, he was a true Christian soldier and gentleman.

"Some say Marion Galt was born two hundred years too late, but I say he was born right on time. Because without Marion, many of us would not have known the chivalry and nobility of a Confederate commander. Without Marion, many of us would not have become reenactors. Some scoff at Civil War reenactors and say we participate in a misguided play-acting hobby. But Marion knew it was no hobby. It was his calling. He was devoted to his men, and his men were devoted to him. Everybody loved Marion. He even had some Yankee friends."

A few chuckles emerged from the sniffling congregation.

"But for those of us who were fortunate enough to serve under Marion Galt, he will live on in our memories the same way the rest of the Southern heroes of the Confederacy live on."

The chapel bell rang out thirteen times for the thirteen Confederate states, and the pallbearers rose as the only black man on the premises stepped up to a side podium. For a large, prepaid sum of cash, the gentleman of color started singing "Carry Me Back To Old Virginny." The bearers lowered the lid on the pine box and covered it with the Second National Flag of the Confederacy, the "Stainless Banner." The flag displayed a Southern Cross canton on an all-white field.

The attendants carried the casket down the aisle and out of the chapel and placed it on a caisson drawn by four white horses. The mourners followed as a rich baritone flowed over the flock.

"There's where I labored so hard for old massa,
Day after day in the field of yellow corn,
No place on earth do I love more sincerely
Than old Virginny, the state where I was born."

Carter and Wendell, shabbily dressed for the occasion but managing to wear shirts and shoes, stood across from the front of the chapel under a black oak. They examined each person as they came down the gray steps onto the circular brick walkway. When Raleigh came out the door, both Flood brothers recognized him. Wendell raised his arm to point, and Carter smacked it down before he could get it all the way up.

When Gordon came out of the chapel, he moseyed over to the side lawn for a quick smoke before joining the procession. He settled by a hemlock tree and pulled out a cigar.

Two men in suits with open-collared white shirts approached Gordon. One was tall and lean with sharp features in a tailored blue suit. The other one was older with swarthy skin and a pock-marked face, built like a fire-plug, wearing a rumpled suit and smoking a cigarette.

The short one reached into his pants pocket and whipped out a gold-plated jeweled Zippo. "Let me light that for you, Mr. Barrett."

"No, thanks. I prefer matches. Do I know you gentlemen?"

The short one continued to do the talking and did his best to stand face-to-face with Gordon, even though he was a head shorter. "Sy Meyer is an associate of ours, and we understand you have some gold coins."

Gordon shrunk back. "What are you talking about?"

"We know the coins are worthless to you, since you're holding them illegally. As a favor, we're going to take them off your hands. Just deliver the coins to Sy's by the end of business today."

Gordon gulped. "And if I don't give them to Sy?"

"You don't want to be holding services here for your nephew anytime soon, do you?" he said, as they all looked across the way to Hezekiah, who stood out in the milling crowd of mourners. "Just get the gold to Sy and everything will be fine." He patted Gordon on the back and looked at his sidekick. "Let's go, Bob."

The two men walked away and Raleigh came over to Gordon. "Come on. We have to get in line."

Gordon stood there stunned.

"Who were those two guys?" Raleigh asked.

Gordon whispered, "We've got even more problems. We've got to talk about this."

Raleigh turned his back to Gordon in anger, spitting epithets under his breath. It took all of Raleigh's self-control to turn back around and say, "Right now we have a funeral procession to get in. We'll talk after the graveside service."

A fife and drum corps led the cortege, striking up the funeral march to start the two-and-a-half-mile walk to Hollywood Cemetery. A color guard followed, rigid in reverence. A six-horse gun team toted a limber and cannon. Infantry strode in reversed arms and mounted officers galumphed along. The four white horses hitched to the caisson carrying the coffin departed, guided by two riders filling the saddles of the horses on the left side. Marion's horse without a rider came after with Marion's empty boots placed backward in the stirrups. The ladies in black crinoline crinkled behind. Those taking their cars followed the horses and the marchers. Jimmy, who didn't want to walk in the procession, drove Gordon's Delta 88. Carter and Wendell, and Sy's business associates, were the last in line.

The solemn column headed down the Boulevard along the median of crepe myrtles, sprouting pink, papery blooms in the late morning heat. They turned at the Stonewall Jackson statue for Marion's last ride down Monument Avenue. Passerby pedestrians and held-up motorists paused in homage, curiosity, annoyance, or incredulity.

The column marched straight until it arrived at Harrison Street, then cut through VCU, passing the monument to the Richmond Howitzers. A bronze artilleryman held a sponge and rammer, referred to by the students as the tampon man.

The cavalcade wound its way around the university and entered the broken streets of Oregon Hill, a white working-class neighborhood and student ghetto, sung about in the unflattering 1992 pop song by the Cowboy Junkies. The neighborhood had been named in the 1840s after the Oregon Territory, because to Richmond residents at the time, the area seemed as far west of downtown as the territory. Oregon Hill had its heyday between the Civil War and World War II, serving as a quarter for the workers of Tredegar Iron Works and Albemarle Paper Company located below the hill on the James River.

The historic neighborhood had been saved from VCU's expansion plans. Some wondered if rescuing all the dilapidated Italianate firetraps with their rickety wooden porches from the wrecking ball was worth it. Even with restoration progressing, Oregon Hill still seemed far removed from the rest of the city.

The procession continued to the entrance of Hollywood Cemetery. The head of the column stopped just inside the gates of the cemetery, giving the marchers, covered in sweat, a chance to rest and take a drink of water from their canteens. Those who drove parked their cars outside the gates and would walk the rest of the way to the gravesite.

Carter peered over the steering wheel. "Just one way in and one way out. We'll wait for them to come out."

In a few minutes, the dead march started up again, but this time only muffled drums sounded. They marched past the stone mortuary chapel now serving as the cemetery's office and down the hill into the city of the dead where every blue-blooded Richmonder wanted to reside someday. Richmond had been the capital of the Confederacy, and Hollywood Cemetery was its shrine. It was the final resting place for the president of the Confederate States of America Jefferson Davis, twenty-five Confederate generals including George Pickett and Jeb Stuart, and over 18,000 Johnny Rebs. Also buried here were two other presidents: James Monroe and John Tyler.

The 135-acre garden cemetery was named after its numerous holly trees. Hollywood was designed to be as much a park as a cemetery, with impressive views of the James River and the Richmond skyline. In the late nineteenth century, families gathered here to picnic and tend their relatives' gravesites. The pastoral memorial remained one of Richmond's more popular "parks." Tall ancient trees shaded carriage lanes, winding over hills and dales covered with artistic memorials of stone, bronze, and iron.

At the bottom of the hill, the procession crossed a bridge that once bordered a pond that was drained and filled shortly after World War II. The caravan moved on up Confederate Avenue, where Confederate flags dotted graves.

At the top of the hill, they took the horseshoe curve around to the cemetery's largest memorial, a granite-block pyramid. Forty-five feet at the base and ninety feet tall, the monolith was consecrated to the Confederate dead and watched over them.

The monument was not only an engineering feat because it was mortarless, but also a financial wonder because it was erected four years after the war ended when the South had little money. The perilous job of climbing the pyramid and guiding the capstone into place, hanging from a crane prone to breaking, went to a convict. Legend had it that the prisoner was rewarded with his freedom for the daring deed, but most likely, he was placed back in his cell.

The stream of mourners passed the cold stack of stones. One of the larger blocks of the pyramid, polished on one side, had carved into it *Numini et patriæ asto*, "They stood for God and their country."

The sorrowers went down a short hill and back up another to a newer section of the cemetery. They had delivered Marion Galt to his final resting place, but Marion had one last reenactment to attend. For this event, Marion would not portray a general, but a captain. Captain William Latané was the only Confederate to die on Jeb Stuart's famous ride around the Union Army of the Potomac in 1862. His death, greatly mourned in Virginia, was one of the first of many more to come.

A photographer set up his equipment and the reenactors took their places to redo *The Burial of Latané*, the oil painting by William Washington, hanging on loan in the Virginia Museum of Fine Arts. A Lost Cause icon, the painting became emblematic of the collective grieving for the losses of a Confederate nation, portraying devoted women and loyal slaves.

A white woman, playing Mrs. William Brockenbrough, who had taken in Latané's body, and white girls, playing residents of Westwood and Summer Hill Plantations, lined up to the right of the coffin containing Marion. Paid black reenactors, playing faithful slaves, lined up to the left of the box. The photographer snapped the picture as Mary Beth stood in the center. She portrayed Mrs. Willoughby Newton, performing the burial service in the absence of a minister who had been unable to cross the Union picket line. Her five-year-old niece stood by her side, holding a wreath of flowers. Mary Beth clutched an open Book of Common Prayer, looking up to the heavens with moon eyes and a confined hairstyle.

To compensate for the bright day and the bare lawn of the cemetery, the photographer planned to go back to his office and use Photoshop to darken up the picture and fill in a lush landscape as a background, the same way William Washington had done with his brushstrokes.

Once the shoot was complete, Mary Beth read from the prayer book. When she finished, seven infantrymen loaded their Enfields "by the nine steps" and fired, then repeated the process twice more. To complete the ceremony, the drums and fifes broke into the Irish jig "Merry Men Home from the Grave" and led the sobbing crowd away from the burial pit back to their cars.

Gordon's party split from the herd and slipped down into a dale where a weeping willow grew. They parted the slender hanging willow branches like hippie door beads to enter a bottom acre filled with small grave markers and a few larger markers scattered among them. This was the section of the cemetery reserved for the Confederate veterans who had lived at the Old Soldiers' Home on the Boulevard. The small stones, with just enough room to inscribe a number and C.S.A., were provided when the Confederate veterans died, in most cases, well into the twentieth century. The larger stones, standard US government-issued markers like the ones in Arlington National Cemetery, were replacements for the smaller ones, usually put there by a soldier's descendants. The larger markers served as a postmortem welcome back into the Union for the Rebels who had died many years after the war had ended, and in deference to the Confederacy, the US stones bore the emblem of the Confederate Southern Cross of Honor.

The reenactors gingerly stepped between the graves and through the smell of fresh cut grass, keeping a respectful silence as they walked up the hill to the edge of the cemetery, where Pickett's grave overlooked the Gettysburg dead.

Six years after the war was over, the Confederate dead still lay hastily buried in farmers' fields around Gettysburg. The Rebels weren't allowed to be buried in the national cemetery established on the Gettysburg battlefield. So in 1872 and 1873, the remains of 2,935 Confederate soldiers who had died at Gettysburg were brought back to Richmond and reinterred on this hillside.

General George E. Pickett's grave marker loomed over some of the men who died in the infantry assault named after the general. The seventeen-foot-high cupola of granite and gray bronze, crowned with an urn protected by sculpted angels, was meant to be placed at the high-water mark of Pickett's Charge at Gettysburg. But the proposal to have a monument dedicated to the Confederates inside the Federal lines wasn't exactly what US officials had in mind in 1887, so the marker was placed the next year over the runner-up location, Pickett's grave.

The reenactors gathered beside Pickett's memorial as the hum of expressway traffic rose from the man-made valley beyond the cemetery's fence. Gordon stared at the monument. He had always thought it to be rather large for a guy who was a loser among losers. Pickett graduated last in his class at West Point, and just before the final Confederate lines were broken at Petersburg, he abandoned his men at Five Forks to attend a shad bake. After the war, Pickett fled to Canada, then returned and sold insurance. To make up for the general's shortcomings, his wife, Sallie, lionized him through her speaking engagements and books, making him out to be God's gift to the Confederacy.

Raleigh ended the reverential silence, anxious to pick up the conversation from the Confederate Chapel, asking Gordon again, "So who were those two guys?"

Gordon took his eyes off Pickett's monument, looked at his pards, and confessed. "On Monday when I left the boys to run errands, I took the double eagle I had been carrying around to Sy's Coins to find out how much I could get for it. I told Sy Meyer, the coin dealer who runs the shop, how many coins we had to sell. Seems Sy is connected to other business interests. Those two guys who showed up in the chapel yard today demanded I deliver the coins to Sy by the end of the day. They know the gold is hot and threatened . . ." Gordon looked at Hezekiah. "They threatened me."

"So are these wise guys?" Pat asked.

"I don't think they're legitimate businessmen."

Raleigh's sweat glands in his brow cranked up. "So now we have a mob after us, along with a militia, and black militants. Who's coming after us next?"

"The IRS?" Gordon said, only half-jokingly.

"It's not funny, Gordon." Raleigh was infuriated. "You blew our cover again to another bunch of psychopaths who want our gold." Raleigh puffed out his cheeks in rage. "What were you thinking? Were you going to go to the coin dealer and sell the gold on your own?" Raleigh turned to the others and pointed to Gordon. "I am tired of this scalawag running the show."

Gordon struck back. "Beats being a racist."

Raleigh threw down his officer's gloves. "I am not a racist. I'm a Confederate American."

"You're delusional, Raleigh. I think you're about one step away from joining the militia that's after us. Look around. All of the Confederates are dead. All we have left here is the low-water mark of the Confederacy."

"You are disrespectful of this place of honor."

"This isn't a place of honor. This is a place of tragedy because these men fought the good fight for a bad reason."

Raleigh felt like he had been slapped in the face but held his temper. He stretched out his arm in a Confederate salute to the Gettysburg dead. "A lot of people would like to revise history.

They would be happy if the Confederacy was erased from our memories and from our history books, like it never happened. But it did happen, and I want to make sure it's never forgotten that these men performed their duty faithfully. I want to make sure people remember these men because they showed courage we will never know, fighting for their families, their homes, and their sweethearts."

"I want people to remember this war too, Raleigh. But to remember it for what it was. Like most wars, it was a rich man's war and a poor man's fight. It was more about greed than glory."

"Stop insulting my ancestors."

"They're my ancestors too."

"Then honor them and show some pride."

"Pride in what?"

Raleigh took a swing at Gordon. Once again, Pat broke it up.

Raleigh blurted, "All I want now is my share of the gold."

Gordon roared, "You don't have a share, Raleigh."

"If I don't get my share, I'll turn the rest of you in."

"Calm down, Raleigh," Pat said, exasperated. "If you turn us in, you go to jail too." He glanced at his watch. "It's almost time to meet Sterling at the Jefferson. Please, let's just go see what he's got to offer."

CHAPTER 18

G ordon let Jimmy drive everybody in the Delta from the cemetery with Raleigh giving full instruction along the way. When Jimmy turned onto Cary Street, in the distance they could see the twin Italian clock towers of Richmond's grand hotel, the Jefferson. The hotel was constructed in the 1890s by Lewis Ginter, the richest man in Virginia at the time. Ginter had made his fortune as the first person to mass-produce and mass-market packs of cigarettes. He wanted to build "the finest hotel in America."

Designed by Carrère and Hastings, the same architectural firm that created the New York Public Library, the Jefferson Hotel was considered one of the country's best examples of Beaux Arts eclectic architecture. The style started off using classical columns and arches, but steadily got out of hand, adding a little bit of every architectural feature through the ages. The result was garishly splendid.

Through the years, the hotel survived fire, bankruptcy, and neglect. It was almost torn down in the 1970s to be replaced by a new Federal Reserve Bank building. But the Fed decided to build elsewhere, and in the 1980s, investors pumped $34 million into the hotel, returning it to its original grandeur.

With Raleigh's direction, Jimmy parked the car on the street beside the five-star hotel. They entered the establishment from Main Street, tramping into the Rotunda, an opulent and mis-named rectangular lobby with a soaring ceiling. A stained-glass skylight hovered in the center, the size of a small swimming pool, illuminating the interior. Around the perimeter, stout, stacked pairs of Corinthian columns of concrete and plaster, with a brown marble faux finish, and fruited and flowered adornment, supported the mezzanine and the roof.

On the left side of the majestic space, Hark sat in T.J.'s Lounge, dressed in a dark suit and a red bow tie. He spotted the reenactors proceeding to the Grand Staircase. A myth had grown up around the stairway when it was covered with red carpet and had no middle railing that it was the model for the Atlanta mansion's staircase in *Gone with the Wind*. The tale had been debunked, but the legend lived on. At the foot of the stairs, an elderly lady was trying to talk her husband into carrying her up the stairway as Clark Gable had whisked up Vivien Leigh in the movie. The old man pleaded back trouble.

Gordon's troupe ascended the stairs while Hark kept his eye on them. At the same time, the Flood brothers walked into the hotel through the same entrance as the reenactors. A security guard detained them, thinking they were maintenance men who should have been using a side service door.

At the top of the stairs, the reenactors entered the Palm Court Lobby, housing a life-sized marble statue of Thomas Jefferson. The statue stood underneath a circular skylight of stained glass. The disk formed a dazzling blue-and-white halo above the head of the founding father.

Through most of the first half of the twentieth century, alligators lived in marbled fountains beside the Jefferson statue. The inside fountains were now gone, and the only alligators left were in the form of a few bronze sculptures in and around the hotel. Without the risk of live reptiles, the reenactors congregated in front of Mr. Jefferson.

Ballard McMullen, chatting with the front-desk clerk, recognized Hezekiah and Jimmy. The hotel's black concierge also took notice of the men in Confederate uniforms and saw their presence as inappropriate and unnerving here in the New South. She strolled up to the reenactors, hoping to shoo them away from their prominent position.

"May I help you gentlemen?"

"We're just waiting for someone," Gordon said.

"Perhaps you would be more comfortable waiting down in the lounge."

"No, we're fine right here."

"Then perhaps you'd like to take a seat."

"We're fine, thank you. Nice place you have here."

"Yes, well, thank you." The concierge went back to her desk, flustered she hadn't accomplished her aim.

From their vantage point, the reenactors could see through the windows in the doors facing Adams Street and spotted Sterling, pulling up in his Jaguar into the circular drive. As Sterling stepped out and gave the keys to the valet, two dark sedans pulled in, one from the front and one from the back, blocking the Jag. Men jumped out of both cars and grabbed Sterling, bending him over the hood of his car and slapping handcuffs on him. One of the men peered through the glare of the glass doors and saw the reenactors. "They're in here," he shouted to the other men.

Raleigh turned toward the stairs and shouted, "Run!"

The man busted through the doors, flashing his badge, and yelled, "Nobody move, FBI."

The reenactors dashed down the Grand Staircase on the double-quick, with Raleigh clanging his sword on every other step. Bringing up the rear, Gordon lost his balance and fell down the stairs, but not as gracefully as Vivian Leigh's stunt double. As Gordon lay huddled up in a heap at the bottom of the staircase, the other reenactors, who didn't see him fall and weren't looking back, headed for the exit.

Hezekiah was the last one to reach the Main Street door, but before he had a chance to go through it, Sy's short and stubby business associate reached out and grabbed his arm. "It's safe this way. Don't say a word and you'll be fine." A bewildered Hezekiah stumbled out a side exit with the man, away from all the excitement.

Hark followed the rest of the reenactors who had made it out the door. The Flood brothers didn't even notice the reenactors fly past them because they were too busy arguing with the security guard holding them up. The argument turned into a full altercation, blocking the way of the cadre of FBI agents running after the reenactors. The agents knocked down Carter, Wendell, and the guard in their pursuit of the reenactors. The guard was out cold, but Carter and Wendell bounced back on their feet. The Flood brothers now wanted to fight the FBI agents who had mowed over them, but on second thought realized they should leave, using the service door the security guard had originally suggested. Ballard watched the whole thing from the mezzanine.

Once outside, Raleigh shouted at Jimmy, "Give me the keys."

Jimmy was breathless. "Where's Hezekiah and Gordon? They were right behind us."

"For God's sake, Raleigh," Pat said. "We can't leave Hezekiah and Gordon."

"Gordon's a big boy and Hezekiah is Gordon's responsibility. Get in the car," Raleigh screamed. "The FBI has them. We've got to save ourselves."

Raleigh revved up the Delta, and Pat and Jimmy reluctantly jumped in. They sped away, but not before Hark got a good look at their car, then ran to his own to follow them. The FBI agents spilled out onto the street but were too late to catch anyone.

Back in the Rotunda, hotel guests gasped and gaped at the spectacle. Lying on his back, Gordon opened his eyes and began making out the gold-leaf coconut palm fronds on the ceiling.

"Gordon Barrett?"

"Yes," Gordon said in a daze.

"I'm FBI Special Agent Richard Howard. I'm going to need you to come in for questioning."

CHAPTER 19

G ordon sat in the stale interrogation room at the branch office of the FBI on the north side of suburban Richmond. Across the table sat Agent Howard in a coat and tie.

Richard Howard was a pale, physically fit man with good hair who looked like he hadn't been with the bureau that long. "We know you have the gold."

Gordon rubbed the bump on the back of his head. It was starting to go down. "Sounds like you're from New England."

"Vermont. We know you and Raleigh Fuqua have been contacted by three separate groups, trying to extort the gold. The Compatriots, a neo-Confederate militia; the Gabrielites, a black separatist group; and the Greek mafia."

Gordon blinked. "Oh, they're Greeks?"

Howard looked over at Gordon. "They're probably connected to the gang down at Virginia Beach. That was the brothers Lichas and Bob Papadopoulos you talked to outside the Confederate Chapel." Agent Howard pointed his finger at Gordon like he was pointing a gun. "These are very dangerous fringe groups, not to mention Sterling Overstreet."

Gordon snorted. "What's so dangerous about Sterling, and why did you arrest him?"

"Mr. Overstreet is not so much dangerous as crooked. You don't have to worry about him anymore." Howard's grim face almost released a smile. "We picked him up on so many violations of the Archaeological Resources Protection Act that you won't be seeing him for a long time."

Gordon shook his head. "He was going to sell the gold for us."

"He was going to sell it for himself. The guy has been traf-ficking in stolen battlefield relics for years. When you walked into his office, he knew he'd be able to retire in the Caymans." Howard cocked his head. "Has anyone else contacted you about the gold?"

Gordon balked, then thought it might be in his best interest to let him know. "My nephew and Raleigh Fuqua's son were approached by a man from Brazil. His name is Ballard McMullen. He said he represented a wealthy client wanting to buy the coins."

"It was probably one of Mr. Overstreet's prospective buyers. I'm sure the buyer didn't trust Overstreet, so he sent somebody up to cut Sterling out as the middleman. Mr. McMullen is most likely not a threat, but we'll follow up on him." Howard stood up, gripped the table's edge with both of his hands, and looked down at Gordon. "We've been trying to nail the Compatriots and Gabrielites on domestic terrorism charges, and the Greeks on, well, take your pick. But now we have a chance to make a triple play. With your cooperation, we can bring in all three of these groups at once."

Gordon banked his torso forward with his chin up. "And what do I get in return?"

"We'll make sure you're not prosecuted."

"What happens to the gold?"

"It becomes the property of the United States government."

"No, it gets donated to my favorite charity."

"We don't make deals like that."

Gordon dipped back in his chair. "Then I can't help you."

Howard leaned almost all the way over the table, staring Gordon straight in the face. "Do you and your friends really want to go to prison?"

Gordon, feeling like he didn't have much to lose, tendered what little leverage he had. "Prosecute us and the big fish get away."

Howard backed off. "Maybe something could be worked out."

Gordon saw an opening. "There's nothing to work out. I'll cooperate with y'all, and I get to donate the gold to whatever charity I want, and you don't prosecute us."

Howard swayed back in for the kill. "A yawl is a boat. Look, you dumb hillbilly, I don't know who you think you're dealing with, but we don't operate that way."

"I prefer people of mountain culture, and if you don't make fun of the way I talk, I won't make fun of the way you talk." Gordon smirked. "You must really hate being stuck down here in the swampy South. I'm sure you think everything is better up North, and if you ever want to get your stiff ass back up there, you'll probably want to cut a deal with me. I bet there's a big promotion in it for you. They'll let you work where the real action is, international terrorism in DC or New York, away from this small-potatoes town. I know you have your career path all mapped out. Here's your chance to complete your detour."

Howard raised his eyebrows but stayed on course. "Maybe the Fuquas or your nephew will be better at cooperating than you are. And we'll go easier on them."

"You're not going to get anything out of my pards."

"Your pards? What's a pard?"

"It's short for pardner. It's what some Civil War soldiers called their buddies. And my buddies aren't talking, and you don't even know where they are."

"We can find them in a minute."

"Go ahead then," Gordon bluffed.

Howard straightened up. "I don't think you understand how dangerous these groups really are. You may think the Compatriots and the Gabrielites are just alienated screwballs, but that's the profile of terrorists, and they're just a truckload of fertilizer away from taking many American lives. And if that happens, you'll be an accessory and spend the rest of your life in prison. If you cooperate, we'll give you protection from them and immunity from prosecution. I would take it if I were you."

"Nice threat, Dick, but it still sounds like you need me to get to them, and that's going to cost you."

Howard knew he had to move and didn't have time to find and bring in Gordon's pards for questioning. "Fine, let's get down to business. We need you to lure all three of these groups to a set location with the promise of the gold so we can arrest them for extortion."

Gordon dealt. "The Compatriots and the Gabrielites wanted the gold three days ago. But we haven't heard back from either of them." Gordon snickered. "Probably because I pulled the battery out of my phone, and they don't know where we're staying."

"And where are you staying?"

"I'm not that dumb of a hillbilly." Gordon kept a poker face even though he was surprised Howard didn't know about Pat and Pat's farm, because he knew about everything else.

Howard drew an exasperated breath. "Look, we've already established we're working together. We don't want you. We just want to bring in the terrorists and the mobsters. When did the Greeks want the gold delivered to them?"

"By the end of business today at Sy's Coins on West Grace."

"Sy Meyer?" Howard asked, a little taken aback.

"Yeah. You know him?"

"Let's just say Sy has been a person of interest for a long time. You can call Sy and let him know about a new pickup time and place."

"And what time and place would that be?"

"It should be someplace you're comfortable, a public park is fine, but we want to be able to clear out anybody who happens along."

"How about the Cold Harbor Visitor Center parking lot?"

"That would probably be all right. We'll have to do it as soon as possible." Howard looked at the calendar on his BlackBerry. "We'll need about four days to prepare. It's Wednesday now, how about Sunday evening at six o'clock?"

"That's June 27."

"So?"

"Nothing. It's just the anniversary of the Battle of Gaines's Mill."

Howard found the historical trivia annoying as he pulled out one of his cards to give to Gordon. Handwritten on the back was a phone number. "Is this your cell phone?"

"Yes."

"Put your battery back in your phone. We'll forward the calls from Fuqua's home phone to your phone so you can set up the appointment with the Compatriots for Sunday night. I'm sure you'll also be hearing from the Gabrielites soon, so you can do the same with them."

"That's all right with me, only if I get to donate the gold to Civil War battlefield preservation and you won't prosecute us. I'll need that in writing."

Howard reluctantly nodded.

CHAPTER 20

With plenty of daylight left, Agent Howard drove Gordon back downtown to the Jefferson.

"Are you sure you want me to drop you here? I don't think they want to see you back in the hotel."

"Yeah, this is fine. I'll call you once I hear from the Compatriots and the Gabrielites, and I'll call Sy. But if I think you're following me or triangulating my position with my phone on, the deal is off."

"Don't worry, Mr. Barrett. I have no need to follow or track you. We both need each other to get what we want. You have my number. I'll wait to hear from you."

Gordon watched him pull away, then waited for a minute to see if he could spot any of Howard's fellow agents lurking around. He didn't see anyone suspicious, so he walked around the block to where his car had been parked. He pulled out his cell phone to call Pat's house, but before he had a chance, the phone rang. Gordon answered, "Your humble and obedient servant, Gordon Barrett."

"Mr. Barrett?"

Gordon slowly responded to the breathy voice of the lady Gabrielite, "Yes."

"We were disappointed we didn't see you at Young's Spring Monday evening, but we did see you at the Jefferson Hotel today. It looks like you're in trouble with the law. We'd like to give you one more chance, Mr. Barrett. Meet us at Young's Spring this evening at eight with the gold."

"I'd feel more comfortable meeting you someplace a little more open, say the Cold Harbor Visitor Center parking lot."

"That would be a setup, Mr. Barrett. If you want to keep living, you'll meet us at Young's Spring and you won't bring the FBI along with you."

"If you want the gold, you'll meet me at Cold Harbor Sunday evening at six."

"We'll see you much sooner than that, Mr. Barrett. Death or liberty."

Gordon heard a click. As soon as he hung up, the phone rang again.

"Your humble and obedient servant, Gordon Barrett."

"Fuqua?" a gravelly voice said abruptly.

"No, he's not here right now. Can I take a message?"

"Fuqua has something he wants to give me, but I haven't been able to catch up with him. Would you tell him he can bring it to me tonight at ten at the gates of Marlbourne, the way he was supposed to Sunday night."

"I talked to Mr. Fuqua about this already, and he'd like to meet you at the Cold Harbor Visitor Center at six Sunday evening to give you the gold."

"So you know about the gold. You must be one of his buddies I saw him with today at the Jefferson Hotel. You tell Fuqua if he doesn't bring the gold to me tonight, I'll be coming after him and you too."

The phone slammed in Gordon's ear.

Gordon blew a puff of air out of his mouth and thought, Who wasn't at the Jefferson today?

The phone rang. "Here we go again. Your humble and obedient servant, Gordon Barrett."

"Mr. Barrett, I met you today at the Confederate Chapel."

Gordon recognized the voice. "So you would be Lichas Papadopoulos?"

"Yeah, smartass, so you know my name. Listen, you over-sized piece of crap, I have your nephew. Say hello."

"Gordon?" Hezekiah's faint voice came from the background.

"Hezekiah?" Gordon's voice thundered through the phone line.

"As I told you this morning, if you don't want to be holding funeral services for your nephew, you're going to want to bring the gold to Sy's today. Once we know Sy has the gold, we'll let your nephew go."

The phone died and Gordon reeled. He managed his panic, but it took all his concentration to punch the speed-dial button for Pat.

Pat answered.

"They have Hezekiah," Gordon blurted out.

"Gordon?"

"Yeah. They have Hezekiah."

"Who has Hezekiah?"

"The Greek mob."

"What? I thought he was with you. Did you get away from the FBI?"

"They picked me up for questioning and I cut a deal for the gold. They dropped me back at the Jefferson, and I just got a phone call from one of the Papadopoulos brothers."

"Who?"

"One of Sy's business associates that I told you about at Hollywood. He told me if I didn't bring the gold to Sy today, he would kill Hezekiah."

"Then let's take the gold to Sy."

"Come and get me. We'll dig it up and deliver it."

"Maybe we should call the FBI?"

"They're useless. They need four days before they can do anything. If we get them involved, they'll get Hezekiah killed."

CHAPTER 21

Bob Papadopoulos held his Kimber to Hezekiah's head and pulled the trigger. The magazine was empty, but the boy still flinched. He couldn't cry out because his mouth was taped, but his eyes expressed his horror.

"Stop messing with the kid," Lichas said as he whiffed on a cigarette.

"I'm just having a little fun with him before we have to kill him."

Lichas looked at Hezekiah. "Don't worry, kid, he's not going to kill you here. It would dirty up the house too much." Lichas laughed and looked at Bob. "Let's go get some supper."

"Is food all you ever think about?" Bob said.

"No, I think about money too."

"We can't leave the kid."

"Sure we can. He's tied up nice and tight. He's not going anywhere. We can make a quick run over to the Mediterranean Bakery. We won't be gone long."

Bob looked at Hezekiah, raised the barrel of his gun to his lips, and blew his breath across it. Then he prissily placed the pistol back into his shoulder holster. "I guess he'll be okay." He winked at Hezekiah. "Don't worry, kid, we'll take care of you later."

A few minutes after the Papadopoulos brothers left their house, Momma Papadopoulos, who lived two blocks away, walked up the driveway. Lichas and Bob's mother looked like a homeless person wearing a blue headscarf and an old dark floral print dress. She saw Lichas and Bob's Mercedes wasn't there but decided to let herself in anyway. She knew her boys didn't like her going into their house when they were gone, but she felt it was her duty to check on things. She chatted incessantly to herself as she opened the front door and found the house reasonably clean. But no matter what condition she found her sons' home, she was always disgusted by it.

"When are my boys going to take wives? They need wives to straighten up around here and to keep them straight. You would think something has turned them off to having a woman run their lives. I just don't know what it is."

She went into the living room and found Hezekiah gagged and bound to a chair. "Good lord, what kind of crazy game are my boys up to now? This kind of thing wouldn't be going on if their father hadn't died when they were so young."

She gently took the tape off Hezekiah's mouth. "Are you all right?"

Hezekiah moved his head down, then up in a deliberate fashion, still terrified.

"Where are Lichas and Bob?"

Hezekiah slowly said, "They went to get something to eat."

She looked at Hezekiah's red hair and freckled pale skin. "Are they ashamed of their friends because they're not Greek? I didn't raise my boys to be prejudice. Just because you're obviously some kind of albino doesn't mean you should be treated like this. As long as you're in their house, you are their guest. And to have left you here all tied up, what were they thinking? And look how skinny you are." Momma loosened the ropes.

"If my boys are too rude to take you out to eat with them, then I'll feed you myself." She finished untying Hezekiah. "You watch TV while I go into the kitchen and cook you something. You relax. And don't think my boys aren't going to hear about this when they get home."

Momma disappeared into the kitchen, and Hezekiah disappeared out the front door. He ran down the neighborhood street of little brick houses as fast as he could toward what looked like a large commercial building in the distance. The road dead ended. He leapt a guardrail bordering the parking lot of Regency Square Mall and sprinted across the hot asphalt to the mall entrance. He dashed into the first store he saw, searching for a phone, and twisted his way to the register in the back through the racks and shelves of expensive clothes and the blown-up photos on the walls of bare-chested young men holding scantily clad young women.

"Can I use your phone?" Hezekiah breathlessly asked the young man with short, tousled, highlighted hair behind the counter.

The store manager eyed him up and down. "Well, yes. Yes, you can. What in the world are you wearing?"

"It's the shirt and pants of a Confederate soldier," Hezekiah said, still shaking from his ordeal.

"No kidding? We're always on the lookout for the latest trends, and I love those cloth suspenders. Hey, Kristen," the manager hollered into the back storeroom behind him, "come out here and look at this." The young man reached across the counter, grabbed a little piece of Hezekiah's shirtsleeve, and rubbed it between his fingers. "Is this all cotton?"

"Yeah, it's what they wore in the 1860s," Hezekiah said impatiently as he eyed the phone out of reach below the counter.

"How retro. It feels like a high thread count and looks hand-stitched too. This must have been imported from Malaysia."

"No, it's American made. May I please use your phone?" Hezekiah pleaded.

A blond girl, emerging from the back, asked with amazement, "Oh my God, you don't carry a phone? What's going on here, Stephan?"

"Kristen, feel this."

The girl reached out and pinched Hezekiah's other shirt-sleeve. "Oh, I like this."

"Me too, and I like what's in it." Stephan almost growled at Hezekiah.

"Me too." Kristen raised her eyebrows and rubbed the shirt cloth more firmly.

"Would you mind taking off your shirt?" Stephan asked, losing his concentration for a moment.

"I just want to use your phone."

"Of course, but we'll trade your shirt for any one we have in the store. Kristen and I are working on our own line, and your shirt could be the style we need to define our look. It could be a big breakthrough for us. Don't you agree, Kristen?"

"Oh, yes, it's simple, yet sexy. I love this look, and it looks great on him," Kristen said as she ran her free hand down one of Hezekiah's suspender straps.

Hezekiah nervously looked behind him. "Could I please use your phone?"

"Certainly." Stephan put the phone on the counter, and Hezekiah grabbed the receiver. He punched in a number and said with a quiver, "Gordon?"

"Hezekiah," Gordon cried out. "Are you okay?"

"I'm okay. I'm at Regency Square. Can you come get me?" Hezekiah chuckled uneasily as the two store clerks continued pawing him to the driving beat of the piped in music.

"What's so funny?"

"Nothing."

"We were worried to death about you. You got away from those men?"

"Yeah, can you meet me in the food court in the mall?"

"Pat's driving me. We're on our way."

"I don't think they're looking for me yet, but would you hurry?"

"Don't worry. We'll be there as soon as we can."

Hezekiah hung up the phone.

"Look, I saw him first," Stephan said.

Kristen flipped her hair back. "Well, let's just ask him who he likes best."

CHAPTER 22

Gordon drove Jimmy and Hezekiah to the Richmond National Battlefield's Chimborazo Visitor Center where the two boys volunteered every Thursday. Although rattled from Hezekiah's abduction the previous day, Gordon and Raleigh agreed it was better for the boys to keep to their schedule, because they were probably safer at the visitor center than at the farm. The gold delivery to Sy had been aborted, and the treasure remained secure, buried in Pat's cornfield. Raleigh and Pat were back at the farm still digging in, just in case they were attacked before the FBI-sponsored Cold Harbor operation on Sunday that Gordon had gotten their buy-in on. Gordon was planning to rejoin them as soon as he dropped the boys off.

They cruised with the top down through the hot morning air, listening to a punk rock version of "The Bonnie Blue Flag." Gordon turned down the music as he turned at Thirty-third and East Broad Streets into the well-groomed Chimborazo Park. During the Civil War on this forty-acre plateau stood the largest military hospital in the world, looking more like a town than a medical facility.

The Confederate Chimborazo Hospital consisted of over one hundred long wooden whitewashed single-story buildings, originally built as barracks. Almost as many teepee-shaped Sibley tents were pitched. But still it wasn't enough room to prevent overcrowding, with the hospital having to accommodate at times almost four thousand patients. Over the course of the war, the convalescent hospital cared for 75,000 soldiers.

Nothing was left of the huge hospital complex. Soon after the war, most of the buildings were torn down for firewood. The only building on the grounds today was a boxy, light brown brick Greek Revival built in 1909 as an outpost for the US Weather Bureau that now served as an NPS visitor center and a Civil War medical museum. Outside flew a plain, dull yellow pennant designating a military hospital. The place was a memorial to a war where twice as many people died on sick beds than on battlefields.

Gordon stopped his car by the sidewalk, leading to the visitor center. "Okay, don't leave the building until five o'clock. I'll be right here to pick you up. Jimmy, you have your cell phone and all of our phone numbers on speed dial?"

"Yeah, Gordon, you've already asked me that about six times," Jimmy said as he and Hezekiah got out of the car.

"If there is trouble of any kind, call me. And if you can't get me, call your father or Pat." Gordon didn't pull away until he saw the boys go safely in the door.

Rather than going directly back to the farm, Gordon couldn't resist taking in the Chimborazo Hill overlook for a minute. The 162-foot hill was ambitiously named after the 20,565-foot inactive volcano in Ecuador.

He drove over to a terrace, teetering on the edge of an ancient canyon cut by the James River. The view of a rail yard, warehouses, and the urban-renewal housing of Fulton Bottom wasn't much, but the topography was powerful. From this vantage point, Gordon caught a glimpse of the river where in 1607 Captain Christopher Newport led an expedition, ten days after going ashore at Jamestown, to the falls of the James. On the fall line, Chief Powhatan's son Parahunt welcomed Newport and his twenty-three men, including John Smith.

Within seventy years, the English had cleared the land of Native Americans for tobacco production and established a feudal system, where the plantation owners were the kings and the slaves were the serfs. It would be another 188 years before this medieval model was overthrown. Even so, 150 years after the Civil War began, Gordon felt the plantation mentality was alive and well. The region's power brokers still maintained an intense fascination with property and seldom displayed a social conscience unless it benefited their businesses. The establishment insisted on a low-wage, low-tax, and low-service economy where private interests prevailed over public needs.

From the start, Richmond was doomed to be a second-shelf city, weighed down by the limited growth potential of a closed, oligarchic society. In the end, it was the matter of race stunting the city's growth. When slavery didn't work out for the South, separation of the races became Virginia's focus. Richmond was able to fend off school integration with Massive Resistance until 1970, in defiance of *Brown v. Board of Education of Topeka*, handed down in 1954. When the legal firewall broke, white people fled to the rural surrounding counties to maintain their separation geographically. Whitey was safe in the suburbs, protected by a Virginia law preventing cities from annexing neighboring counties.

By the 1980s, middle-class blacks followed the same flight pattern, producing a full-fledged economic apartheid, leaving the city mostly black and poor and the counties mostly white and affluent. The migration created a new separate and unequal society that integration had tried to correct. It left the counties and the city noncooperative and hostile toward each other, with both sides paying the price for not sharing resources and services. The racism cut both ways and dragged on the economy. What was driving old Dixie down these days was Dixie itself.

The tensions between the localities made it difficult to agree upon the best way to promote the Richmond region, a medium-sized metropolitan area of 1.2 million people. Obvious to

Gordon, Richmond's history as the heart of the Confederacy was the prime tourist attraction. But R-town boosters were reluctant to market their jewel on the James as a Civil War destination. They didn't want to appear backward and downbeat or make anyone uncomfortable by concentrating on a dark past. Richmond was Charleston with a guilty conscience.

Even with all its faults, Gordon embraced his adopted city. But there would always be those who made him feel like an outsider, letting him know he was just an interloper. Gordon didn't take it personally. He chalked it up to Richmond's native white population, heavily weighted toward English ancestry, leaving a legacy of a large segment of the citizenry stiff, elitist, and worshipping the past. But time was taking the old capital of the Confederacy onward. Despite itself, young people were flocking into Richmond. This clubby town of churches and debutantes was becoming a cosmopolitan city, while maintaining one of the best short tracks on the NASCAR circuit.

As Gordon contemplated the view and the sweep of history, his phone rang.

"Your humble and obedient servant, Gordon Barrett."

"Mr. Barrett, this is Sy."

Gordon stiffened with fear. "Yes?"

"You were very lucky, Mr. Barrett, to have gotten the boy back. They would have killed him, even if you had given them the gold. I like you, Mr. Barrett, so I am calling you to give you one last chance to prevent any bloodshed. If you come in this morning and drop off the coins to me, we'll just forget the whole thing."

"I can't deliver the gold to you today, but you can pick it up Sunday night at six at the Cold Harbor Visitor Center parking lot."

"Did you concoct that with the FBI? We're not fools, Mr. Barrett. I was hoping I could reason with you, but if I can't, you will be the biggest fool of all. You, your nephew, and your friends will all wind up dead. It's not worth it. You might as well deliver the gold to me because you're not going to be able to unload it. What would you do with the money anyway?"

"We'd buy Civil War battlefields as a memorial for the soldiers who died in the war."

For a moment, there was silence on Sy's end. "Do you know where the Hebrew Cemetery is on Shockoe Hill?"

"Yes."

"Can you meet me there in about ten minutes?"

"Are you bringing the Papadopoulous brothers?"

"No, just me."

"What do you want to meet about?"

"I have something else to tell you."

"Why don't you just tell me over the phone?"

"I think you'll understand better at the cemetery."

Gordon hesitated. "Okay, I'll meet you."

Gordon got back in the Delta and headed west on East Broad Street, wondering if he should have left the boys and whether he should call Raleigh and Pat to let them know what he was doing. He knew Raleigh's response would be negative, so he decided not to call. He wanted to hear Sy out, hoping Sy could offer him another option.

He coasted down steep Church Hill, then moved across the paved-over rich bottomland where Shockoe Creek used to run. Shockoe was a bastardized version of the American Indian name for the big flat rock at the mouth of the creek, where it flowed into the James River. The rock was nowhere in sight, and the creek now ran underground as part of the sewer system, but the name remained.

Gordon started up Shockoe Hill, passing the site of the city gallows where Gabriel was executed in 1800 for planning his slave insurrection. Conveniently located beside the gallows was the African Burial Ground. Most of this eighteenth- and nineteenth-century black cemetery was covered over when I-95 was constructed.

Still riding on Broad Street, Gordon gazed skyward at the big downtown buildings. Broad Street fifty years ago was the commercial center of the city and downtown Richmond's unofficial dividing line between whites and blacks. To the segregationist holdouts, the south side of Broad Street was still the white side, and the north side was still the black side. The line wasn't as clear as it used to be, but poor black people still waited for the bus along Richmond's main thoroughfare.

He turned north on Third Street, snaking around the city's maze of one-way streets to latch onto Fourth. He went over a bridge, crossing the interstate, and was traveling outside the comfort zone of many white folks in Richmond. He found Hospital Street and parked his car behind a clean white Cadillac along a high brick wall, protecting Shockoe Hill Cemetery, Richmond's first municipal cemetery.

Once St. John's churchyard had filled up, the business moved over to Shockoe Hill in 1822. Across the street was the Hebrew Cemetery. Richmond was home to one of the six original synagogue communities in America. When the Hebrews filled up their own cemetery at the base of Church Hill, they expanded to Shockoe Hill before the Gentiles in 1816.

Gordon put on his slouch hat and got out of his car. In the Hebrew Cemetery, he saw the back of a hunched-over figure walking with a cane and wearing a white, wide-brimmed canvas hat and a blue-and-white-striped seersucker suit. Gordon looked around to see if the man had brought anyone along. He saw no one else, crossed the street, and opened the gate to the cemetery. He walked

up the brick pathway as Sy reached out to place a pebble
of remembrance on the top of a tombstone among other
pebbles that had been left.

Attached to the front of the grave marker, the only one in a
large grassy plot, was a memorial tablet with a Star of David at
the top that read:

To the glory of God

And

In memory of

The Hebrew Confederate soldiers

Resting in this hallowed spot

Below the epitaph, the soldiers' names were listed, followed by:

Erected by

Hebrew Ladies Memorial Asso.

Richmond VA.

Organized 1866

At the base of the stone lay a wreath of red roses and milky magnolia blossoms. In front of the wreath were three hand flags, their
small staffs plunged into the ground. The American flag stood
on the left, the Israeli flag in the middle, and the Confederate
battle flag on the right.

Sy nodded to Gordon, then turned to walk out of the fenced-in
plot, closing the gate behind him. Gordon met him and shook
his hand. Sy gave Gordon a fatherly look. "You're still dressed
like a Confederate soldier? It's too hot today for wool, my boy."

"It's jean wool. It's a cotton-wool blend, not that hot."

"Regardless, you should dress a little more sensibly in this
heat or you'll get a stroke. You need to get yourself a nice light-
weight, light-colored suit like mine."

Gordon yielded politely to the sartorial suggestion.

Sy reached back and wrapped his weathered hand around the railing of the cast-iron fence. Although the ornate ironwork was rusting, it exhibited exceptional artistry. Iron had been molded into fence posts in the shape of four stacked mussel-loading rifles, their barrels shrouded by a Confederate battle flag and a kepi on top. The fence sections between the stacked arms were formed into crossed swords with laurel wreaths hanging from them.

For a few moments, Sy and Gordon stood in silence in the shade of an old elm, surveying the Jewish Confederate Soldiers' Section of the cemetery, a rare burial ground for Jewish soldiers outside of Israel.

Sy broke the silence. "Thirty Confederate Jewish soldiers are buried here. These boys were from all over the South—Texas, Louisiana, Mississippi, Georgia, the Carolinas, and, of course, Virginia. Thirty soldiers." Sy held the railing tight. "Not so many, when you consider 750,000 soldiers losing their lives in the American Civil War." A tear rippled down his cheek. "But the death of one solider or one civilian in war is one too many. Each one had family members enduring their loss. Life is too precious to be wasted away fighting to preserve unjust economic and social systems."

Sy let go of the rail, pulled out a handkerchief, wiped his eyes, and blew his nose. "When I get back, I'll have to call my business associates to let them know you won't hand over the gold. And they're not going to wait to meet you at Cold Harbor. They'll be coming after you as soon as I get off the phone, and you'll be in great danger."

"So why are you telling me this?"

Sy nodded his head toward the soldiers' graves. "For them. I wanted to give you a chance to get away and maybe cash that gold in and buy those battlefields for these forgotten men." His head and hands shook a little, and then he looked back at Gordon and handed him a slip of paper. "Here's the phone number of a dealer in New York who will give you top dollar for those coins. You tell him Sy sent you."

Gordon took the slip. "There's a Brazilian in town who wants to buy the gold."

"South Americans." Sy shrugged. "You never know where they're coming from, but you always know they're going to low-ball you. I'd give my guy a call."

As they walked out of the graveyard, Gordon looked across the street at Shockoe Hill Cemetery. In the distance, among the lawn of tombstones, he saw a woman in heavy mourning dress. He turned to Sy and pointed. "Do you see that?"

Sy squinted underneath his white hat. "See what?"

"Over there. A woman in a black crepe bell skirt and black veil."

Sy pressed his eyes against the horizon. "I don't see anyone. I think this heat is starting to get to you. You've got to get out of that uniform. At least take off the jacket. You're making me hot just looking at you."

Gordon pulled at a button on his shell jacket. "I think I'll go pay my respects to the folks across the street."

"Be careful," Sy said, as they crossed the road together.

Sy walked back to his Cadillac, and Gordon entered the gates of Shockoe Hill Cemetery, city owned and city neglected. Unmown grass and vandalized stones predominated the cemetery.

Gordon walked a short way up a pea gravel–covered lane, then cut across the lawn. He looked back across the street over the wall of the cemetery and admired an imposing brick building with three pedimented pavilions looming over the northern edge of the burial ground. The structure, built just before the war, was to be Richmond's almshouse but instead was pressed into service as a hospital for the Confederacy, initially for Union prisoners of war. In the summer of 1864 when Federal troops shelled and

burned Virginia Military Institute, VMI relocated to the almshouse and stayed there until the evacuation of Richmond the
following April.

Gordon continued on, passing the grave of John Marshall,
the great chief justice of the early nineteenth century who had
placed the Supreme Court on equal footing with the other two
branches of the US government by issuing court opinions estab-
lishing judicial review. But Gordon was more interested in visiting a tomb lying farther into the boneyard.

He entered a parallel lane. An arrow-shaped, metal sign
pointed the way to the grave where he wanted to pay homage.
Written in white paint on the black background of the sign was
the name. He strolled down a path between the headstones and
saw a large rock, shaded by a magnolia and a tulip tree, marking
the grave of the North's most successful spy during the war. The
"witch," as she was referred to by neighbors in her later years,
was buried standing up due to lack of space in the family plot.
Someone had left a small plastic American flag flower arrangement that had fallen on its face. The bronze plate embedded in
the rock read:

> Elizabeth L. Van Lew
> 1818–1900
> She risked everything that is dear to man —
> friends, fortune, comfort, health, life itself, all
> for the one absorbing desire of her heart — that
> slavery might be abolished and the Union pre-
> served. This boulder from the Capitol Hill in
> Boston is a tribute from Massachusetts friends.

Gordon thought about Elizabeth Van Lew and the truth in the
inscription. She was a forty-three-year-old spinster when the
war broke out and lived on Church Hill across from St. John's

Church. Her mother and father were from the North but made their money in the South. They had sent Elizabeth to school in Philadelphia. Elizabeth's father had died before the war, leaving his family a fortune, and she spent her inheritance running an espionage ring inside the capital of the Confederacy.

During the war, she was in constant communication with Union generals, hid Union soldiers in her home, and cared for Union prisoners. When Grant was headquartered at City Point in present-day Hopewell, Elizabeth Van Lew provided him everything from troop movements to a copy of Richmond's newspaper the *Daily Dispatch* every morning for breakfast reading. When Grant heard Richmond was evacuating, he ordered troops to do two things: maintain order in the city and provide for Miss Van Lew's safety. Once the Union Army occupied the city, large American flags flew over two prominent places, the state capitol building and Elizabeth Van Lew's mansion. Grant had tea with her when he visited Richmond in October of 1866 to thank her for her efforts during the war and appointed her postmaster of Richmond when he became president in 1869.

In her last years, she was a penniless pariah and received financial support from Massachusetts veterans and the family of the late Colonel Paul Joseph Revere, the great-grandson of Paul Revere, whom she had provided aid and comfort while he was a prisoner of war in Richmond. It was the Revere family who had sent the granite boulder to mark a grave that had originally gone unmarked for a death that had gone unmourned by the people of Richmond.

Eleven years after her death, the City of Richmond tore down her Church Hill mansion to build the Bellevue School. In the elegant home before the war, the Van Lews had entertained luminaries from the church, the state, and the arts. Poe had recited "The Raven" there. Richmond had saved so many of its older buildings, but it wouldn't save the home of a Yankee spy.

Gordon nervously looked over his shoulder past the west brick wall of the cemetery at the Gilpin Court housing project. The project was Richmond's oldest, largest, poorest, and most notorious. Gordon thought Elizabeth had worked hard to free the slaves, but some of their descendants, it seemed, had not progressed that far. Gordon reached down to prop up the flower arrangement beside the boulder and heard the crunch of crinoline and fallen magnolia leaves. He looked up, and from behind the tulip tree, the woman in black appeared.

"Don't touch that with your filthy Confederate hands."

"Whoa, whoa, whoa, and how do you do?" Gordon threw up his hands. "I'm Gordon Barrett. Who are you, ma'am?"

The woman brushed back her veil over her bonnet, revealing her face. "My name is Bet Van Lew."

"So you do Elizabeth Van Lew as your civilian reenactor impression?"

"No, my name is Bet Van Lew. Elizabeth Van Lew was my great-great-great aunt."

"Get out of town. You're kin to Crazy Bet and you're named after her?"

"She wasn't crazy. It was a disguise."

"I know. I know." Gordon studied her profile. "I see the resemblance." Then he pinpointed her. "I saw you at Marion's funeral and at Berkeley Plantation. I wondered where I had seen you before, but I hadn't, I had seen Elizabeth Van Lew's photograph." As Gordon looked her over, it dawned on him. "Were you spying on me when I was over at the Hebrew Cemetery?"

She clutched the jet cross hanging from her necklace. "I know you have the Confederate gold, and the FBI and I will make sure it goes into the hands of the United States government."

Gordon's jaw dropped. "You and the FBI, huh." He whipped out his phone from his trouser pocket and pressed the button for Agent Richard Howard.

"Dick, Gordon Barrett. I thought we had a deal. I thought you weren't going to follow me."

"What are you talking about?" Howard asked, annoyed. "I'm not following you."

"But your informant, Ms. Bet Van Lew, is. I'm standing here right beside her."

"What?" Howard gulped, knowing he had been found out.

"So what did you intend to do?" Gordon asked. "Use us as human shields, then take the gold?"

"We can't let you keep the gold," Howard conceded.

"Sure you can. We've already been over this. Here's the new deal. We not only want to give the gold for battlefield preservation and be free of prosecution, but I want Sy Meyer to have immunity, since he is helping me cash in the gold."

"Are you nuts?"

"Don't do anything he says, Richard," Bet screeched as she reached for Gordon's phone and Gordon stiff-armed her.

"If you hurt her," Howard warned, "all you'll get is a federal prison cell."

"She's the one trying to hurt me." Gordon fended Bet off as she tried to claw him as he backed away. "So listen up. Both the Gabrielites and the Compatriots have contacted me, and I told them both to meet me at Cold Harbor on Sunday night. Sy is going to let the Papadopoulos brothers know to meet us there too. But none of them are going to wait until Sunday night. They're all out looking for us now, and my pards and I are risking our lives for you. We just want you to hold up your end of the deal, because we're holding up ours."

"I think I'm going to need you to come back in and see me so we can regroup."

"Like I'm coming back in to see you so you can arrest me."

"If you don't come back in and talk to me, Mr. Barrett, I can't promise you immunity or protection."

"If we can't settle this over the phone, Cold Harbor is off."

"We're at Shockoe Hill Cemetery," Bet screamed to be heard.

"Got to go now, Dick." Gordon hung up, popped the battery out of his phone, then turned to Crazy Bet. "Ms. Van Lew, it was a pleasure to meet you."

"It's Miss Van Lew."

"Well, Miss Van Lew, I must be leaving before the FBI sends a car around for me. May I escort you out of the cemetery?" Gordon offered his arm.

"Piss off."

"That must be out of character for Elizabeth Van Lew to say. She would never be so ill-mannered."

"Oh, blow it out your arse."

"Good day then." Gordon tipped his slouch hat and walked briskly back to his car, leaving Crazy Bet in the field of the dead. He drove back over to Broad Street to a payphone and called the number Sy had given him.

"Benjamin Coins," the voice answered on the other end.

"May I speak to Mr. Benjamin?"

"I'm sorry. He won't be back until Monday. May I help you?"

"No, I'll call back then."

CHAPTER 23

P at and Raleigh were up to their ankles in mud, reinforcing the newly dug trench around the farmhouse with fascines, when Gordon returned and reported what had happened at the Hebrew and Shockoe Hill Cemeteries.

Raleigh erupted, pulling himself out of the ditch. He threw his hat down on the ground, cutting a shine. "The deal is off with the FBI? We've got no protection? We've got no immunity? These crazy white people and crazy black people and crazy Greek people are all out to kill us for gold the FBI is just going to take away from us anyway?"

Pat crawled out of the hole, caught Raleigh by the arm, and jerked him. "Snap out of it. Why don't we start thinking about what we're going to do to them rather than what they're going to do to us?"

Gordon smiled. "Right, let's quit thinking about what Bobby Lee is going to do to us and think about what we are going to do to Bobby Lee."

Raleigh regained his composure and took a long breath in and out. His thin lips trembled. "You all made your point, but if you're going to talk like Ulysses S. Grant in the Wilderness, remember what he told a reporter that same day, 'If you see the president, tell him, from me, that, whatever happens, there will be no turning back.'"

Raleigh, resuming his role as captain, pointed down to the edge of the property. "The creek is rising. The abatis, cheval-de-frise, and tripwires are all in place, and the fort will be finished tomorrow. We're fully committed here and there is no turning back. We should move the gold."

"Why?" Gordon questioned with an aggravated voice, still thinking it was just another scheme for Raleigh to cash in for himself.

"In case we have to abandon the position," Raleigh clarified. "If no one can find our gold, then we still have bargaining power."

"All right, but where?" Gordon asked.

Pat suggested, "The Confederates buried the body of Colonel Dahlgren in Oakwood Cemetery to hide it."

Gordon thought about it. "We could stick it back in the corner of the Confederate section of the cemetery. Nobody ever goes back there except the maintenance crews to cut the grass."

"Okay," Raleigh said. "Let's move it there."

In the late afternoon, they dug up the gold from the waist-high cornfield and loaded it into the back of Pat's truck. They picked up the boys from the visitor center and put them in the back with the gold.

Pat crossed over Broad Street to Chimborazo Boulevard, a big name for a narrow, two-lane street, covered in Belgian blocks in need of repair. The road cut through the Oakwood-Chimborazo Historic District, a blend of assorted architecture mixed in with the dilapidated.

"Where you going?" Raleigh asked.

"Taking a shortcut to the cemetery," Pat said.

Raleigh was ill at ease. "You could get us killed going through this neighborhood. Turn around and go to the front entrance. It's bad enough going that way, much less this way."

Pat reasoned, "If we go through the back entrance, we don't have to go by the cemetery office, and we're right there at the Confederate section."

"It's not that bad, Raleigh," Gordon reassured, crowding them with his girth sitting in the middle of the cab seat. "If we stay on the beaten path and you don't scream any racial slurs out the window, we should be fine."

Raleigh pursed up.

During the crack cocaine wars of the mid-1990s, Richmond was known as Murder City, and this was one of the parts of town helping it earn its nickname. The crime rate was down, but the image lingered, and city leaders hoped to come up with a better promotional slogan than "Richmond: Safer Than It Used to Be."

Pat hung a right at a tiny worn triangular park onto Oakwood Avenue, passing houses with black folks sitting on their porches, escaping from the heat inside their homes. A half-mile down, they entered through the twin iron gates of Oakwood Cemetery, anchored by square stone pillars, capped by sculpted upside-down giant acorns with oak leaves on their sides.

Oakwood's claim to fame came during the war when the Confederates secretly buried Federal Colonel Ulric Dahlgren here. Dahlgren died on March 2, 1864, leading a cavalry raid on Richmond and carrying orders to assassinate Jefferson Davis and his cabinet. The discovery of the orders ignited an international controversy and may have fueled John Wilkes Booth's desire to assassinate Abraham Lincoln. Stirring the pot, the Confederates defiled the body before putting it in the ground. But the young colonel was retrieved a month later by Elizabeth Van Lew's spy ring and reburied on a Unionist's farm ten miles northwest of Richmond. After the war, the body was removed again and returned to Dahlgren's father, Admiral John Dahlgren, the inventor of the Dahlgren gun.

During the war, thousands of Union soldiers who weren't sons of admirals were buried at Oakwood, mostly the Belle Isle prison camp dead. After the war, 3,200 of them were removed and buried at the Richmond National Cemetery, four miles away on Williamsburg Road. The only Civil War soldiers left at Oakwood were Confederates. Seventeen thousand lay on seven-and-a-half acres, eight thousand unknown.

Richmond's first Memorial Day was held at Oakwood Cemetery on May 10, 1866. Robert E. Lee was invited to speak but declined, writing back to the Ladies' Memorial Association sponsoring the event, "The graves of the Confederate dead will always be green in my memory, and their deeds will be hallowed in my recollection."

Unfortunately, this place didn't match Lee's remembrance. This wasn't the pastoral setting of Hollywood Cemetery. Most of this cemetery's namesake oak trees had been cleared, leaving a field of stones out in the sun, with grass not cut as often as it should have been.

Once through the gate, Pat turned right on Confederate Drive. The graves were marked with small cubes of marble, rising about six inches out of the ground, providing only enough room to engrave three identification numbers on their sides to mark three separate graves. The stones at first were unimpressive, but once a visitor realized that each tiny monument represented the graves of three Confederate soldiers, the gravity of the ground kicked in. This field of little stones went on for a quarter of a mile, with only a few Confederate flags breaking up the monotony. The miniature marbles made the Confederate soldiers beneath them seem less significant, but these small grave markers were all the South could afford at the turn of the twentieth century.

Pat followed the long, curved, flat lane past the obelisk and two cannons in the middle of the dead. The road started to gently slope, disclosing even more miniature tombstones. On the left was a bandstand, once used for the large Memorial Day celebrations. The last one was held in 1966, one hundred years after the first one, before the whites moved out of the neighborhood and the blacks moved in. Below the bandstand a plaque read:

1861–1865
Lest we forget
The sacrifices and devotion of the
Women of the Confederacy
Lee Chapter 123
United Daughters of the Confederacy

With Confederate dead now on both sides of the road, the pavement dropped off and turned into dirt and gravel. Pat took the left fork over a low concrete curb, following it into a grove of southern red oaks and pignut hickories. He stopped under the trees at the head of a turnaround circle adjacent to a woods fringed with blooming mimosas disseminating their honey-fruit scent.

They jumped out of the truck, and squirrels scampered in the trees, giving the pards a small scare. Gordon and Pat pulled the chest of gold out of the truck bed with Hezekiah and Jimmy pushing on it. Gordon and Pat lugged the weighty box in fits and starts over a knoll. Jimmy and Hezekiah brought up the rear with picks and shovels, as Raleigh provided instruction. They weaved between the stones to the end of the plots where there was a grassless zone in the shade.

Raleigh dashed off more orders. "Hezekiah, I want you to go back over by the truck and keep a lookout. Jimmy, you can help us dig. All we need to do now is find a spot where we don't hit any remains."

Gordon pointed. "This is a vacant plot here."

"How do you know?" Raleigh asked.

"I've talked to the head groundskeeper before on grave locations."

"You have?" Pat smiled, amused, grabbed a shovel, and started digging.

The cicadas in the trees ripped around them as they dug. The ground, hard from lack of rain, made their work difficult. Once the task was accomplished, Gordon raked over the site, trying to disguise that the ground had been broken.

Raleigh was calm but exhibited his sweaty brow. "Let's get out of here."

"Sounds good," Gordon said. "This is the fourth cemetery I've been in during the last two days. I'm starting to question my social life."

Pat leaned on his shovel. "Yeah." He paused and looked back over the mass of little stones. "Let's get out of this lonely place."

CHAPTER 24

Late Friday afternoon, the Flood brothers traveled the twenty-two miles south of Richmond on I-95 to cross the Appomattox River. The Petersburg skyline on the right looked, for the most part, remarkably the same as it did during the Civil War. Before the war, the future of Petersburg was bright as the second largest city in Virginia and the seventh-largest city in the South. The town bustled, competitive with Richmond, as a manufacturing center and transportation hub. Alas, Petersburg's "golden age" of the 1850s was never to return. Petersburg became more of a victim of time rather than a victim of war. Grant's bombardment of the city did minimal damage, and the economy recovered after the war. But as the years went by, the jobs and the brains drained to other cities.

It had been two days since Carter had received his invitation to Cold Harbor for Sunday evening. He had spoken to Garnett, and Garnett had advised him against going. They both suspected it was a setup. They had agreed to keep looking for the reenactors and still had all weekend to find them before resorting to a rendezvous at Cold Harbor. Garnett wanted to reconvene with Carter and Wendell before continuing their manhunt. He had asked them to meet him at the Crater and to bring some barbeque.

The brothers took the Crater Road exit. About a half-mile farther south, they came to a commercial intersection where a statue stood at the foot of the Merchant's Tire & Auto parking lot. A likeness of Colonel George W. Gowen of the 48th Regiment of the Pennsylvania Volunteers was erected by the citizens of Schuylkill County, Pennsylvania. It was a rare statue of a Northern Civil War soldier in the South.

Carter and Wendell raised their middle fingers in defiance of the permanent occupation. They drove on through the scruffy commercial district in the rush hour traffic. Integration and white flight had left Petersburg with an African American population of almost 80 percent, the highest of any municipality in the state. High poverty and crime rates, bad schools, and short life spans made Petersburg the stepchild of Metro Richmond.

A mile down the road, Carter and Wendell found their destination and turned in at a tin sign shaped like a fireplace, outlined in busted white neon, proclaiming King's famous BAR • B • Q Number 2. They got out of the truck cab and into the heat, and found refuge through the restaurant's carry-out door. Their mouths watered as they spied over the counter the pork shoulders in the open kitchen. The slabs of meat warmed over an oak fire after being pit cooked out back for six hours.

Once their orders were filled, they drove back the way they came, giving Colonel Gowen the bird again on the return trip and eating as they went. They passed the one-way exit gate of the Petersburg National Battlefield.

"Damn, the Crater is right over there, but they won't let you go in that way." Carter's craggy voice faded out, then tuned back in. "So now we have to drive all the way around. Garnett sure as hell better appreciate this. He could have just called to tell us what he had on his mind. When I told him we should meet someplace a little more convenient, this wasn't what I meant." Carter continued to drive the three miles around to the battlefield entrance, where they stopped at the contact booth to pay the entrance fee.

Carter pulled away. "What really burns my ass is having to pay to get on our own land." He quickly circled the visitor center parking lot to start the tour drive through one of America's most significant Civil War battlefields.

Grant and Lee only faced each other for eleven months of the four-year civil war. Nine and a half of those months were at Petersburg. During the war, Petersburg became Richmond's lifeline. Its railroads connected the capital of the Confederacy to the rest of the South. Grant couldn't capture Richmond, but he could cut the capital off from its supply center. To execute this stranglehold, Grant laid siege to Petersburg. Lee held the line, and the misery of modern trench warfare was born.

The Flood brothers drove along the siege line past Fort Stedman, where Lee led his last offensive, checked by Grant before checkmated at Appomattox Court House. Beyond the earthen fort, at the beginning of the nine-month Siege of Petersburg, the 1st Maine Heavy Artillery took the heaviest regimental loss in a single action during the war, losing over 70 percent of its men in ten minutes.

The brothers rode through the rolling countryside, with barn swallows swooping in the air and bluebirds sitting on cannons, until they reached the last stop on the battlefield drive. Carter parked the truck just as they finished their meal in transit. Wendell grabbed the lone full white bag. Instead of taking the meandering walkway, they made a beeline across the football field–sized meadow, where they found Garnett leaning over a split-rail fence, holding a brown bag and looking into a large, grassed-over hole in the ground.

Garnett saw the white bag with the grease stains Wendell was holding. "Give me that barbeque. I didn't think you all were ever going to show up. Did you get it with slaw?"

"I got it with slaw," Wendell said, handing him the bag. "How else am I going to get it?"

Garnett took a seat on the bench beside the fence and sat his brown bag down. He opened the white bag, reached in to pull out a french fry with the skin on, and took a bite. "A little cold."

"Maybe it would be warm," Carter said, "if we didn't have to drive all the way around Petersburg to meet you."

Garnett gobbled down the rest of the fries despite his initial critique, then opened the brown bag beside him, pulled out a fifth of Rebel Yell about two-thirds of the way gone, uncapped it, and took a belt. "It's important to come here so we can remind ourselves about the first place in Virginia where the North used the mud people against us and what happened." Garnett grabbed his barbeque sandwich from out of the bottom of the bag and stood up with the sandwich in one hand and the bottle of whiskey in the other. He sat the bottle on the fence post and unwrapped his sandwich from its white-paper covering as the three men watched over the pit, greatly reduced in size by man and erosion over the years. This was the Crater.

A 511-foot tunnel from the Union defense line was dug to this spot by a regiment of Pennsylvania coal miners. The miners placed 320 kegs containing 8,000 pounds of gunpowder directly underneath the Rebel trenches. Barely before sunrise on July 30, 1864, the powder was ignited, producing a mushroom cloud and a 170-foot gap in the Confederate line. Instead of Union troops moving around the breach, they marched into the freshly created 30-foot deep hole for what they thought was a ready-made fortress, but in reality was a deathtrap. Some of those Union troops were black, the first black troops to be deployed in Virginia for a major engagement. The Southerners were out-raged that the Negro was used against them in this fashion and shot the Union soldiers in the Crater like fish in a barrel. The white Union soldiers were allowed to surrender, but not the black ones. The Confederates' battle cry was "Take the white man! Kill the nigger!" Some white Union soldiers killed their black counterparts in fear of being killed if caught with them. An operation that could have shortened the Petersburg siege by eight months turned out to be what Grant called "a stupendous failure," chalked up to poor planning, training, and execution, combined with drunken officers.

"Have a drink," Garnett offered.

Wendell grabbed the bottle from the post, while Garnett took a big bite out of his small, spicy sandwich. The bun was stale, but the minced barbeque covered with green slaw was moist and potent with a superior tang.

Garnett began to talk with his mouth full. "Southerners are the superior white race." The meat juice ran down his chin, but he didn't bother to wipe it off. "We are descended from the Norman barons of William the Conqueror, known for their ability to fight, and we will win this time around." He took the bottle from Wendell, tippled it, and passed it on to Carter. "The mud people keep growing in number, while our numbers dwindle. The government has given the mud people our jobs and our women, attempting to make these inferiors our equal. But they will never be our equal by the natural order.

"It is time for us to fight again to preserve our culture, our rights, and our values. We are the true patriots defending our land and liberating our state. The invaders will be repelled, and we will be vindicated. It is time for, in the last written words of Edmund Ruffin, 'deliverance & vengeance for the now ruined, subjugated, & enslaved Southern States!'" He swallowed the last bit of his sandwich and cleared his throat. "Time for dessert."

Garnett reached over to the white bag he had left on the bench and pulled out a half-sized Styrofoam cup and a plastic spoon. He lifted off its lid, revealing a piece of fatback floating on top of barbecued beans. He swiftly scooped out the fat meat and spooned it into his mouth. "Ah, that's the best part." Then he ate the beans, buoyed in a soup of shredded slivers of barbeque. "Nothing better than King's beans."

Garnett reached for the bourbon from Carter and held the bottle by its body. "I checked the plates on the Delta 88 you followed to the Jefferson Hotel that Fuqua was riding in. It belongs to a Gordon Barrett."

Carter fished a cigarette out of his pack. "That was the guy telling me to meet Fuqua at Cold Harbor."

Garnett took a drink and gave the bottle to Wendell. "I found out Fuqua and Barrett have a friend who owns a farm somewhere out in the East End. I'm having a little difficulty locating it. I've got a feeling they're hiding out on that farm. If we can find the farm, I think we'll find Fuqua and the gold."

Wendell drank the last of the liquor, capped the empty bottle, and placed it on the fence post. He looked down into the Crater. "When we find these men with the gold, there will be no quarter for them either. We will 'kill 'em. Kill 'em all.'"

Garnett nodded his approval and took off his black army beret, exposing his perspiring shaved head. He balanced the beret on the bottle's neck with the Confederate battle flag insignia facing them. He stepped back, then stretched out his right arm with his palm open to the sky. Carter and Wendell followed by raising their arms in the same fashion. Garnett led the Pledge of Allegiance to the Confederate flag. "I salute the Confederate flag, with affection, reverence, and undying devotion to the cause for which it stands."

CHAPTER 25

P etersburg had two Memorial Days, the US Memorial Day in May and its own Memorial Day on June 9. The latter began in 1865 and placed Petersburg in the field of over two dozen other towns claiming to be the birthplace of Memorial Day, originally called Decoration Day. In 1865 Nora Davidson, a local schoolteacher, and her students strewed garlands on soldiers' graves to commemorate those who had died defending their homes in Petersburg on June 9, 1864.

In 1864, all of the able-bodied men were off to war, and the town's militia of 125 old men and young boys held off 1,300 Union cavalrymen until reinforcements arrived. They prevented a quick Federal victory, forcing the longest land siege in North American history. A commemorative service was held every June 9 at Blandford Church and Cemetery about a mile northwest of the Crater.

Ballard McMullen was still in town hoping to purchase the gold coins from the reenactors. Driving his rental car, he had picked up Julius Bohannon at the Virginia Historical Society thirty minutes earlier, and they rode through the entrance of the Blandford churchyard. The colonial brick church, completed in 1737, sat on the highest hill in Petersburg and was the oldest building in the city. The church eventually fell into ruin, but in the early part of the twentieth century was restored and converted into a Confederate memorial.

Julius adjusted his bow tie in the side mirror. "The church is closed for the day, but you really need to come back to see its

Tiffany windows. It has a Tiffany dedicated to every Confederate state except Kentucky." He shook his head and elevated his eyebrows behind his large horn-rims. "Kentucky never fully committed." Julius raised his palm to his lips, then moved it out and down slowly, almost as if blowing a kiss. "But at this time of the day and the year with the sun in the west, the green robe of St. Matthew is just on fire in the Florida window."

They motored around to the back of the church and down the hill through the memorial granite arch for the Confederate dead, with the inscription on the front "Our Confederate Heroes" and on the back "Awaiting The Reveille." Blandford Cemetery housed approximately 30,000 reinterred Confederate dead, mostly from the Siege of Petersburg, more Confederate graves than anywhere, most unknown.

Once past the arch entrance, there were mass graves by Southern state on both sides of the road, marked only by two-and-a-half-foot-high rectangular stone pillars etched with the name of the state. Julius studied a map. "I think we need to go back."

Ballard drove the car up Memorial Hill to a bandstand once used for the June 9 ceremonies. He turned around on A. P. Hill Avenue and maneuvered the car back through the arch and up the hill to the cemetery's older section. Confederate flags marked several graves, left over from the just-passed ninth of June observance.

"I appreciate you coming out here with me today," Ballard said.

"I'm always happy to aid a fellow Petersburg descendant with genealogical research."

Ballard had called the Virginia Historical Society for information on his family tree and was referred to a curator. Julius took the call and was exuberant to have a descendant of a Confederado on his hands, and offered his assistance in Ballard's ancestral grave search. Besides, Julius couldn't resist a man with a Southern-Portuguese accent.

They had almost reached the top of the hill when Julius instructed, "Just pull over to the side."

The two men left the comfort of the air-conditioned car. Ballard put on his straw hat and followed Julius. Julius, wearing a full suit, stepped up from the sunken road onto the cemetery lawn with a grunt of exertion, then offered Ballard a hand up. The pungent smell of boxwoods and cedars sifted through the air as a mockingbird sang. It was a perfectly serene place if you ignored the sound of the traffic on Crater Road and the sight of a cell phone tower rising over the dead. They walked between two elaborate iron fences, surrounding family squares. Blandford was well known for its decorative cast- and wrought-iron fences, part of the funerary art of the Victorian era. They continued walking through the cemetery to a square unprotected by a fence.

"Here he is," Julius proclaimed.

In front of them, a small, rectangular stone was cut with the words "Harold McMullen, Died 1865." A small Confederate battle flag stood by the stone.

"It's him," Ballard said excitedly, pointing at the flag, "and someone remembered. It's my great-great-grandfather's older brother. He wanted to go to Brazil with his younger brother but died of smallpox before they could leave. Harold was much older than my great-great-grandfather and had fought in the Mexican War, but both brothers fought together in Mahone's Brigade during the Civil War. And their father fought in the War of 1812, marching from Petersburg to protect northwest Ohio and Indiana from British invasion. And his father fought in the Battle of Petersburg during the Revolutionary War."

Ballard choked up for a moment, then continued. "Three generations of McMullens provided for the founding and freedom of this nation, but in the end, the McMullens lost their country and felt they had to leave. My great-great-grandfather wrote in a letter, 'If only the abolitionists had left us alone, we would never have left for Brazil.'"

Ballard stepped back from the grave, still looking at the stone. "History is a funny thing. Most people aren't interested in it. They look at history as mythical stories that have no bearing. But we're all a part of history, because it affects how we live our lives today. I'm a Brazilian citizen because of a war fought 150 years ago."

Julius put his hand on Ballard's shoulder. "Our ancestors suffered so we could have better lives."

Ballard shrugged. "At least different lives." He overturned the somberness of the moment by changing the subject. "I must tell you, Mr. Bohannon, I find this phenomenon of Civil War reenacting fascinating. I was wondering if you knew any Civil War reenactors you could put me in touch with."

"As a matter of fact, I know several reenactors. One in particular, a Mr. Pat McCandlish, I would highly recommend. He is a beautiful man, and I'm sure he would be happy to answer any questions you might have if you tell him I referred you. He also has a friend Gordon Barrett who would be helpful to you as well."

"Do you know where I can find them?"

"Pat has a farm in Varina. Gordon may be harder to locate. I should have their phone numbers on file, since I have assisted them both with research at the Society. In fact, I saw Pat earlier this week with a young lady." Julius sighed in resignation. "He may be busy with her. You may have better luck catching up with Gordon."

Julius picked a piece of lint off the front of Ballard's shirt and brushed it with his hand, then looked into Ballard's dark eyes. "I'm restoring a place in Old Towne Petersburg, away from the rabble of Richmond. Would you like to come and see it?"

CHAPTER 26

About a mile northwest of Blandford Church lay Old Towne Petersburg. Because of a fire in 1815, most residents and businesses rebuilt with brick, leaving Petersburg with a historic district noteworthy as any in Virginia. Petersburg most likely would do another phoenix act in the future, prompted by a real estate boom caused by the expansion of Fort Lee to the east. Already colonized by artists, Old Towne Petersburg was filling up with antique stores and boutiques, a sure sign the philistines wouldn't be far behind.

Among these historic buildings, just down from the Siege Museum on Bank Street, was Alexander's. From the outside, it looked like it was closed, but on the inside it was alive with diners. Against a wall sat the Papadopoulos brothers.

"Why did we have to come all the way to Petersburg to eat?" Bob asked.

"Because you can't get a souvlaki sandwich in Richmond like the ones they make here," Lichas replied, "and the price is right."

"The price is right? You make me sick with your penny-pinching. You have more money than anyone I know."

"Yeah, and tomorrow I will have more."

The meals came and Lichas's souvlaki was wrapped in a hot pita and smothered with wet feta cheese on top.

Bob looked down at his brother's supper. "Why can't you get a real meal, like my veal ala Greca? Did you ever think of ordering something you eat with a knife and fork?"

"This sandwich is a real meal. Take a bite." Lichas pushed the sandwich into Bob's face.

"I don't want a bite."

"You don't know what you're missing."

Lichas crammed the sandwich into his mouth, but most of the feta cheese went on his face and hands.

"Oh, for the love of God," Bob said. "Use a napkin. You're eating like an animal. You're my older brother. You should be setting an example."

"I am setting an example for you, but you're not following it. Look at you with that suit and tie. You could pass for Anglo. Sometimes I think you're ashamed to be Greek."

"Let's just drop it and try to enjoy our supper." Bob paused, wanting to reach over and wipe the feta off his brother's face.

With a full mouth, Lichas talked into his souvlaki as if it were a microphone. "I got a call from Virginia Beach this afternoon. Turns out one of the dress-up boys has a farm out in Varina. That's probably where they're hiding out."

"So we can go out there tomorrow and finish the job?"

"Yeah, too bad Momma messed it up for us the first time." Lichas lowered his voice. "Now we have to take care of them all, but business is business. After this is over, maybe I'll go out to Nevada for a vacation. Maybe swing by Arizona and New Mexico. Someplace where the air is clear, not heavy and dirty like it can be here in the summertime."

Bob started delicately cutting into his veal. "We should get an early start tomorrow."

Lichas kept stuffing the souvlaki into his pie hole and talking at the same time. "You know I always sleep in on Saturday and after I wake up, I'll need to eat a big breakfast. I can't go to work on an empty stomach."

Bob didn't see the point arguing with Lichas. He knew the result would be the same. "Fine. We can leave around eleven."

CHAPTER 27

Below the streets of Old Towne Petersburg lay Pocahontas Island. The misnamed little peninsula on the Appomattox River was originally the site of a Native American village but became the first free black settlement in Virginia and one of the largest in America. Inspired or feeling guilty after the American Revolution, numerous Virginia planters emancipated their slaves, some of which were their children. Many of these former slaves flocked to Petersburg because of the availability of jobs. Before the Civil War, thousands of freed men and women called Pocahontas Island home. Joseph Jenkins Roberts, a leading figure in the Back-to-Africa movement and the first president of Liberia in 1848, grew up here.

Despite the historical and cultural value of Pocahontas Island, in 1971 the white-majority Petersburg City Council tried to zone its residents out of existence. The council zoned the island as light industrial, preventing homeowners from obtaining loans for renovations. The idea was to have the houses deteriorate enough so they could be condemned and the residents would be forced to move. The island's inhabitants hired a lawyer and reversed the decision in 1975.

Fewer than one hundred residents held on, mostly elderly, living in meager homes on the island's five streets, sharing the spit of land with a heating oil company, warehouses, and the South Central Wastewater Authority. The community's center-piece was the Pocahontas Chapel. The original wooden structure was moved here by barge in 1868 from City Point and used as a Freedman's Bureau School. In 1993, a tornado blew the small white chapel down, and it was replaced by a sturdier replica, topped by the surviving little steeple holding the original church bell.

This evening behind the chapel, a celebration was going on. Dancers in chromatic costumes moved to the beat of African drums, and the smell of fried fish permeated the air. Away from the jubilee on the north side of the island, Fattah sat between Leela and Hark in lawn chairs beside the river. The Appomattox was about sixty yards across here, just down from its fall line and just above the roar of the I-95 traffic crossing it. Fattah and Hark cooled out in shorts, sandals, and dashikis. Leela relaxed in a caftan with matching pants and head wrap.

The Gabrielites toasted with applejack in snifters. Hark drew his glass away from his nose. "We know they're somewhere in the East End, since I was able to follow them from the Jefferson almost to the end of Main Street before I lost them. They have to come in and out of the city. The primary way back into town is on Main Street, so all we have to do is stake out the east entrance of town and we'll probably catch them"

"We'll start the stakeout tomorrow morning," Leela said.

"They won't be going anywhere before then, and I won't hesitate to use my heater when we find them."

Fattah nodded his approval, handed his glass to Leela, and stood up. He looked across the water to Colonial Heights, the white flight suburb of Petersburg, shook his fist, and said, "Colonial Whites." He took a couple of steps down the riverbank and pivoted, putting him at eye level with Leela and Hark, and started speaking softly and steadily.

"Young's Spring has run dry, but it's time again for the waters to rush forth. Gabriel's Rebellion failed, but ours will succeed. We don't have to break into an armory because we're already fully armed. There is no Tom or Pharaoh to betray us. And the rain won't stop us this time. Rather we will rain down upon the white man never to be enslaved again."

Fattah pointed upstream to the old railroad bridge abutments in the river. "The Richmond and Petersburg Railroad used to run across this water. Another train also rolled through. It was the same train that ran a thousand miles away from here, out of Missouri and through Kansas and Nebraska and on into Iowa. It was the Underground Railroad." Fattah turned to face the river, speaking with a louder but still steady voice and raising his fist back up. "But it is no longer a time to run away. It is time for the avenging angel to draw near again, and as it is written in Hebrews 9:22, 'And almost all things are by the law purged with blood; and without shedding of blood is no remission.'"

CHAPTER 28

R aleigh turned off his backhoe and climbed down. With his back to the late afternoon sun, he walked up to join his pards resting on the porch. They had been working most of the day on the fortifications around the house.

"That's it. We're done," Raleigh said, looking over their handiwork.

"It's a thing of beauty," Pat admired as he wobbled in a rocking chair, drinking a glass of lemonade and feeling confident they were safe in their fortress.

Over the past four days, Raleigh had dug a six-foot trench behind the fraise around Pat's house and had taken the dirt to build a six-foot earthen wall between the trench and house. Gordon hadn't been able to borrow cannons on such short notice with no questions asked, so they placed Quaker cannons, black-painted logs, around the parapet. In front of the fortress, along the side of the hill, were layers of abatis, cheval-de-frise, and tripwires. And beyond these obstacles at the bottom of the hill, the dammed creek created an inundation, preventing entry from the main road. Pat had tested his pontoon bridge for a crossing, then disassembled it so the enemy couldn't use it.

"We'll be ready for them if they come," Raleigh said as he wiped his brow with his forearm. "There's only one thing left to do."

Jimmy, frustrated from having been overly supervised by his father all day, asked exasperatedly, "What's that?"

"To make sure we're clear on everything, we need to hold a council of war."

"It's going to have to be later tonight," Pat said as he took another sip of lemonade. "I'm taking Ann out to dinner."

Raleigh's mustache buckled. "Don't you think it might be a good idea to stay home, since we've been receiving death threats and one of us was kidnapped? Oh yeah, and I forgot to mention, we're wanted by the fricking FBI."

"Settle down, Raleigh," Pat said. "I'll be careful. It'll be all right. The enemy is close, but not that close."

"I hope you're right," Raleigh said, remaining unconvinced.

Gordon, leaning on the banister, raised his eyebrows. "Another date with Ann? Where you all going?"

"The Half Way House."

"Isn't this date number three? The consecration date. You should get further than halfway."

Pat took out the ice cube he had just stored in his cheek and threw it at Gordon. Gordon dodged the projectile.

Hezekiah interrupted the horseplay, hemming and hawing, "Gordon, can you drop me in Ashland at Kim's?"

"Sure. Everybody's got a date for Friday night except the fat boy," Gordon replied. "Oh yeah, sorry, Raleigh, Jimmy."

Raleigh stared in disbelief. "We're on high alert here and all you all can think about is gallivanting around town?"

"Why not get in one last night of exquisite lovemaking before the big battle." Gordon clawed at his own chest through his shirt with his fingertips while forming a Q with his open mouth and tongue as his head and eyes cocked skyward.

"You disgust me." Raleigh turned away.

The phone inside the house rang, and they all turned nervously toward the sound.

"I'll get it," Pat said as he rose and went inside the house. He came back out and handed the cordless phone to Raleigh. "It's for you."

"Who is it?"

"Linda."

Raleigh made a face and took the phone. "Hi, Linda. How did you know I was here?"

"I knew if I just started calling around to all of your worthless reenactor friends I would eventually find you."

"So you found me. Calling to give me another tongue-lashing?"

"Let's drop the hostilities for a minute, Raleigh. Gayle is sick. I checked her into the VCU Medical Center."

"What's wrong with her?" Raleigh voiced true alarm.

"She was having chest pains. They ran some tests, and we're waiting to see what they show. She's resting right now, but she wanted me to call you to see if you would bring Jimmy down to see her this evening around seven thirty. The doctor said it would be okay for you to stay an hour."

"We'll be there."

"They're going to move her, so check the front desk for the room number."

"Oh, have you called her work?"

"Yeah, I've already talked to her boss. He seemed a lot more concerned than you are."

Raleigh contained his emotions from the slight. "Thanks, Linda," he said and hung up.

Raleigh looked over at Jimmy. "Son, your mom is sick. We've got to go downtown to the hospital tonight to see her."

"What's wrong with her?"

"They don't know, but I'm sure she'll be fine," Raleigh reassured Jimmy.

"I hope it's nothing serious," Pat said.

"They're running some tests. Linda told me we could visit for an hour." Raleigh paused, then got back on task. "The White House of the Confederacy is right beside the hospital. We can have our council of war there, say around nine in the garden, after Jimmy and I finish visiting."

"Are you sure with Gayle sick?" Gordon asked. "We could postpone the council."

"There's nothing I can really do. We'll be down there anyway, so we might as well meet at the Gray House."

CHAPTER 29

Gordon chauffeured Hezekiah down Ashland's Railroad Avenue that turned into Center Street, where the train tracks ran in the middle of the road. Mineral springs were discovered in Ashland, and in the 1840s, the Richmond, Fredericksburg, and Potomac Railroad developed the town as a resort. But the springs no longer existed, and left beside the tracks were turn-of-the-twentieth-century homes, a commercial center built after a fire in 1893, and Randolph-Macon College.

Out of New York, a stinking trash train of dirty green and gray containers caught up with Gordon and Hezekiah as they rode down Center Street. Trash was one of the state's leading imports, making Virginia for garbage rather than for lovers. The train rumbled beside them, so close Gordon could almost touch it.

The locomotive blasted its whistle as Gordon pulled his car up to the curb beside the sidewalk next to Kim's house. Kim sat on a swing, suspended from the limb of an old walnut tree. Hezekiah waved to her and jumped out of the convertible without opening the door.

"I'll pick you up at eight. I'm going to turn my phone back on until then in case you need me. Watch your back," Gordon hollered from the driver's seat, but he wasn't sure Hezekiah heard him over the roar of the train that was still passing. He pulled away as Hezekiah ran to meet Kim.

Kim, in her summer dress and elfish haircut, hopped out of the swing to greet Hezekiah.

"I've never seen you in a modern dress," Hezekiah sputtered. "You look good."

Kim blushed. "You're wearing your uniform. There's no reenactment this weekend, is there?

"No, but I may be in a battle."

She giggled. "What are you talking about?"

"I can't really tell you."

"Oh, it's top secret. Has your uncle Gordon gotten you in trouble again? Do you need some help?"

"Uncle told me not to say anything."

"Okay." Kim backed off, a little worried. "If you need some help, let me know." She pointed toward a picnic table beside the swing. "My mom and I baked some peanut butter cookies. You want some?"

"Sure." Hezekiah grabbed a couple of cookies as another train whistle blew in the distance.

"That's my dad. Let's go down to the sidewalk and wave."

Kim's father, Jeff Dansey, was a train engineer, driving the Amtrak to and from Washington, DC, and Richmond twice a day. When Kim and Hezekiah reached the sidewalk, they could see the train stopped a half mile away, dropping off and picking up passengers at the Ashland station. The depot, with mirror-image sides for black and white waiting rooms, was a remnant of segregation and a favorite location of train spotters. When the express started back up, Kim stepped out in the middle of the empty street and waved to her father as he pulled by. He gently blew a couple of short toots and waved back wholeheartedly from atop the front of the engine. Kim's dress fluttered around her light, lithe form from the wind produced as the train swept past, and she and Hezekiah kept waving until the last passenger car was gone.

CHAPTER 30

Gordon pulled out of Ashland intending to make a black powder run to Bob Moates Sports Shop on Richmond's South Side in case he and his pards needed extra. His cell phone rang.

"Your humble and obedient servant, Gordon Barrett."

"I need to talk to you in person without the FBI."

Gordon knew the voice. "How can I trust you not to bring them with you?"

"You can't, but I have a deal for you, and I think you're going to be interested. Meet me at Grant's headquarters in an hour." She hung up.

Gordon thought, even if she brings the FBI, we still have the gold hidden for leverage. Might as well see what she has to say. Looks like the fat boy has a date after all.

He drove the Delta across the Varina-Enon Bridge over the James River onto the Bermuda Hundred Neck, the peninsula between the James and Appomattox Rivers. Across the peninsula in the spring of 1864, Confederate General Beauregard's men dug an eight-mile earthwork called the Howlett Line, "bottling up" Federal General Butler's troops who had landed on the tip of the neck. The Confederate line prevented Butler from joining Grant to take Petersburg.

Gordon took Route 10 east and crossed the Appomattox River into the City of Hopewell. If Petersburg was the stepchild of Metro Richmond, Hopewell was perhaps the cousin to avoid. Hopewell had been thrown up almost overnight when DuPont came to town in 1913 to build a dynamite factory for the World War I demand. The city sat on prime waterfront real estate at the confluence of the James and Appomattox, but the air and water had been heavily polluted by industry. The most insidious case was the dumping of the pesticide kepone into the James River from 1968 to 1975, closing the commercial fisheries for thirteen years. Hopewell had cleaned up most of its act, so passersby were no longer forced to roll up their car windows and hold their noses as they rode through town.

Gordon hung a left at the Beacon Theatre and headed to City Point where the rivers came together. Between June 1864 and April 1865, City Point became the largest supply base of the Civil War, with over 100,000 troops, and one of the busiest ports in the world. Cabins and tents of the Union Army blanketed the area, and the army built a half-mile of wharves, serving as many as two hundred ships a day. When the ships unloaded, the goods were placed on railcars. The US Military Railroad Construction Corps had built an eight-mile line to the Petersburg front, supplying a cornucopia to the Federal forces, while the Confederates starved in their trenches a few hundred feet away.

Today, the grounds of City Point were empty except for Appomattox Manor, a plantation house built in 1763, overlooking the blue wide water. Besides the big house, there was only one other structure on the property that stood out, a two-room cabin. The small, simple structure of vertical beams and logs, chinked with concrete, was a reconstruction of Grant's headquarters. Grant had lived here with his wife and youngest son while he commanded the entire Union Army via telegraph.

After parking his car on Pecan Avenue, Gordon straddled the short split-rail fence bordering the park service site and walked across a large lawn with his slouch hat shading his eyes from the sun, still a long way from setting in the summer sky. He cut through an old grassed-over lane lined with crepe myrtles to get to Grant's cabin. From behind the cabin, Bet Van Lew emerged. She had changed her dress from heavy morning to full mourning, allowing white trim and a white collar.

Gordon looked around. Once he saw that she was alone, he tipped his hat. "Grant's headquarters. That was cute."

"I knew you would know where to come," Bet said, "and the FBI wouldn't, if they were listening in. They're good at law enforcement, but they don't know much about the Civil War."

"So what did you want to talk about?"

"Mr. Barrett, I didn't know you wanted the gold to save Civil War battlefields. I realized the FBI was using me, and I'm not working for them anymore, but I can help you."

"So how would you like to help me?"

"Cold Harbor is back on."

"What do you mean?"

"I threatened the FBI to go to the media with how they botched the capture of domestic terrorist groups just so the government could confiscate gold that you wanted to donate to charity." She tilted her head. "They saw it my way. The Cold Harbor operation is back on for Sunday. Be there at five. The sting will be at six."

"I'm not sure if I want to thank you or not." Gordon half-frowned.

"You should. I got the total deal for you. You and your friends get immunity, Sy gets immunity, and you get to donate the gold to buy your hallowed ground. But it's not a cakewalk. I'll give you all the assistance I can, but these groups are treacherous. I know. I've investigated them all."

"So what made you come over to the other side?"

"At first, I thought it was my duty to help the FBI, the same way my ancestor Elizabeth Van Lew helped General Grant, but I realized we're living in another time. That gold could go a long way in preserving battlefields, and that goes a long way to preserve the memory of my great-great-great aunt. If the FBI recovers the gold, it just gets locked away forever in a government vault and doesn't do anyone any good. We're the last generation that can save Civil War battlefields, and it's our duty to do so if we can."

"Okay," Gordon said skeptically. "So what's really in it for you?"

"Five percent of the gold's sale proceeds go for the restoration and maintenance of Shockoe Hill Cemetery."

"You just said having the gold go toward Civil War battlefields would go a long way in preserving the memory of your aunt. Isn't that enough?"

"Having the cemetery restored and maintained where Elizabeth Van Lew is interred would go even further." Bet thrust up her chin. "Look, Mister, my ancestor died an outcast in Richmond to save America and to abolish slavery. We already have a statue of Lincoln in town. Why not restore the cemetery holding the grave of one of the most influential women of the Civil War? Five percent or I'm not going to be able to offer you my services."

"And what exactly are your services?"

"I make sure the deal with the FBI sticks. So are you in?"

Gordon bowed his head, stuck his hands in his pockets, and brushed the grass with his right foot like an animal looking for food. Then he looked back up. "Okay, 5 percent, but I've got to clear it with my pards." Gordon looked her over. "You know there are other fabric colors besides black."

"I'm in mourning."

"Perpetually?"

"The war was a catastrophe for the country, one that could have been avoided. England didn't have to have a war to abolish slavery, and we shouldn't have had one either. All those children who lost their fathers, all those parents who lost their sons, and for what?"

"Now, there's something we can agree on." Gordon looked out over the water. "You know, Lincoln, Grant, and Sherman met here for the first and last time on—"

"March 27 and 28, 1865," they said together, then smiled at each other.

"Not many people really care about our history," Bet said.

"There are some of us who care," Gordon gazed at Bet.

Bet's face lit up underneath her black straw hat.

"I'm sure you know," Gordon said, "the last meeting of the Trinity of the North took place here on the beach below us. Would you care to stroll down to it, Miss Van Lew?" Gordon offered his arm.

"That sounds lovely, Mr. Barrett." Bet latched on.

They ambled along the bluff and down to the beach as a bald eagle soared in the upper reaches of the blue sky and cumulous clouds hung on the horizon.

CHAPTER 31

Pat drove Ann in his F-150 out to eat. She wore a blue dress, and he wore his best civilian reenacting clothes, a long black coat and vest with a white shirt and black cravat. They crossed the James River on the Interstate 95 bridge, heading south into the industrial pit of Richmond. To the left, the eternal methane flame burned above the Richmond Wastewater Treatment Facility, and to the right sat huge, dirty white oil storage tanks. The six lanes of interstate traffic scrunched together, divided only by a thin concrete barrier. Looming overhead were billboards and transmission lines. Trucking distribution centers and warehouses hugged the road. Farther down, they passed the Philip Morris plant, where Marlboros were made. The manufacturing facility, marked by a 144-foot pop-art pylon, proudly advertised its cigarette brands.

Pat kept a close eye on his rearview mirror, making sure he wasn't being followed, then exited onto the Jefferson Davis Highway. The pike was part of US 1, the major north–south route of the East Coast before the interstate was built. About a quarter of a mile up the highway on a hill among the seedy businesses was an out-of-place white colonial manor with red shutters and a double veranda on the back. A signboard on a high pole announced, "Half Way House Restaurant, est. 1760, FINE DINING." General Butler had used the Half Way House as a headquarters, and the structure barely escaped destruction by Confederate shelling.

Pat eased his truck into the restaurant's parking lot under a shade tree. They walked up the back drive to the house, went down the stairs, and opened the red door with a pineapple doorknocker. They entered the basement, escaping the sticky summer heat. The cool low-ceiling cellar bore walls of exposed bricks, beams, and mortar. The waitress promptly sat them in Windsor chairs and lit a tall, stout candle on the side of their table, providing a little light in the dim space.

Ann stared at the menu with sticker shock. She noticed the cheapest thing on the menu was the colonial chicken. "I see they serve colonial chicken. I really had my heart set on a Civil War chicken."

Pat smiled and thought, *I like this gal. She has a sense of humor.* "The crab cakes are some of the best I've ever had, but they're not associated with any time period or war."

Ann's eyes sparkled over the candlelight. "When you told me you were taking me to the Half Way House, I thought we were going to a rehab center. So why do they call it the Half Way House?"

"Because we're half the way there."

"Pardon me?"

"Uh, halfway between Richmond and Petersburg. It was a stop on the stagecoach road that used to run by here."

Changing the subject, Ann reached over to hold Pat's hand. "So when are you going to show me your farm?"

"The place is a wreck. I've got a lot of construction going on right now."

"What are you building?"

"Fortifications."

"So you're a little boy still building forts? Are you expecting an attack?"

"Possibly this weekend," Pat said, knowing she would think he was kidding. "After dinner, I'd like to show you a real fort."

She had the lamb chops, and he had the crab cakes. They shared their entrées and a bottle of wine. After finishing their dessert of strawberry shortcake, they drove up the Jeff Davis Highway, following the national park signs for Drewry's Bluff, also known as Fort Darling. They parked in an empty parking lot, and Pat took off his coat and vest but left his cravat on. They got out of the truck and walked hand in hand down a wide asphalt path that turned into a brown-pebbled trail, leading to the edge of the fort overlooking the James River, seven miles downstream from Richmond.

"Do you take all your dates to Civil War battlefields?"

"No, but this is one of my favorite spots. It's peaceful as long as there are no boaters or Sea-Dooers on the river."

"Nice view. Beats the heck out of looking at another pile of dirt."

Pat looked a little hurt.

"Sorry," Ann said. She put her arm around his waist as they looked out from the high bluff over the long, skinny, flat stretch of river, ending in a bend.

"Didn't Jimmy Dean, the Sausage King, live around here somewhere?" Ann asked.

"Yeah, Big Bad John lived across the river, down around that turn. His piano-shaped mausoleum overlooks the water. But long before Jimmy Dean showed up, the *Monitor* came up the river during the war."

"The *Monitor* that battled the *Merrimack*?"

"The Confederates raised the USS *Merrimack* after the Federals burned the frigate to the waterline and sunk it so it wouldn't fall into enemy hands. The Confederates covered the hull in iron plating, and the ship became the CSS *Virginia*."

"I like a man who has command of the facts. Don't stop," Ann teased.

Pat smiled. "In March 1862, the *Monitor* fought the *Virginia* to a stalemate at Hampton Roads in the famous first ironclad ship battle, making wooden warships obsolete. Two months later, when the Confederates evacuated Norfolk, they blew up the *Virginia*, clearing the way for the *Monitor* and four other Federal gunboats to come up river and capture Richmond. But this was as far as they got."

Pat pointed. "Down there the Confederates had blocked the waterway with pilings and sunken boats. The Federals opened fire on the bluff but were no match for the eight Confederate cannons pouring down on them from this ninety-foot cliff."

"Wow," Ann said, actually interested.

"The Federal gunboats retreated back downriver. The Yanks would eventually get to Richmond, but not this way." Pat took a breath. "I know a wealthy reenactor, Hiram George, who built his own replica of the *Monitor*. My friend Gordon Barrett takes care of it for him. If you'd like, I could take you for a ride sometime."

Ann's enthusiasm for the battle was waning as she turned to face Pat. "So would you like to show me the inside of the fort?"

Pat took her by the hand, and they walked down into the breastworks, gently crushing last season's oak leaves as they sauntered. Above the mossy mounds, the wood thrushes called as they found a hidden sunken room in the earthen fortress and kissed.

CHAPTER 32

It was dark by the time Raleigh and Jimmy came out of the entrance of VCU's Critical Care Hospital built on the rim of Shockoe Valley at the end of Clay Street. They crossed over to the small brick plaza of the Museum of the Confederacy and walked between the anchor and a section of the propeller shaft of the CSS *Virginia*. The museum housed the largest collection of Confederate artifacts and memorabilia, including Jeb Stuart's plumed hat and the original oil painting of *The Last Meeting of Lee and Jackson*. The depository was the pride of some but the shame of others, at times seen as the museum *for* the Confederacy instead of the Museum *of* the Confederacy.

Raleigh and Jimmy continued to the right of the museum into a garden, sat on a bench beside an iron fountain, and faced the back of an antebellum mansion with triple-sash windows and four pairs of Doric columns. The White House of the Confederacy, the residence of Jefferson and Varina Davis during the Civil War, was a National Historic Landmark, but not for the nation Jeff Davis intended. During the war, many Richmonders preferred calling it the Gray House from the color of its stucco exterior because they didn't want it confused with Lincoln's residence.

Pat walked into the garden with his cravat untied, looking relaxed after leaving Ann at her apartment. Gordon and Hezekiah were close behind. Gordon carried a box of Country Style Donuts under his arm.

Raleigh shook his head. "You brought donuts to a council of war?"

"When the going gets tough, the tough get donuts." Gordon opened the box, took one, and then offered up the rest. With half a donut in his mouth, Gordon asked, "How's Gayle?"

"They think it's stress. The doctor says she probably just needs to rest, but they're going to run some more tests. There's nothing we can do for her right now except let her get some sleep. We'll go back to the farm with you after we're finished here and check on her tomorrow." In the shadows of the floodlights focused on the house, Raleigh stood up, pulled a scroll from his frock coat, and unfurled it. "I drew my own map of Pat's property. Let's look it over and discuss what we're going to do if we're attacked."

"I've got something else we should talk about first," Gordon said. "I met with Bet Van Lew earlier this evening, and Cold Harbor is back on."

"The FBI informant?" Raleigh's mustache and eyebrows approached each other. "The Cold Harbor Operation is back on?"

"Miss Van Lew is on our side now, and the deal is back on."

Pat tensed up. "How did this come about?"

"She had a change of heart and persuaded the FBI it was in their best interest to go on with Cold Harbor."

"Do we still get immunity?" Raleigh asked.

"Do we get to buy battlefields with the gold?" Hezekiah inquired.

"We get the immunity and we get to buy the battlefields. But there is one thing. Miss Van Lew wants 5 percent of the gold proceeds to go to the restoration and maintenance of Shockoe Hill Cemetery."

"What?" Raleigh put his hand to the side of his head as if a headache had struck.

"Van Lew revived the deal with the FBI and can break it again," Gordon assessed. "I think she's worth it."

Pat scratched the back of his neck. "Can we trust a spy?"

"I think we can," Gordon said earnestly. "I think her heart is in the right place, and I think this is our best shot."

Raleigh wrinkled his lips. "Fine," he said in resignation. "Now I guess the only thing we have to worry about is if someone shows up uninvited at the farm before Cold Harbor. If someone does show up, the fortifications will slow them down enough for us to get out of there."

"That's it?" Jimmy asked. "That's all we have to meet on? After all that work on the fort, don't you want to plan to stand and fight instead of just retreat?"

Raleigh avoided eye contact with his son. "I like to think of it more as a countermarch. There is no need to kid ourselves. We've been over this before. Even if we fought it out on the existing line, the best we could hope for is a delaying action before we would have to retreat. They'll have twenty-first-century weaponry."

"Your father is right," Pat said, looking at Jimmy. "But if we withdraw, where do we go?"

"We can go to my great-aunt April's out in Hanover Town," Gordon said. "She lives so far out in the boonies no one would think to look for us there."

Raleigh smirked. "I'd forgotten about the non-mountain side of your family."

Gordon let it go. "She's got plenty of room and always likes having company. I'll call her and let her know we may be coming."

Raleigh looked around to make sure they didn't have any intruders, then unrolled his map. "Hezekiah, hold this end. Jimmy, stand up and hold this end." The boys stretched out the parchment, and Raleigh pointed at Pat's house marked on the map. "Gentlemen, here's the situation. We will be positioned here at headquarters. There are only two ways in and out, the front creek entrance and the back farm road. From the watchtower, we should be able to spot the enemy easily at either entrance. As soon as we see them, we'll abandon our position. We won't have much time. If they show up at the front entrance, they'll realize quickly they won't be able to cross the impoundment and will be looking for another way in. And we'll have to skedaddle out the back entrance before they find it."

"What if they come in the back way?" Hezekiah asked.

"The back entrance has a locked gate, which should slow them down enough, so we can lay the pontoon bridge across the creek and get out the front way."

"What if they show up at both entrances?" Jimmy asked.

"Then maybe we will fight it out," Raleigh said.

Jimmy smiled.

Gordon jumped back in. "Let's say we are able to retreat. Whatever exit we have to take, once off the property we can head over to Hanover Town and stay there until Sunday afternoon."

Jimmy tightened his grip on the map. "If we have to retreat, we probably want to stay off the main roads as much as possible."

Raleigh looked at Jimmy proudly. "Good idea. I'll map out the safest route to get over to Gordon's aunt's house so we won't be detected. Gordon, if it's okay with you, I'd like you to drive your Delta since it has the most room."

Gordon nodded in agreement.

"We need to pack our haversacks tonight and put them in Gordon's car, so if the invader comes, all we have to do is get in the car and go."

Pat grabbed one end of his cravat and yanked it from his collar. "I guess all we can do is go back to the farm and wait. I need to make sure Shiloh has plenty to eat and drink, in case we do have to leave the farm, and I need to get out of this suit and put my uniform back on. I'll take the watch tonight."

"We'll see you all there." Raleigh fidgeted. "Jimmy, I'm a little hyped up. I'd like to sit here for a minute."

The others left, looking around as they headed out and making sure they weren't being followed.

Raleigh and Jimmy took a seat back down on the bench.

Raleigh looked over at the Museum of the Confederacy. "Did you know they're going to break up their collection? Send it off to other museums."

"I heard something about that."

"The museum can't afford to keep it here anymore because their visitation is too low. They say people can't find the museum, hidden back here behind the hospital. I hope it's that and not that people don't care anymore."

Raleigh cast his eyes back on the Gray House. "I don't like to think about it much, but Lincoln was here. Two days after the evacuation of Richmond, the city still smoldering from its fires, Lincoln showed up in a rowboat on the James River just south of Seventeenth and Dock Streets. There was no Union honor guard to receive the president of the United States, but there were plenty of black folks to greet the Great Emancipator once he came ashore. There was no carriage to take Lincoln to the Confederate White House, commandeered to serve as the Union Army's headquarters in Richmond. So Lincoln decided to walk the mile up Shockoe Hill to the house with his small escort of sailors and his twelve-year-old son, Tad, picking up more and more liberated slaves as they went. The parade was a painful sight for many white Richmonders." Raleigh looked down at the ground, then back up at the house. "When Lincoln arrived, the housekeeper, who had been left behind by the fleeing Davises, showed him into the library." Raleigh pointed to the first-floor window on the left. "Lincoln sat in Jefferson Davis's chair and drank a glass of water. That was five days before Appomattox and eleven days before Lincoln would be dead."

Jimmy stared at the pennies shining in the bottom pool of the little fountain in front of them, but his dad kept staring at the house.

"Oh, what a place, what a place," Raleigh reveled and pointed over to the first-floor window on the right. "In the dining room over there, Davis, Johnston, and Lee held a council of war on how they could defend Yorktown and stop McClellan from coming up the Peninsula."

Raleigh pointed to the right-corner room on the second floor. "That was the nursery. It was bedlam with the three young children the Davises brought with them to this house. Varina Davis liked that room the best. She could overlook a garden with fruit trees and take in the sweeping view of Shockoe Valley. No fruit trees now, and no view with these hospital high-rises in the way. Some people wanted to move this grand house, but it would be like moving the Cold Harbor battlefield because there are too many subdivisions around it. You can't change the spot where the history took place.

"Varina bore two children in this house, the youngest one, Winnie, became known as the Daughter of the Confederacy. When Winnie grew up, she was engaged to a Yankee, but Varina talked her out of marrying the Northerner, and Winnie died single at thirty-four." Raleigh shrugged, then pointed over to the right end of the porch balcony. "Five-year-old Joe Davis died when he fell from that balcony. The death of that little boy was hard on Jefferson Davis. Winnie and Joe along with the other four Davis children are buried beside their parents in Hollywood Cemetery." Raleigh stopped talking for a minute to think about the death of the little boy and tried to remember Jimmy as a little boy but couldn't remember, and tears started flowing.

Raleigh turned to Jimmy, and Jimmy saw his father crying. Raleigh resumed. "When I was a kid, my heroes weren't ball-players or Jedi Knights. They were Robert E. Lee and Stonewall

Jackson. I guess they still are. I love reading about the war, visiting places associated with it, and being a reenactor." Raleigh looked back at the house. "This country's real treasure isn't the gold we found, but places like this, preserving our history. They make me feel important, make me feel like I'm part of something bigger. You probably think I'm pathetic, but studying the war gave me adventure in my boring life and, I guess, kept my mind off my own problems and responsibilities."

Jimmy uncomfortably switched his weight on the bench. "Let's go, Dad."

"Your mom and I got married too young. We had you too soon after. I guess I ignored you both and spent my time building my business and reenacting. My business grew and I worked my way up to captain, but I almost lost you and your mother along the way. I can't redo those years, but I can start being a better father and husband right now."

"Dad, don't worry about it."

"I'm going to make it up with your mom. She's a good woman, and you don't know how much I love her. You and your mother are my treasure. You and your mother are my gold."

CHAPTER 33

Gordon relieved Pat from his nightshift in the watchtower and spent all morning keeping his eye on encroaching development rather than an encroaching enemy. At noon, Hezekiah climbed up into the crow's nest to relieve Gordon as the sun beat down on them.

Gordon started scaling down the ladder when Hezekiah pointed in a frenzied fashion. "Look."

On the ladder, Gordon was unable to rotate his head far enough to see what Hezekiah was pointing at. "Look at what?"

"Somebody's coming up the driveway."

A black Mercedes appeared on the other side of the flooded creek, and two men got out.

"It's them, Uncle." Hezekiah shook with fear, seeing his captors again.

Gordon jumped back onto the top of the platform, determined this time to protect his extended gene pool. "You go down first, Hezekiah. Double-quick," he barked.

Lichas and Bob looked across the moat at the defenses of pointy sticks and dirt piles. Lichas, eating a slice of pizza, stopped in mid-chew, boggled by the bastion. "What the hell is this all about? Are those cannons up there?"

Bob looked beyond the brim of the fortifications and saw the second story of the farmhouse and the top of the watchtower behind it. He discerned two figures climbing down a ladder from the tower and reflexively whipped out his Kimber from his shoulder holster and took aim. Before he could fire, Lichas pushed Bob's arm toward the ground and the gun went off.

Bob protested. "Why'd you do that?"

Lichas smacked Bob on the back of the head. "Before we shoot them, we'll need to ask them where the gold is."

Raleigh, Pat, and Jimmy heard the shot and ran out of the house. Gordon and Hezekiah were already on the ground.

"It's the Greeks," Gordon frantically told them.

Raleigh stayed cool. "Let's do it like we drilled."

They scrambled into the pre-packed Delta and raced down the back road.

Lichas heard the car's tires chucking up gravel. "We can't go across, but they can't either. There must be a back way out." They jumped into their car, and Bob put it in reverse.

The reenactors stopped to unlock the gate, then slipped out, making their way over to Highway 5, and connected with Battlefield Park Road as a roundabout path to Aunt April's. Confident they had escaped, they sailed down the road marking the line of the outer eastern defenses of Richmond during the war. Battlefield Park Road offered the surreal scenery of Civil War earthworks mixed in with suburban houses. The fortifications, dappled by the summer sunlight, were a constant reminder to the neighborhood that the war was in their backyard. Gordon pushed the Delta past the Confederate forts of Gilmer and Johnson.

"I have to pee," Jimmy said.

"Hold it," Raleigh snapped.

"I can't." Jimmy twitched in the backseat, thrashing around, unable to find an empty soda bottle or cup.

"Just pee in your canteen," Pat suggested.

"I'm not peeing in my canteen!"

"Take it easy," Gordon said. "I'll stop at Fort Harrison, and you can use the bathroom there. We have time. The Greeks aren't catching up with us anytime soon."

Gordon pulled into Fort Harrison's parking lot and passed a couple of parked cars with empty bike racks. No one was there to actually visit the fort. He whipped around to face the road and came to a stop. Jimmy burst out of the car and darted through a breastwork entrance toward a log cabin serving as a visitor center.

Fort Harrison, a military crest, sat on the highest point between Richmond and Norfolk. During the war, the fort offered a commanding view for keeping tabs on enemy forces. It was first occupied by the Confederates and later by the Federals. The trees had grown up around it so the view was gone, but the fort remained a monument to manual earthmoving for the slaves who had built it.

A few minutes later as the reenactors still sat in the car waiting for Jimmy, they spotted the black Mercedes coming down the road. The sedan kept going, to the reenactors' relief, but before passing out of sight, it halted in the middle of the road.

"Christ, I knew we shouldn't have stopped," Raleigh said. "Jimmy, what is keeping you?" He reached for his replica LeMat revolver. "Let's go get him."

They all bounded out of the car just as Jimmy came back through the earthwork. Raleigh swung Jimmy back around, directing him to the side gate of the fort with the others following. "We're going this way."

As Bob pulled in beside the Delta, Lichas caught sight of the reenactors running through an opening in the bulwark. The brothers got out with guns drawn. Feeling no need to run them down, thinking they had them trapped, they slowly walked over to the fort. But once inside the fort, there was no trace of them, just a flat, grassy compound seventy yards wide and fifty yards long with a few trees providing little shade from the sunlight, piercing the humid, windless air. Blocking their line of sight on the far border was a traverse, an inner wall of dirt constructed to thwart artillery shells. Lichas stayed on the straight path, and

Bob took the path to the right. They proceeded cautiously around the inner fortress wall from opposite sides, only to find a second traverse with no sign of the reenactors.

Lichas gritted his teeth and mumbled. "I'm starting to feel like a rat in a maze."

They crossed through breaks in the second inner wall and still didn't see them. They paired back up, walked over to the edge of the fort and onto the top of a rampart, looking out over an eighteen-foot drop-off with a forest on the other side.

Raleigh shot his revolver from the woods and screamed, "Stay off the earthworks. They're fragile."

The gangsters hit the ground. "What kind of nuts are these guys?" Bob said. "And they got my suit dirty."

"They're in the woods. We just have to go down in there and get them," Lichas said, brushing dirt from his cheek.

"I'm not going in there," Bob said. "There's poison ivy in there, snakes, ticks, biting flies, God knows what else."

"Shut up, you *muni*," Lichas said. "You cover me from up here, and I'll sneak around to the bottom and flush them out."

Lichas walked around to the left to access the outside of the wall while the reenactors walked in the opposite direction to slink back into the fort.

Bob heard something behind him, looked, and spotted them. He shouted at Lichas, "Hey, back up here. They're getting away."

Bob took a shot at them as they ducked behind a traverse and ran to the parking lot. The reenactors leaped into the Delta, pulled out, and raced down Battlefield Park Road. They took a left at Confederate Fort Hoke and followed the Federal line of earthworks paralleling the road leading to Fort Brady. Gordon pulled into the small parking area for the fort.

"What are you doing?" Raleigh said. "They're just going to corner us here."

"Don't worry. I've got a plan."

"I hope it's better than most of your plans," Raleigh said as they furiously unloaded from the car.

Gordon led them into Fort Brady, built by the Federals after they had captured Fort Harrison in 1864.

A few minutes later, Bob and Lichas found the car.

"Not another fort," Bob said. When he got out, he shot the Delta's tires. "They won't get away this time."

The mobsters followed the pebbled-over asphalt path into the fort. Fort Brady was much more compact and shadier than Fort Harrison. It overlooked the James River and had been manned by the 1st Connecticut Heavy Artillery. The artillery's job was to cut off Confederate naval attacks from Richmond on the Federal supply base at City Point.

Once inside the circle of earthworks, the brothers discovered another traverse in the middle of the fort with a trail going between the inner mound of dirt and the outer breastworks. They split up again. Lichas took to the left and Bob to the right. Bob walked the short trail around the fort and met back up with Lichas.

Bob shook his head to indicate no sign of them. Lichas pointed up to the outer earthwork at the end of the fort, and this time he walked carefully up the rise, crouching behind a tree at the top for cover. He looked from behind the tree and through the foliage, laying his eyes on the grayish green river below. Beside the river was a long tin shed. He took a closer look. It was a marina.

Lichas waved to Bob to join him on top of the parapet. "They're down there. Let's go get them."

"How do you know they're not just in the woods waiting to take another potshot at us? Or they're just going to sneak back around on us again?"

"Because they heard you shooting out their tires and know they can't go back to their car. Let's go down and get them before they get away."

They stepped down the other side of the earthwork and followed an unmarked trail through the brush to a twenty-foot clay cliff. They followed the cliff along its edge as it trailed off to the marina parking lot and walked onto the dock.

Lichas pointed out to the river. "That's them. I recognize the funny hats. What the hell are they riding on?"

Bob used his hand as a visor. "I don't know, but they're too far away to shoot."

Lichas looked up at Bob. "That's a good little brother, practicing some restraint."

"Can I help you, gentlemen?" A voice came from behind them. It was the dockmaster.

"Yes, we're going to need a boat," Lichas said.

"Are you members of the yacht club?"

"Yes and here's our membership card." Bob brandished his gun.

Lichas and Bob tied up the dockmaster, hijacked a ski boat, and were soon out on the river, closing in on a strange, slow-moving craft. There was no longer anyone on the deck of what looked like a black metal raft with a small sawed-off silo in the middle. As the brothers pulled alongside, the vessel was dead in the water, but the silo revolved slowly.

Bob automatically shot off a couple of rounds at the silo, but they just bounced off the iron armor of the ship. The silo kept turning until Bob and Lichas saw a cannon face poking through a gunport. Their jaws dropped. Then they heard the order, "Commence firing!"

The ski boat took a hit and the Papadopouloses catapulted into the river. The wise guys at first were buoyed by their silk suits but were rapidly weighed down by them. Gulping the dark water, they struggled to slip off their saturated jackets. As soon as they regained their breath, they cursed the men on the weird watercraft and threatened vengeance while trying to stay afloat. Realizing that survival was more important than revenge for the time being, they turned to swim to shore as the ship that shot them into the water cruised away at six knots.

Hiram George had commissioned this diesel-powered version of the *Monitor* after seeing the full-scale replica of the famous ironclad at the Mariners' Museum in Newport News. Hiram's *Monitor* was eighty-six feet long, only half the size of the original, because even Hiram couldn't afford the full-sized model, and the ship just had room for one cannon in the turret instead of two. He had given Gordon the key and told him he could take it out anytime he wanted in exchange for helping him with the maintenance.

Gordon's gun crew crawled out of the turret on a ladder, as Gordon in the little pilothouse got on the phone to Hiram.

"Hiram, this is Gordon. How you doing?"

"I'm fine. I'm at the New Market Heights commemoration."

"Oh, yeah, I forgot that was today."

"What's going on, Gordon?"

"I've got the *Monitor* out this afternoon."

"Are you having a good cruise?"

"Yeah, and I've got Hezekiah, Pat, Raleigh, and Jimmy with me. They're really enjoying the ride."

"That's super. I'm glad you're all having a good time. How's the *Monitor* running?"

"A-1 as always, and we tested the gun and it's working great. But I do have sort of a problem."

"What's that?"

Gordon hesitated, then said nonchalantly, "We've got some guys chasing us who want to kill us, and if we go back and dock the *Monitor*, they probably will."

"Stop messing with me, Gordon."

"I'm not kidding, Hiram."

"So you can't go back and dock my *Monitor* because some guys are trying to kill you." Hiram sounded more disappointed than surprised. His voice lowered. "Is this over a gambling debt?"

"No, it's nothing like that. I can explain it to you later, but I need your help now."

"Gordon, I'm tired of bailing you out, especially when it involves my expensive toys."

"It's for a good cause, Hiram."

Hiram bit his lip. "Yeah, I'm sure it is. Look Gordon, why don't you just meet me at Deep Bottom Park. I'll take the *Monitor* on down to Jordan Point and dock it there until the coast is clear for you. You can take my truck and pick me up."

"Well, that's another thing, Hiram. If you would let me borrow your truck, and we could have someone pick you up at Jordan Point."

"Borrow my truck? What do you need my truck for?"

"To make a clean getaway."

"Who are you, Jesse James? Who are you trying to get away from?" Hiram demanded in frustration.

"I'll explain it all to you when I see you at Deep Bottom."

"You know, Gordon, this is really testing our friendship." Hiram abruptly hung up with Gordon still hugging his phone to his ear.

Gordon guided the *Monitor* into Dutch Gap. To the starboard was the Dutch Gap Cutoff, the canal started by General Butler's men in 1864 to bypass the Confederate fort Battery Dantzler on the James River, holding the northern end of the Howlett Line. The cutoff, improved after the war, was now part of the main shipping channel.

Ruffled by Hiram's rebuke, Gordon didn't notice a freighter, heading up to the Port of Richmond, bearing down on them. The freighter didn't see the "cheesebox on a raft," pulling out in front of it.

The foursome on deck screamed at Gordon to get out of the way.

Gordon saw the danger and pressed on the throttle, but it was already at full speed. All he had time to do was shriek an expletive.

The freighter missed by inches. The rusty hulk's wake splashed over the *Monitor's* deck, and the crew held on, sucking in the exhaust from the merchantman, praying not to be swamped.

Gordon managed to stabilize the ironclad, and Raleigh walked around to the front of the pilothouse, the shape and size of a washing machine box protruding above the foredeck with horizontal slots to give the captain a 360-degree view. Raleigh bent down and shouted through a slot, "How many times do I have to tell you not to drive and talk on a cell phone at the same time?"

Gordon whispered back through the slit to assure himself and Raleigh, "We're going to be all right. Hiram is going to meet us at Deep Bottom." He maneuvered the *Monitor* on down the river through the dwindling wake of the freighter.

The danger had passed, and the mates relaxed as much as they could on the hot black deck, looking out over the water with the US jack flapping on the forward, displaying thirty-four white stars on a blue field. The James River was still beautiful after centuries of abuse. This stretch of water between Richmond and Hopewell was one of the most polluted in the state, but also one of the most historic. Here early Virginia history was early American history. On the high bluff to the right at the abandoned "Citie of Henricus," Pocahontas and John Rolfe married in 1614.

They floated under the almost-mile-long Varina-Enon Bridge that Gordon had driven over the previous day to get to Hopewell. Gleaming cables flowed down from two center towers supporting the bridge, looming 150 feet above them, tall enough for the big oceangoing ships to limbo. They traveled another mile and a quarter down the river, then ported, leaving the main dredged channel of commerce into the original river's course around Jones Neck. The neck, formed from a curve in the river, was a thumb-shaped island of swamp forest and tidal flat surrounding a marsh. Once in this backwater, the quiet, flat, murky river came alive with fish jumping and pickerelweed blooming purple along its banks. Great blue herons filled the sky and a din of insects rose. They traveled to the bottom of the oxbow to the dock of Deep Bottom Park where Hiram waited for them.

He greeted them with, "So what in God's name is going on?"

Gordon walked up the landing with Hiram while the others tied up the vessel. "It's a long story."

"I'm listening."

Gordon anxiously told Hiram about the gold, how they were going to lure mobsters, white militiamen, and black militants to Cold Harbor tomorrow evening for the FBI, so the FBI would let them donate the gold to buy Civil War battlefields. But the mob had decided to go on the offensive.

Hiram mulled over Gordon's far-fetched story. "So how do you know the militia and militants aren't coming after you now rather than waiting for tomorrow night?"

"I'm sure they are out looking for us. That's why if we could borrow your truck, I think they'd have less chance of finding us."

"Where are you going to be until tomorrow evening?"

"We're going to hide out at my aunt April's."

Hiram eased up, finding it hard to be mad at Gordon. "I want you to give my regards to your aunt April. She's a lovely woman. My mother enjoys visits with her so much." Hiram reached into his pocket. "I'm doing this against my better judgment. Here's the key to my truck. Take it as long as you need it. Be careful, and call me to keep me posted or if you need anything else. And don't worry about sending someone down to pick me up. I'll get back home on my own."

"Thanks, Hiram, you won't regret it."

"Uh-huh."

Hiram took the *Monitor* downriver, and the reenactors took Hiram's Toyota Tundra with the boys in the truck bed up to Highway 5, originally called New Market Road.

CHAPTER 34

B eside the historical highway marker for the Battle of New Market Heights, Powhatan Dubel's outfit, the 5th United States Colored Infantry Regiment, was sponsoring a commemoration of the battle as part of Dixie Days, even though it was over three months until the actual anniversary of the combat.

At dawn on September 29, 1864, six regiments of the US Colored Troops (USCT) charged the Confederate line held by Gregg's Texas Brigade along New Market Road. The attack was an effort to force Lee to move more of his troops to the outer defenses of Richmond instead of reinforcing Jubal Early in the Shenandoah Valley. The black troops fought through a blizzard of bullets to take the heights. It was the first time in the Civil War a force consisting mostly of African Americans achieved a victory. For their effort, fourteen black soldiers received the Medal of Honor. Not until the Invasion of Normandy on June 6, 1944, would that many Medals of Honor be earned again in a single battle.

Unlike the celebrated 54th Massachusetts made up of free blacks, portrayed in the movie *Glory*, the USCT were mainly runaway slaves known as contrabands. They proved they could fight and win when they took this strong Confederate position. On the Battle of New Market Heights, General Butler wrote, "the capacity of the negro race for soldiers had then and there been fully settled forever." But it would take another eighty-six years before black and white troops were fully integrated, occurring during the Korean War.

Powhatan, out of his state trooper attire and in his Union uniform, led the ceremony. He wasn't named after the American Indian chief but after Powhatan Beaty, a hero in the Battle of New Market Heights. Powhatan and his men paid tribute with a rifle salute. As the reenactors fired the volley, Carter and Wendell Flood happened to be driving by in search of Raleigh Fuqua and company. Carter slammed on his brakes.

"Those nigras are shooting at us," Wendell shouted. He stuck his Glock out the window, blindly pointing it over the roof of the truck cab, and started spraying bullets at the line of soldiers.

The 5th USCT took cover from Wendell's poor aim. Gordon, driving toward the scene, saw the front of the gray utility truck with the discharging pistol and slammed on his brakes.

Raleigh leapt out of the Tundra and screamed at Jimmy in the truck bed, "Get out!"

"Where are you going?" Gordon clamored.

"Away from here. I'm tired of my son and myself being shot at." Raleigh grabbed Jimmy by the arm, and Jimmy's cell phone dropped out of his pocket. The two started running back down the road.

"Stop shooting," Carter squawked at Wendell. "It's just nigra Civil War reenactors." He shook his head. "Just one more thing they took from us."

Wendell stopped shooting and Carter pushed on the gas pedal. Gordon, seeing the utility truck moving, mashed on his accelerator with hopes of avoiding gunfire in his direction. As they went by each other, Carter got a good look at Gordon and Pat in the cab, and Hezekiah in the bed.

The pards couldn't help but notice the jumbo Confederate battle flag painted on the side of the utility truck. "I've seen that truck before," Gordon muttered to himself. "Oh man." He glanced over at Pat. "That truck passed us when Powhatan pulled us over last week. They must have been following us because they saw us find the gold. That has to be the Compatriots."

"What about Raleigh and Jimmy?" Pat asked.

Gordon stomped on the brake, almost pitching Hezekiah into the open back window. "Do you see them?"

Pat looked back. He saw the utility truck continuing down the road, but no sign of Raleigh and Jimmy. "No."

Gordon cried out over his shoulder, "Hezekiah, do you see Raleigh and Jimmy?"

"No."

Gordon pulled his slouch hat over his eyebrows. "They must be hiding in the brush. They should be okay. They can get a ride back with Powhatan. We'd better get out of here before the Compatriots figure out who we are and circle back for us."

"Then go, go, go," Pat said.

With his goal still on getting to his aunt April's in Hanover Town, Gordon tried to regain his bearings and sped west on Highway 5 toward Richmond, the same way the Yankees marched into town in 1865. At the city limits, the highway turned into Main Street and dipped to parallel the James River at Rocketts Landing, then spiraled back up.

Leela, Fattah, and Hark sat in Leela's red Lexus. Parked in a car detailing lot above the intersection of Williamsburg Avenue and East Main Street, they faced the inbound traffic, waiting patiently for the reenactors to appear. The Gabrielites studied each car as it went by, keeping an eye out for Gordon's butternut Delta 88 but easily recognized Gordon as the driver of a gold Tundra.

Gordon also recognized Leela. She started her car and pulled out in pursuit.

Gordon glanced in the rearview mirror and saw her coming. He shouted through the back window. "Hezekiah, lay down."

"What for?"

"Lay down. Someone's after us."

Hezekiah looked back, saw the red Lexus, and stretched out in the bed of the truck.

"Who is it now?" Pat asked.

"Gabrielites."

Gordon turned sharply left on Twenty-first Street, barely missing an oncoming semi. Leela tried to follow, but the big wheeler blocked her path along with the subsequent traffic. She watched as Gordon darted two blocks down to Dock Street and hung a right. He followed the road through a hulking flood-wall door, passing a revamped portion of the James River and Kanawha Canal. Under the spaghetti mesh of trestles and over-passes, Gordon took Fourteenth Street to cross the low-slung, quarter-mile-long Mayo's Bridge. It was the same path taken by Confederate soldiers evacuating their burning capital.

Hezekiah swiveled around on his stomach to peek above the tailgate. They were halfway across the river. He rotated again and rose up to the back window. "The red car is catching up. It's starting to cross the bridge."

Gordon pressed on the gas harder to reach the other side, where the colossal, abandoned Southern States Cooperative feed mill straddled the south bank. "Don't worry. We're going to lose them."

They went through another floodwall door and the road curved, putting them over the river and momentarily out of sight from their pursuers. But to their horror, as if on cue, beside the Richmond Railroad Museum, a train started crossing the road and blocked their escape route.

"Park it," Pat commanded and pointed to the right. "Let's get on the floodwall."

Gordon pulled the truck to the back of the floodwall trail parking lot to ditch the vehicle, hiding the Tundra behind other cars.

"Hiram's going to kill me," Gordon said as he opened his door.

"Let's go," Pat yelled as he hopped out.

They scaled a couple of short, open wooden fences as fast as they could with Gordon bringing up the rear and hit the start of the not-so-scenic portion of the Floodwall Walk. The asphalt pathway ran beside a chain-link fence, bordering the derelict Manchester Canal in an industrial area. Transmission wires hung over their heads, and the smell of formaldehyde filled the air. They ran up the stairs attached to the side of the floodwall. Once on top, they looked back and didn't see anyone coming up the path behind them.

"I think we shook them," Gordon said, out of breath. "They must of thought we beat the train and didn't check the parking lot. If they had, they'd be on us right now."

Walking instead of running, they pressed on but kept turning around to make sure they weren't being followed while ignoring the best view of the James River and Richmond. The white-water pitched in the foreground and the skyline perched in the background. To the left and right, railroad and highway bridges crossed the river, and ospreys fished overhead.

"Give me your phone," Pat asked Gordon. Pat had inadvertently left his mobile at home after leaving in a hurry as they retreated from the Greeks. "I'll call Ann to give us a ride." Gordon handed him his phone, and Pat punched in the number and waited. "No answer. I'll try again in a minute. I'm still worried about Raleigh and Jimmy."

"I'm sure they're all right," Gordon said. "They'll catch up with Powhatan, and he'll give them a ride out to Aunt April's. I'll just give Jimmy a call on his cell to make sure." Gordon took the phone back from Pat. "It's rolling over to his voicemail." Gordon winced. "I'll leave him a message."

They continued along the top of the serpentine floodwall, impaling the riverbank. The Corps of Engineers completed the massive concrete wall in 1994 at a cost of $143 million. The campaign for the wall began in 1972 after Hurricane Agnes delivered a devastating flood to the city, the second one in three years.

"Hey, there's the top of the state capitol," Hezekiah said, sightseeing. He pointed across the river to the pediment tucked in behind the high-rises. In the nineteenth century, the state capitol building was Richmond's most prominent landmark, featured in many Civil War photographs. Today the temple on top of Shockoe Hill stood obscured and dwarfed by modern architecture.

They followed the trail, going under the Manchester Bridge. Once under the bridge, the floodwall turned into a levee, reinforced on the sides with seawall stone. The shade of the bridge offered welcome relief with a breeze flowing down from the river as the automobile traffic resounded above them.

The trail looped around and up to an overlook with a view of a row of brown granite abutments evenly placed across the river. The abutments had supported a bridge for the Richmond and Petersburg Railroad. When the original Confederate capital moved from Montgomery, Alabama, to Richmond in May of 1861, Jefferson Davis, the Confederacy's provisional president, rode a train across the bridge into the city. Crowds of enthusiastic supporters received him at the station and in the streets. Richmond gaily accepted the capital of the Confederacy, an enticement they were promised in exchange for Virginia to secede.

Hezekiah, Pat, and Gordon stood at the edge of the overlook built over the first abutment, now a rock climber's challenge referred to as the Manchester Wall. Pat held out his hand for Gordon's phone. "Let me try Ann again." He dialed the number and got her. She would soon be on her way to pick them up to take them to Hanover Town.

CHAPTER 35

After Raleigh and Jimmy fled from the scene at New Market Heights, they dove into a muddy ditch to evade the gunfire coming from the gray utility truck. As they watched the Confederate battle flag on the side of the truck pass, Raleigh put it together. Once the truck was out of sight, they pulled themselves out of the mud.

"Give me your phone," Raleigh said to Jimmy. "I need to let Gordon know I spotted the Compatriots."

Jimmy patted down his pockets but couldn't feel his cell phone.

"Did you lose your phone again?" Raleigh demanded to know.

"I had it just a minute ago."

Raleigh was fresh out of fits and thought he would rather conserve energy than give Jimmy another futile chewing out. He realized they had bigger problems and decided they needed to march east. He didn't want to go back and catch a ride with Powhatan because that might mean exposing their situation to more law enforcement, making things worse. With too many of the wrong people looking for him and his son, he thought it best to hide out for the night.

Raleigh set his sights on the Malvern Hill battlefield, five miles away. When they reached the less-traveled Long Bridge Road, they turned onto the narrow lane, the back door to the battlefield the deaf and hapless Confederate General Theophilus Holmes had taken in 1862.

Three miles into their forced march, Raleigh was on the verge of heat exhaustion. Jimmy wasn't faring much better. They were traveling light since they had left their weapons, haversacks, canteens, and other accoutrements in Gordon's Delta back at Fort Brady, but Raleigh was still wearing his long underwear in the heat to maintain his authenticity as a Civil War soldier. Raleigh was feeling dizzy but snapped to attention when he heard a motor. They hadn't seen a vehicle since starting down the Long Bridge Road, so Raleigh was alarmed. "Do you hear that?"

Before they had a chance to take cover, a truck appeared around the corner.

Catching only a glimpse of a gray truck, Raleigh screamed, "Run, Jimmy, run!"

A tow truck was upon them before they even had a chance to sprint, and a young man who looked Polynesian pulled up beside them with his window down, eating a fried bologna sandwich.

"Your car must have broken down. Can I give you a tow?"

Raleigh's face fell with relief, seeing it wasn't the Compatriots. He tried to act like nothing was the matter. "No, we're just doing a march."

"You're kidding? You don't want a ride?" the man asked, working a mouthful of bologna and white bread that moved his broad nose up and down on his circular face.

"No," Raleigh said, covered in dirt and sweat.

The man looked Raleigh and Jimmy over. "Oh, you fellows must be Civil War reenactors."

"Yeah, that's right," Jimmy said, rankled.

"Whose side you on?"

"The South's," Raleigh proclaimed, but not really in the mood to educate the public at this time.

"You both look like you could use something to drink."

"That would be great," Jimmy said.

The man got out of his truck, not bothering to pull over to the side. He was a giant, rounded and muscular in all places. He pulled out a cup attached to his orange plastic water cooler strapped to the front of his wrecker. "Here, have some water."

Jimmy went first, waiting impatiently as the little stream of water came out of the cooler to fill the cup.

"I'm Lester Littlefeather. Oh, I don't mean to be rude," he said, chewing with his mouth open. "Would you like a bologna sandwich? Mumma made me a whole bunch."

"A sandwich would be good," Raleigh said, not having eaten since breakfast, "but I think I need a little water first."

"I'll take a sandwich," Jimmy said.

Lester reached into his cab, pulled out a couple of sandwich bags, and passed them out to Raleigh and Jimmy. "You know, my great-great-great-grandfather fought in the Civil War."

"Yeah, whose didn't?" Jimmy said as he ravenously broke into the sandwich bag.

Raleigh glared. "Jimmy, don't be disrespectful. This gentleman is offering us his hospitality."

Jimmy's comment didn't seem to bother the tow truck driver. He kept on talking. "Yeah, Great-Great-Great-Grandfather was Choctaw and fought in the Battle of Pea Ridge in Arkansas. The Indians and the Confederates were fighting a shared enemy, the federal government. That was the battle where the Cherokees scalped and mutilated live and dead Union soldiers. Both the Rebels and the Yankees got real upset at the Indians. But it was a war, what did they expect?" He shrugged his shoulders. "They called us savages, but after what the white eyes had done to us, who were the real savages?" They chewed on that.

Jimmy's interest swung. "You're a Choctaw Indian?"

"Poppa is Choctaw. Mumma is Chickahominy. They met at a powwow in Oklahoma. She liked the way Poppa danced. So you sure you don't need a ride?"

Raleigh had lost both of his heel plates in their flight and felt the blood blisters forming on his feet. He worried the next truck coming around the corner might be the Compatriots. "Sir, would you mind giving us a ride to Malvern Hill?"

"No problem. Hop in. I'm on my way home to New Kent and that's not that far out of my way."

CHAPTER 36

To become less vulnerable from attack by the British during the Revolutionary War, in 1779 the Virginia General Assembly decided to move the state capital inland from Williamsburg. Hanover Town lost the bid to Richmond by a slim margin. At the time, Hanover Town was a busy port on the upper Pamunkey River, but within twenty years, the river silted up, preventing ships from reaching its docks. Fifty more years went by and the town disappeared. Aunt April's ancestors stayed.

Ann pulled into the part-grass, part-dirt driveway of a large white farmhouse with black shutters, brick chimneys on both sides, and a black tin roof. Ann and Pat jumped out of her old VW Beetle to release Gordon and Hezekiah from the backseat.

Pat looked over the low roof of the car to Gordon. "I'm going to stay with Ann tonight. Call her when Raleigh and Jimmy surface, and we'll talk about getting things straight for Cold Harbor tomorrow." He and Ann hopped back into the bug, waved good-bye, and pulled away.

Gordon and Hezekiah walked up to the opened front door. Blue snowball hydrangeas blossomed on both sides of the stoop. Gordon knocked on the screen door. There was no answer and the door was unlocked, so they went in.

"Aunt April, are you here?" Gordon called out.

They received no reply and walked through the central hall past the sweeping staircase in the un-air-conditioned house to the screened-in porch on the back.

"Why hello, Gordon, how are you doing?" There she sat, a tiny, frail, and ancient woman with short gray hair and gold wire-framed glasses holding round lenses, sipping her afternoon sherry.

"Aunt April." Gordon walked over, clasped her hand, and kissed her on the forehead.

"Hi, Aunt April," Hezekiah said, bending over to hug her and kiss her on the cheek.

"Just look at you, Hezekiah, growing up to be such a fine-looking young man. Forgive me for not getting up." She looked at them together in their Confederate uniforms. "I see you're still concerning yourself over the Late Unpleasantness. You know the Yankees burned my grandfather's house on this spot. But he just rebuilt. The Yankees are gone, Clarence is gone, and I'm still here. Would you boys care for a sherry?" She raised her glass slightly.

"Not right now, Aunt April," Gordon said.

"You boys look like you could use some freshening up and something to eat."

"It would be great if we could get cleaned up."

"That would be fine. Now, I thought Pat, and Raleigh and his boy were coming with you?"

"Pat's with his girlfriend, and I hope Raleigh and Jimmy will be here later."

"Well, if they do come, I have plenty of room, and I always enjoy seeing all of you."

After a shower, supper, and a fresh change of socks, Gordon and Hezekiah joined Aunt April on her back porch. They took in the view of the cut hayfield below. Bales waited for collection, placed like giant game pieces on the stubble. But the country serenity was interrupted by a ringing phone.

"Gordon, would you like to get that for me? I'm right settled."

"Sure." Gordon walked into the living room and answered the phone.

"Hi, it's Bet."

"Miss Van Lew. How did you get this number?"

"Mr. Barrett, I understand Raleigh and Jimmy Fuqua are missing."

"How did you know that?"

"I'm a spy, remember? Meet me at that new dance club in Shockoe Bottom across from the farmers' market at eleven this evening. I would very much like to see you again, and by then I may have some more information on the Fuquas." Bet cut the call.

Gordon walked back out to the porch. "Aunt April, that was a friend who wants to meet us downtown tonight. I need to ask another favor of you. I'd like to borrow your car."

"Oh, Gordon, I need my car to get to church. But if you'd like to borrow Clarence's Falcon, it's out in the barn. Sandy, my handyman, takes it out every now and then. It's a little beat up, but Sandy says it runs just fine, and since Clarence has been dead for thirty-five years, I'm sure he wouldn't mind if you drove it."

"We should be back tonight. I'm not sure though. If Raleigh and Jimmy show up, would you please have them call me?"

"That's fine, boys. I'm usually up. Don't sleep much at night, you know, when you get old . . ."

As soon as Gordon and Hezekiah left, Aunt April called Mary Beth. "I think Gordon and Hezekiah are in trouble, which means your Pat may be in trouble, too."

Aunt April could hear the lump in Mary Beth's throat over the phone.

"He's no longer my Pat. I'll never be his darling." She choked back her tears.

"I'm sorry, dear, I didn't know. I'm sure it's for the best. It's always better for these things to shake out now rather than years later into a marriage. Both people need to click to get on. I'm sure a beautiful and charming young lady like yourself will find someone much better suited to you."

"You think so?"

"I'm sure. You see, Mary Beth, my fiancé was killed in World War II, and I thought I would never find anyone else. But after the war, I met Clarence. And you know, Mary Beth, there was no one I could have gotten on better with than Clarence. So love can bloom more than once."

"Yes, well." Mary Beth swallowed hard. "I suppose you are right. I do have an admirer, but I can't think about that right now when our brave Southern men in the field are threatened. I must put my duty to my country above my personal feelings. I'll call an emergency meeting of the United Daughters of the Confederacy so we can come to the aid of our men."

CHAPTER 37

B etween the downtown high-rises and Church Hill lay flood-prone Shockoe Bottom, the original center of the City of Richmond. Before the Civil War, the Bottom was full of tobacco factories, grain and coffee traders, warehouses, and stockyards. At the time, the district was covered in clouds of coal and wood smoke, and the streets were filled with horse manure. But there was something much more odious about Shockoe Bottom. It was the home of a large slave market consisting of a substantial number of slave auction houses and holding pens, making Richmond second only to New Orleans in the antebellum slave trade. The vilest of these human corrals was Lumpkin's Jail, known as the Devil's Half Acre. Here in the Bottom, slaves were cleaned up, bulked up, and dressed up before they were placed on the auction block, splitting up families, in most cases, forever.

In 1841 Solomon Northup, the author of *12 Years a Slave*, after being kidnapped in Washington, DC, was sold in Shockoe Bottom, bound for Louisiana. In 1842, when Charles Dickens visited Richmond, he found the Bottom to be a wicked place. The grime and sewage didn't repulse him anywhere near as much as the cruelty and lack of conscience of the slaveholders he met.

During the Civil War, Richmond's population swelled from 38,000 to over 130,000. The city filled with soldiers, refugees, and opportunists of all stripes. Shockoe Bottom's factories and warehouses were turned into hospitals and prisons. The hospitals were organized by Confederate state with the purpose of housing patients from the same state in the same building. There were the

Alabama hospitals, the Georgia hospitals, and so on. But as far as the prisons were concerned, you could be from any Northern state to qualify for admittance. Those who were lucky enough not to be in a hospital or a prison in the Bottom had access to an abundance of gambling houses, brothels, and saloons. Not much had changed. At night people still streamed on Shockoe Bottom's thoroughfares, looking for the action among the bars, restaurants, and clubs. Cars jammed up along Main Street, people crowded the sidewalks, and a cop stood on every corner.

Gordon found a parking space for the battered brown Falcon under the dark tangle of overpasses in the Bottom, so he and Hezekiah could join the throng. They walked east toward the middle of Richmond's nightlife, following the smell of fried foods and gasoline. Gordon kept looking around for those who might be out looking for him. Above Gordon and Hezekiah loomed the clock tower of Richmond's Main Street train station adorned in terra cotta. Gordon looked up at the clock to check the time with his pocket watch. "Ten thirty. We're early."

As they approached the dance club where Gordon was to meet Bet, they could hear the music pounding out the door. When they entered, the bouncer did a double take at their Confederate uniforms, but made the connection and said, "Scarlett's been waiting for you." He waved them on.

Gordon thought he must be talking about Bet. Once past security, a large hand with red fingernails clutched him by the wrist. He jerked back, fearing an adversary, but instead Gordon looked up to see the Scarlett O'Hara impersonator he had admired at the reenactment last weekend. She dragged him out on the dance floor. "Remember me?" she said in a deep sexy voice as she embraced the man in uniform. "I saw you eyeing me at Berkeley."

"Yes, I do remember you." Gordon took a big gulp. "But I don't have time to dance. I was supposed to meet a lady here."

"And I can be that lady." She held him tighter. "Surely you have time for just one dance."

Gordon conceded amid the flashing lights and propelling house music, as they sallied across the floor among the huge wooden support beams in the converted warehouse.

Hezekiah, left standing by himself, wandered over to the bar.

"I'd like to buy this young Confederate a beer." It was the voice with the Southern-Portuguese accent Hezekiah had heard down by the river. He turned and again met the outstretched hand of Ballard McMullan. "How have you been?"

This time Hezekiah shook his hand.

The bartender took one look at Hezekiah. "This kid's nowhere close to twenty-one."

"My friend only looks young." Ballard laid down a Grant. "Would you please serve him a beer."

The bartender took the $50 bill and placed a beer in front of Hezekiah, much to his delight.

Ballard wiped the foam from his beer off his wide, dark mustache. "Are you and your friends ready to sell the gold? I'll give you much more than you would get anywhere else, but I need to know soon."

Hezekiah nervously took a sip of beer. "You've got to talk to Uncle." He nodded toward Gordon out on the dance floor.

"Oh, yes, of course." Ballard looked on as the TBG gyrated with Scarlett to the beat. Then a belle, in a half-mourning gray dress and hair restrained by black ribbons, cut in between the two more colorful partners.

Scarlet shouted above the music, "I want him back as soon as you're finished with him!"

Gordon fastened an arm around Bet's waist to continue the dance. "I didn't recognize you without your black dress on."

Bet spun out of the grip, took his hand, and led him off the floor. "Let's take a walk around the block," she said with a beckoning lilt.

"I need to get Hezekiah."

"He'll be fine."

"There are people who want to kill us."

"Trust me, I know, and none of them are around here right now." Bet locked arms with Gordon, and they went out the door of the hot club into the warm night, making their way past the unsavory soup of sidewalk cafes and tattoo parlors.

"It's good to see you again, Miss Van Lew. Have you heard anything on Raleigh and Jimmy?"

"Unfortunately, there is no word yet on your friends, but I think they're safe."

"What makes you think that?"

"If the enemy had them, I would have heard."

Distressed by her report, Gordon stopped in his tracks. "I'm going to have to go find them."

"You can't find them tonight. You might as well get a fresh start in the morning. And since everyone is looking for you, you may want to take a more indirect path."

Gordon got the idea, causing him to crack a smile. "You may be right." They started walking again.

"You should also know the guy at the bar talking with Hezekiah is the Confederado who wants to buy your gold."

"What?" Gordon turned around to rush back to make sure nothing had happened to his nephew.

Bet pulled him back. "Don't worry. He's harmless. He just wants to make a purchase. But there is one more thing you should know."

Gordon stiffened up, expecting the worst. "What's that?"

"Scarlett's a drag queen. I really don't think she's your type."

Gordon didn't see that coming. "You're probably right."

They made it up to Twentieth and Main. Across the street sat the Old Stone House, the oldest house in downtown Richmond. The small dwelling, built around 1754, reposed under the dark shadow of a live oak tree and was part of the Edgar Allan Poe Museum. Poe, called "America's Shakespeare," was the child of traveling actors. His drunken father abandoned the family when he was an infant, and his mother died in Richmond of tuberculosis the month before his third birthday. Elizabeth Arnold Poe, Edgar's mother, was buried in St. John's churchyard.

Separated from his older brother and younger sister, Edgar was taken in but never adopted by John and Frances Allan. John Allan was a successful Richmond merchant, but a cold and controlling Scottish man. Poe inevitably fell out with his foster father when he came of age.

Bet eyed the stone cottage. "Baltimore has Poe's body, but Richmond has his angst."

Gordon flashed a broad grin. He loved her historical references and thought he might love her.

They turned down Twentieth, catching the gentle wind coming up from the river, and the screech of a train rolling on the trestle beside the canal became louder.

As they passed an old tobacco warehouse now serving as the Virginia Holocaust Museum, Bet pointed across the street to the two open hatch doors in the seventeen-foot-high concrete floodwall. "There's a site of Yankee suffering."

They went through the near hatch door and sat on brick steps, looking at the train trestle and the dark canal beyond. Below them lit with yellow streetlights ran Dock Street, the same road the Gabrielites had chased Gordon down earlier in the day.

Bet and Gordon rested on the site of the infamous Libby Prison. Libby was probably no worse than any other Civil War prison, since almost all were hellholes. But Libby held Union officers better equipped to tell their stories, making the prison

ignominious, second only to Andersonville. Its real reputation was made when the former three-story ship chandlery was
disassembled after the Civil War and reassembled in Chicago
in 1889 as a museum. Ten years later, the structure was torn
down for good.

With her face shadowed by the floodwall, Bet pointed back
to her left. "It was over there where they popped out of the
ground on the evening of February 9, 1864."

The noise of the traffic on Dock Street reverberated off the
floodwall. Gordon was having a hard time hearing Bet tell the story
in her gentle yet passionate voice. "In the basement of the prison,
surrounded by squealing rats, Yankee soldiers dug in the dark, the
cold, and the fetid air with chisels and broken hand tools stolen
from the workshop. After seventeen days, they had excavated a
fifty-three-foot-long tunnel. One hundred and nine prisoners broke
out. It was the Great Escape of the Civil War. Fifty-nine of those
men made it to safety."

Bet paused and looked at Gordon. "I'll make sure you and
your friends make it to safety." She leaned over and kissed him.

CHAPTER 38

Gordon woke up at his sister's house in Ginter Park on the North Side of Richmond on Sunday morning hung over and sore from dancing. He had decided not to go back to Aunt April's after the clubs closed and was going to heed Bet's advice to take a more indirect route to find Raleigh and Jimmy. He hobbled out of bed with his uniform still on, stumbled into the adjacent bedroom, and gently shook Hezekiah. "Time to get up."

In a few minutes, they lumbered out the door. Neighbors stirred in the old streetcar suburb, getting ready for church. Gordon had other plans. He started up the Falcon, and they rolled down the windows. Even at this early hour, it was already hot, and there was no air-conditioning in the car. They drove down Confederate Avenue, a different street with the same name as the one in Hollywood Cemetery. This road wasn't built for the dead but rather for early-twentieth-century suburban appeal. Its grassy median, bordered by hitching post fences and trees, emulated Monument Avenue on a smaller scale.

Gordon turned north, sailing past the A. P. Hill Monument in the middle of the Hermitage Road and Laburnum Avenue intersection. A statue of "Little Powell" stood on top of a little pillar without a horse. Hill had been shot dead from his mount during the Petersburg evacuation. As part of a real estate promotion, Hill was reburied here from Hollywood Cemetery in 1891. The monument was placed over his remains, eternally exposed to the exhaust of the busy roadways.

"Where are we going, Uncle?"

"You'll see."

When Gordon pulled into the Exxon at the corner of Brook Road and Azalea Avenue, Hezekiah knew exactly where they were going.

On June 12, 1862, this corner was Mordecai farm, the starting point of Stuart's ride around the Union Army of the Potomac. General Lee wanted to call Jackson's troops in from the Shenandoah Valley to attack the Federals threatening Richmond, but Lee didn't know how far north of Richmond the Union line extended. So he asked Stuart to find out.

James Ewell Brown "Jeb" Stuart, called the "eyes and ears of the Army of Northern Virginia," became the most celebrated cavalryman of the Civil War. He was most renowned for this ride around McClellan's army. The exploit turned out to be of little military value but boosted Southern morale to see one of their generals ride a circle around the Federals. It didn't hurt Stuart's reputation to be young, dashing, and dapper in a red silk-lined, gray cape and with an ostrich plume in his hat. Or that he did his work in the attention-getting Eastern Theater, serving directly under the master Lee. Capping off his career, Stuart was fatally shot in combat, becoming a martyr and a legend.

Nathan Bedford Forrest of the Army of Tennessee, nick-named the "Wizard of the Saddle," was truly the best cavalry commander of the Civil War because of his innovative tactics. But Forrest could never compete with Stuart, because he served in the downplayed Western Theater, and Forrest was unable to get himself killed during the four-year conflict, even though thirty horses were shot out from underneath him. After the war, Forrest's military achievements were further discounted by his involvement with the Ku Klux Klan, so the tendency was to remember Stuart and forget Forrest.

Stuart saddled up for his ride around McClellan's men at two o'clock in the morning. Gordon and Hezekiah started at nineish. But first, the Falcon needed gas and Gordon needed coffee.

Gordon looked at the price on the pump. "At these prices we may have to go back to horses." He swiped his credit card. "Pump this for me, would you?"

"Sure," Hezekiah said.

"Do you want anything?"

"Get me a Red Bull."

Hezekiah filled up the gas tank, while Gordon went inside to fill up a tin cup along with a thermos he had borrowed from his sister's kitchen. He grabbed an energy drink for Hezekiah and paid up.

They proceeded north on Brook Road, following Stuart's route, but traveled less than a mile before pulling into the Brook Run Shopping Center. In the parking lot rose a fifteen-foot-high remnant of the earthworks of Richmond's Outer Defenses, saved from development. During the war, Richmond had three rings of earthworks encircling it, protecting the capital of the Confederacy, dug by slave labor. This island of dirt on the edge of a sea of asphalt was part of the third and outer ring, guarding the northern approach into the city. It witnessed Union cavalry attacks led by Stoneman, Kilpatrick, and Sheridan. Today, most whites lived on the outside of the outer defenses rather than on the inside.

Gordon and Hezekiah took the short path up to the top of the earthworks, and Gordon unrolled a map and placed a finger on the chart. "We're here. We'll follow Stuart's path as best we can. We can't follow it exactly because of modern road changes, but we'll go around the enemy the same as Stuart and look for Raleigh and Jimmy. And while we're at it," Gordon chuckled, "maybe we'll gather some intelligence on enemy positions just like Stuart."

Hezekiah gave his uncle a confused look. "Wouldn't it be easier if we drove back to New Market Heights where we last saw Mr. Fuqua and Jimmy and go from there?"

"We'll elude the enemy this way."

"I don't know, Uncle." Hezekiah knew it wasn't the most efficient way to find Jimmy and his father, and he was having a hard time humoring his uncle this time around.

Gordon put his arm around Hezekiah. "Don't worry. We'll find them." He clutched his nephew's shoulder, then released his arm to point back at his map. "This is what we're going to do. We'll head north, bypassing Ashland on its west side, turn southeast traveling through Hanover, New Kent, and Charles City counties, then cut back to Richmond. It should take us about three or four hours to do the 104-mile ride by car. It took Stuart over three days on horseback."

Gordon glanced up from his map to see the tops of apartment buildings for the elderly beyond the fortifications. He paused for a moment of silence. He knew behind the apartments Upham Brook flowed toward Brook Bridge, where Gabriel and his followers had planned to meet and march on Richmond.

Gabriel was a literate, twenty-four-year-old blacksmith born in 1776. He had been exposed to all the talk of freedom but wasn't free. Because his master didn't have enough work for him to do on nearby Brookfield Plantation, he allowed Gabriel to hire himself out with his master receiving part of his hard-earned wages. Gabriel wanted his freedom and his wages in full. It was the year of the Jefferson–Adams presidential election with a bitter split in the Federalist Party between President Adams and Alexander Hamilton. Gabriel was hoping to gain support from Jefferson's Democratic-Republicans. The charismatic black leader of herculean stature saw an opportunity to end slavery in Virginia. Inspired by the success of the Haitian slave revolt nine years earlier, he knew the time had come to make his move.

Gordon pointed toward the stream and told the story Hezekiah already knew. "On August 30, 1800, it started raining. The sky opened up, probably the way it did on the same date in 2004 when Tropical Storm Gaston hit Richmond. The water made the roads impassable, and only a handful of Gabriel's followers showed up for the rendezvous at the Brook Bridge. The insurrection was postponed until the next night. By that time, Gabriel was ratted out but not captured until twenty-four days later in Norfolk. He was brought back to Richmond, tried, and executed at the city gallows. Twenty-six of his co-conspirators also swung for the crime of willingness to fight for their freedom.

"All that was accomplished was to deliver a wake-up call to the white authorities to take action if they were going to keep their 'peculiar institution' intact. The white man subjugated with new laws of brutal repression, showing the Virginia state motto of *Sic semper tyrannis* did not apply to them. Sixty-two years later, Stuart rode north from here in a war Gabriel tried to start." Gordon tipped his hat. "I guess we'd better get going."

Gordon and Hezekiah followed Stuart's trail, crossing over Brook Bridge, passing through motley commercial strips, and traversing the upper reaches of the Chickahominy River. Continuing on Stuart's winding course of back roads, they passed cyclists on the TransAmerica Bike Trail and bumped over the railroad tracks at Elmont, known as Kilby's Station during the war. Stuart linked up with the last of his men at this place. Twelve hundred gray horsemen rode north on their assignment to find the right wing of the Federal Army. But it was just Gordon and Hezekiah now in an old car turning west onto State Route 54 on the outskirts of Ashland, the same as Stuart had done to complete his head fake of going west to reinforce Jackson in the Valley. But Stuart's, and Gordon and Hezekiah's, real objective lay in the east.

The land opened up to fields of corn, wheat, and soybeans, much of it looking like it did in Stuart's day. Gordon thought the landscape begged the question, How long before Stuart's entire ride around the Army of the Potomac becomes Stuart's ride around suburbia?

Gordon turned north, then east on the country roads with an overabundance of Posted No Trespassing and Private Property signs. He saw the rural landscape disappearing as part of a "Manifest Development Destiny," a direct outgrowth of Virginia's English heritage of property rights above everything else, requiring that all land should be privately owned and money made from it. Preserving land to benefit everyone seemed foreign to many native affluent Virginians, insulated in their river houses and country clubs. Gordon pondered while Hezekiah kept his eyes peeled for Raleigh and Jimmy, though the chances of spotting them were nil.

They traveled across US 1 and went under the Virginia Central Railroad trestle. During the war, the line was a vital link to the Shenandoah Valley, "the bread basket of the Confederacy." Turning onto Hickory Hill Road, the sun flashed in their eyes. In the fields on their left, known as the Winston Farm, Stuart's men camped after their first full day of riding.

Gordon and Hezekiah crossed the bridge going over Interstate 95, and the roadway turned to dirt and gravel. The surface forced Gordon to slow down and creep along the vacant road, transecting forests and fields bordering the 3,200-acre Hickory Hill estate. He thought about speeding up, but he knew the Falcon's shocks couldn't take it. He just relaxed at the five-miles-per-hour pace, and the rhythm of the vibrations from the washboard road lulled him and Hezekiah into a halcyon haze. But it didn't last long. Gordon's cell phone rang and he answered.

"Your humble and obedient servant, Gordon Barrett."

"Hello, Mr. Barrett. This is Ballard McMullen."

"Yes," Gordon said and gulped his sloshing cold coffee from the tin cup, leaving no hands on the wheel.

"I didn't get a chance to talk to you last night, but I spoke to your nephew."

"I know."

"I would like to meet you at Hanover County Courthouse. I know you are nearby."

"You do?"

"Mr. Barrett, my client is willing to offer you twice as much for the gold as you would get anywhere else."

"I'll talk to you at the courthouse in a few minutes." Gordon hung up.

"Who was it?" Hezekiah asked.

"It was your drinking buddy, Ballard McMullen. He wants to meet us at Hanover Courthouse."

"He's a really great guy."

"I'm sure he is." Gordon looked out his side window and did an eye roll without Hezekiah seeing him.

They made their way to the courthouse and got out of the car. Gordon felt under the Falcon's bumpers and pulled out a GPS tracker. He and Hezekiah walked around to the front of the colonial brick courthouse. They sat on the step below the middle arch of the courthouse's arcade, taking in the strong smell of magnolias and boxwoods on the green.

"Hello, gentlemen," came the Southern-Portuguese voice from down the portico.

Gordon and Hezekiah stood and entered the cool passageway. Gordon took the lead. "You must be Ballard McMullen."

Gordon and Ballard shook hands on the large stone tile floor of the arcade, while Gordon held the receiver in his palm like a joy buzzer. Ballard recoiled as if it was a shocking device, and Gordon said, "I believe this is yours."

"I just wanted to make sure I could get in touch with you. My client is growing impatient. He would very much like to buy your gold, but he'll have to withdraw his generous offer tomorrow if you can't decide."

"Maybe I don't want to do business with someone who is attaching a tracking device to my car."

Ballard pointed with his thumb at the door that led into the courtroom. "Ever been inside, gentlemen?"

"No," Gordon said, not wanting to change the subject.

"I took a tour this week. As I'm sure you know, this part of Hanover County is best known for Patrick Henry railing against the king of England and the Anglican clergy, but I think it should be better known as the birthplace of Henry Clay."

Gordon raised his eyebrows with a slight interest but was still irritated by the foreigner.

Ballard looked toward the courthouse door with his dark eyes. "Inside they have Henry's portrait right up front, but Clay's portrait is hung to the side. Henry helped create your nation, and Clay prevented it from dissolving. Henry wouldn't compromise, but Clay was the Great Compromiser. They were both men of tremendous public stature. Henry knew when to push, and Clay knew when to back down. Clay clearly knew what happens if you're unwilling to deal. He helped keep America out of a civil war for forty years by cutting compromises on slavery in Congress, long enough for the Northern states to gain enough strength to prevail if war came. In the end, the war did come because the South could no longer compromise over expanding slavery into new states, and the war cost the South everything. The history lesson is, Mr. Barrett, you may want to consider compromising or you may lose everything."

"Thanks for the lesson." Gordon scoffed. "I'm sure we'll be in touch. I know you have my cell number. Let's go, Hezekiah." They walked back to the Falcon.

Ballard called after them. "You're running out of time whether you sell to me or not, Mr. Barrett."

Gordon didn't turn around but instead threw the keys to Hezekiah. "I'm going to let you drive for a while. I need to rest my eyes. These people are wearing me out. Just follow the map while I catch a little catnap."

Gordon fell asleep and Hezekiah tried to read the bad map as he drove. When Gordon woke up, he saw the monument to the 36th Wisconsin Volunteer Infantry beside the road. "Hezekiah, you took a wrong turn. We're off Stuart's route. Pull over and I'll drive."

They switched seats, and Gordon soon had them back on track, passing the Enon United Methodist Church. On the front church doors hung wreaths with small American flags sticking out of them for the upcoming Fourth of July. To the side of the church, the Third National Flag of the Confederacy, the "Blood-Stained Banner," flew, displaying a Southern Cross canton on a white field and a red bar on the fly edge. The final flag of the Confederacy differed only from the second version by the addition of the red bar, making the last flag of the Lost Cause easier to identify at sea and preventing it from being mistaken for a flag of truce. The banner fluttered on a pole beside a small monument to the twenty-seven unknown Confederate soldiers buried in the churchyard who died in the Battle of Haw's Shop, a battle fought mostly along the other side of the church on May 28, 1864.

By the time the Battle of Haw's Shop occurred, it had been almost two years since Stuart had ridden by on his reconnaissance mission. Lee followed up Stuart's ride by driving McClellan from the gates of Richmond during the Seven Days Battles of 1862. It was the Federals' first major attempt to capture Richmond, their main objective only one hundred miles from Washington, DC.

During those heady days of the Confederacy in 1862, a Southern nation seemed possible. But at Haw's Shop in 1864, the Federals' second major attempt to capture Richmond was well underway. This time the Union Army wasn't creeping toward Richmond, up the Peninsula led by the timid General McClellan, but swarmed toward Richmond from the north led by the bold General U. S. Grant. "On to Richmond!" was looking more like a reality than a rallying cry.

Grant was a man, as Lincoln said, who "knew his arithmetic," referring to the outnumbered Confederates and the North's ability to overwhelm the South with soldiers by throwing bodies at the endeavor, and Grant did.

At this point, Ulysses had the cataclysmic battles of the Wilderness and Spotsylvania Court House behind him. Doing a minuet of maneuvers with Lee down the Virginia countryside, he made his way toward Richmond in his Overland Campaign. Grant escaped the trap Marse Robert had laid for him on the North Anna River and crossed the Pamunkey only to have the Confederates greet him here at Haw's Shop.

Haw's Shop was one of the largest and bloodiest cavalry engagements of the war. Over ten thousand horsemen clashed, but most were dismounted because of the heavily wooded terrain. The battle raged for seven hours until George Armstrong Custer's Michigan Wolverines charged the Confederates on foot, wielding their seven-shot Spencer repeaters, putting this one in the win column for the blond-boy commander.

Today, Haw's Shop is called Studley, after the nearby plantation where Patrick Henry was born, and a mile down the road Gordon parked at the Studley General Store. "I've got to use the bathroom. You want to come in and find something for breakfast besides that Red Bull?"

They walked across the store's open front porch. The bell hanging from the door jingled as they entered. Country music flowed from the radio behind the counter, deflecting off the low white-paneled ceiling interspersed with exposed fluorescent lights. Gordon headed for the restroom, and Hezekiah looked around the sparsely stocked shop with the exception of a wide variety of rebel flags for sale across from the register.

A man sat in the back amid the license-plate decor at one of the two tables for the store's deli customers. All you could see of him was his black beret popping up over an open Sunday *Richmond Times-Dispatch* he was reading. He lowered the newspaper enough to peer over and watch Hezekiah. Garnett Pollard, the Compatriot leader, raised the paper back up when Gordon came out of the restroom.

Gordon bought chicken salad rolls for Hezekiah and himself. Once they left, Garnett followed them out but stopped on the porch and pulled out his cell phone. "I found a couple of them. They match your descriptions. One's fat and bearded. I think he's Gordon Barrett. The other one is the tall, redheaded teenager. They're in an old brown Falcon. They just pulled away from the Studley General Store and are going east. You should be able to catch up with them easily. I'm on my way to church, but I will check in with you once I get out of service."

Gordon and Hezekiah approached the turnoff for Summer Hill Road, leading to the farm where Captain William Latané was buried, close to Aunt April's.

"Maybe we should go back by Aunt April's to see if Raleigh and Jimmy are there," Hezekiah said.

Gordon shook his head. "If they had shown up at Aunt April's, they would have called by now."

They kept southeast, crossing the skinny, swampy Totopotomoy Creek. Upstream, after the Battle of Haw's Shop, another fierce round of fighting took place around the creek's banks, naturally called the Battle of Totopotomoy Creek.

From here in 1864, Grant and Lee would move on to Cold Harbor, but Gordon and Hezekiah were still on Stuart's path of 1862 as they moved down the road another mile to Linney's Corner. This rural intersection of Studley and New Bethesda

Roads, now marked by a septic tank cap, was where Stuart had ordered Latané to lead a charge against a company of Federal pickets. Captain Latané, fearless and foolish, trotted fifteen paces out in front of his men on his half-Arabian horse. As gallant as he was, Latané was an easy target and was shot down in the first barrage. The encounter forced the Federals to retreat, but Latané lay dead on the ground. The burial of Latané depicted in art and verse, and reenacted last Wednesday at Marion's graveside service, kept the memory of Latané and Stuart's daring ride alive.

Gordon and Hezekiah, moving on, crossed the commercial strip of Mechanicsville Turnpike and found themselves in the land of the Hanover tomatoes with another two weeks to go before ripening. They continued traveling through the rural and not-so-rural landscape to Old Church. Here under Stuart's command, Fitzhugh Lee, the twenty-seven-year-old nephew of Robert E. Lee, led an unopposed charge into the camp of the 5th US Cavalry. Fitz would later become only one of four ex-Confederate generals to be a general in the US Army, serving the other side during the Spanish–American War. But for now, he had helped answer his uncle's questions about the strength and position of McClellan's right flank.

Old Church became known as Stuart's point of no return in his ride. From here, Stuart could have turned back to rejoin the Confederate army, since he had completed his mission. Or he could go around the Federal Army to gain more intelligence and seize enemy equipment and supplies. Stuart realized backtracking wasn't the path of least resistance, because the Federals were on to him. He also knew the enemy didn't expect him to go on, so he did. And so did Gordon and Hezekiah.

Riding another eight miles in their sidestep course, they came to Steel Trap Road, leading to Garlick's Landing on the Pamunkey River. Stuart's party pillaged the undefended Union depot, robbing sutlers, taking prisoners, stealing horses and mules, and burning everything they couldn't carry off. But Gordon drove on until they came to the tracks at Tunstall's Station, leading to White House Landing, McClellan's main supply base.

John Singleton Mosby, who later in the war made his reputation as a partisan ranger, took Tunstall's Station for Stuart. Gordon and Hezekiah took on across the tracks with the hot morning air blowing through their open windows. Gordon looked in his rearview mirror and saw a truck a quarter of a mile back, approaching fast. The vehicle got a little closer, and he could tell it was the dirty, gray utility truck with rebel flags on the sides that he had passed yesterday at New Market Heights.

He kept his composure, still staring into the rearview mirror. "Hezekiah, it looks like we've determined one of the enemy positions. Time to make a quick skedaddle."

Gordon sped up and turned onto St. Peter's Church Road. He pulled into the drive of the colonial church, the church of Mary Custis who married George Washington in 1759. Gordon took the left fork to the church hall. The Flood brothers were close behind but didn't see Gordon take the turn, and they took the right fork, leading to the church itself. By the time Carter and Wendell spotted the Falcon, their truck was blocked by parishioners going in for the eleven o'clock Eucharist. Gordon turned around, hastily retreating out the church entrance.

Hezekiah looked back. "I think you lost them."

Gordon made it back to the main road, flooring the Falcon for all it was worth when his phone rang.

He picked it up and said in an unfazed voice, "Your humble and obedient servant, Gordon Barrett."

"What's up?" Pat asked. "I hadn't heard from you."

"I just shook the Compatriots off my butt."

"Where are you?"

"Right now I'm hanging a louie at the Talleysville intersection."

"Talleysville? What are you doing in Talleysville?"

Hezekiah and I are doing Stuart's ride around McClellan and looking for Raleigh and Jimmy."

"Raleigh and Jimmy didn't make it to your aunt April's last night?"

"They're MIA."

Pat fell silent for a moment. "We need some help, Gordon, if we're going to find them."

"There's only one person who can really help us," Gordon said as he turned south onto Olivet Church Road.

"Hiram," they both said at the same time.

"You think he's going to talk to you after you ditched his truck yesterday?" Pat asked.

"He doesn't know we ditched it yet. You're going to have to get him out of church at St. Paul's. That should make him even madder, but be careful. You don't know who's watching you."

"Okay, I'll get Hiram to meet us in front of the Dabbs house at one o'clock."

"That's about how long it's going to take us to finish up Stuart's ride. And if I find Raleigh and Jimmy along the way, we won't even need Hiram."

"We'll see."

"Hey, wait a minute. So how was your night with Ann?"

"Piss off. I'll see you at the Dabbs house."

South of the town of Providence Forge, Gordon and Hezekiah took the bridges spanning the two channels of the Chickahominy River. Their crossing was much easier than Stuart's had been. Stuart's men constructed bridges over a flooded Chickahominy and burned the bridges once across to prevent the Yankees, who were on their tail, from following.

On the other side of the Chickahominy was Charles City County, one of the least populated counties in the state, even though it was only fifteen miles from Richmond. They were back in the country of the big plantation houses where the wealth still lay locked up in the land, held by the white minority, outnumbered by African Americans and American Indians.

Surveying this landscape at the top of a fire tower with a pair of binoculars, Fattah Absalom looked for the gold Tundra he had lost going across Mayo's Bridge yesterday. Fattah had a hunch the Confederate sympathizers might be roving around the countryside today, and he would have a chance of spotting them from this perch. Knowing they might have switched vehicles again, he scrutinized every passing car on the lightly traveled road and found himself in luck when he recognized Gordon by his beard and ran down the tower's ladder as the brown Falcon passed. He hopped in the Lexus with Leela at the wheel and Hark in the backseat.

Oblivious they had been detected, Gordon and Hezekiah rolled on into the hamlet of Charles City. Gordon turned west onto Highway 5, "the Big House Highway," where the plantations lined the river and where they had found the gold. They pressed on another five miles, then Gordon turned onto Wilcox Wharf Road. "Let's take a break. If the Compatriots are still close, we'll give them a chance to drive by us." Gordon drove into Lawrence Lewis Jr. Park, fronting the James River. They got out to stretch their legs and walked to a pier to take in the view of the wide water.

From this landing in 1864, Grant ferried most of his infantry south across the river after failing to take Richmond because of the Cold Harbor debacle. He was carrying out an end run to Petersburg. Three miles downriver at Weyanoke Point, Grant ordered the construction of a bridge to advance his remaining men along with artillery, wagons, and animals. Union engineers erected a 2,100-foot bridge in eight hours. They worked from both sides of the river, linking 101 wooden pontoons while fighting strong tidal currents. Once the bridge was up, Grant completed his crossing in four days, and on the fifth day, the longest pontoon bridge ever built at the time was dismantled.

Crossing the river today were huge transmission lines, while pleasure boats plowed underneath them. Black men fished at the end of the pier for catfish, rich in PCBs, in a sun so hot if Gordon and Hezekiah hadn't been steaming in their wool their bare skin would have quickly turned pink.

"Let's get out of this sun," Gordon said.

When they pulled out of the parking lot, they passed a curbed red Lexus. Gordon recognized the car and driver from yesterday. He grabbed the steering wheel tightly and gritted his teeth. "Looks like we found another enemy position."

The Lexus pulled out behind them as a forest green Volvo pulled in between the Falcon and the Lexus and halted. Gordon stepped on the gas and escaped.

With Leela's pathway barricaded, she slammed on the brakes and laid on the horn. Fattah angrily waved a handgun out his window. But the Volvo wasn't moving. Fattah got out of the Lexus and stepped over to the Swedish brick, pointing his gun directly in the driver's face. The driver rolled down her window. Mary Beth was transporting three other officers of the United Daughters of the Confederacy.

"Sir," she unflinchingly said to Fattah, looking past the gun barrel as if it wasn't there. "We're looking for Westover Church, we're running late for service, and we're wondering if you could give us some directions?" Mary Beth feigned.

"I'll give you some directions," Fattah screamed, "Get out of our way!"

The passengers gasped, but not Mary Beth. She stepped out of her air-conditioned car, dressed in layers despite the heat and humidity. She donned a scarf and pearls over an open front sweater, over a vest, over a ruffled blouse with a skirt, slip, hose, and pumps. "Sir, we were only looking for a little assistance. There's no need to be rude."

Fattah's eyes bugged out and his mouth hung open. He turned away and got back into the Lexus. "Back up and go around them," he ordered Leela. "Crazy West End white bitch. Shouldn't she be in a Junior League meeting somewhere?"

CHAPTER 39

P at had borrowed Ann's powder blue Beetle and parked it on the street behind the Governor's Mansion. The state executive residence was a Georgian structure, finished in 1813, painted a pale yellow. Lafayette and Churchill had visited, Stonewall Jackson and Arthur Ashe had lain there in state, and in 1999, Bob Vila filmed the building's makeover.

Pat extended his legs, stepping out of the tiny car, still wearing his Confederate uniform from the previous day when the Papadopoulous brothers attacked his farm. He crossed the road and followed a fence of green-painted, cast-iron spears to an opening where he entered the lush grounds of Capitol Square. Pat walked along the outside of the four-foot-high yellow brick wall, protecting the governor's place from intruders. The governor and his family were out of the country, but the state police were always present, providing security for the grounds.

Powhatan sat in the little glass and wood gatehouse in front of the mansion. When he saw Pat, he popped out of the box, knowing he had a problem on his hands. They stood there, facing off, both tall and in uniform. Powhatan, the broader man, demanded, "What are you doing here?"

"I need a favor."

"I'm working and it's kind of early on a Sunday morning, isn't it?"

"I just need to borrow the key to the Bell Tower for a minute."

"Are you out of your mind? I could lose my job. What do you want in the Bell Tower anyway?"

"I need to ring the bell."

"That bell is rung to call the Virginia General Assembly into session."

"I need to ring the bell to get Hiram's attention, so he'll come out of the church service over at St. Paul's."

"Why can't you just go in and get him?"

"Enemy spies."

Powhatan lowered his voice and moved his face closer into Pat's like a drill sergeant. "Let me get this straight. You want me to risk my job, so you can ring the tower bell to get Hiram out of church, so you won't be detected by enemy spies?"

"That's right." Pat stood his ground. "Just for five minutes."

"Does this have anything to do with those peckerwoods shooting at me and the rest of the USCT yesterday?"

Pat nodded his head. "I need your help, Powhatan. Help your pards out."

Powhatan reluctantly reached inside the gatehouse and handed him the key. "If somebody catches you, tell them you're there for a reenactment."

Pat hurried down the sidewalk before Powhatan changed his mind. He tramped along the backside of the Virginia State Capitol, America's first Classical Revival building, started in 1785. Thomas Jefferson designed it as an absentee architect by mailing the plans from France. The building housed "the oldest continuous law-making body in the New World," and during the Civil War, the white-plastered, neo-Roman temple did double duty as the Confederate Capitol.

Pat walked on. In front of him was Virginia's Washington Monument, an equestrian statue surrounded by statues of other early prominent Virginians on lower pedestals. With hopes of Washington being reinterred here, a tomb was built into the base, and the statue was unveiled in 1858 during the height of Washington worship. On February 22, 1862, Washington's birthday, on the east steps of the monument, Jefferson Davis was inaugurated as the president of the Confederate States of America, elected unopposed for a six-year term. Davis and the rest of the Confederacy embraced the ideals of the Revolutionary fathers as their own. Only one statue of a man on a horse in Richmond stood higher than Washington's, and that was Robert E. Lee's on Monument Avenue.

A squirrel scurried down the wide brick steps, cutting through the capitol grounds, and Pat did the same. The grounds became a refuge for Richmond residents during the burning of the city and after Richmond fell were used as a campsite for Union soldiers. Pat took a right turn at a fountain, surrounded by red roses, to the Bell Tower, partially hidden in tall trees on the edge of Capitol Square. The stout sixty-five-foot square brick tower was constructed in 1824 as a guardhouse and signal tower. Pat let himself in and climbed the stairs to the third floor where a rope, attached to the bell in the cupola, hung down.

He gave two tugs to produce two strokes, then paused, then another tug to produce a single stroke. He continued repeating the two-to-one sequence. It was the same alarm sounded in 1861 to warn Richmond citizens the Federal gunboat *Pawnee* was coming up the James River. The alarm sounded again in 1864 when Dahlgren's cavalry approached the city from the west, and again in 1865 when Richmond was evacuated or liberated, depending on your point of view.

Across the street from Capitol Square, the congregation knelt in prayer at St. Paul's Episcopal Church, known as the Cathedral of the Confederacy. Jefferson Davis and Robert E. Lee had worshipped here, along with many other Confederate officials and officers. On April 2, 1865, in the midst of the service, President Davis received a telegram from General Lee informing him it was necessary to abandon the lines around Petersburg, forcing the evacuation of Richmond.

Hiram always sat in pew 113, two rows back from pew 111, General Lee's reserved seat. Anyone could sit in the Lee family pew now, but in reverence to the general, Hiram always sat back of it.

While kneeling and praying, Hiram heard a bell, opened his eyes, and turned his big-jowled face toward the direction of the sound's origin. His eyes came to rest on the stained-glass window of *Moses Leaving the House of Pharaoh*. The window had been installed adjacent to the Lee pew to represent General Lee's decision to refuse the command of the Union Army and to join the Confederacy.

The bell kept ringing and Hiram looked at his watch. It wasn't on the quarter hour when the bells of St. Paul's rang, and this was a single bell, a little more distant. He stared intensely at the decorative window as if he could see through it and listened more intently, then identified the simple ringing pattern. It was the call-to-arms, and he knew the source had to be the Bell Tower in Capitol Square and something was wrong.

As soon as the prayer concluded, he slipped out of the church, turning a few heads. He hurriedly made his way one block down to the Bell Tower and found Pat coming down from the belfry. "What's going on?"

Pat gave a half-smile, happy to see Hiram had received the signal, but turned serious. "We're in trouble, Hiram."

"Why does that not surprise me?"

"We need your help finding Raleigh and Jimmy."

"They're missing?"

"We lost them yesterday on our way back into Richmond. We ran into the militiamen at New Market Heights, and Raleigh and Jimmy jumped out of your truck, and we haven't seen them since."

"Well, let's form a search party and go find them."

"I asked Gordon and Hezekiah to meet us at the Dabbs house."

Hiram loosened his tie. "We're going to need support. There are a few units still here from Dixie Days I can call up."

"One other thing, Hiram. We need to go down to the flood-wall and pick up your truck."

Hiram bristled.

CHAPTER 40

T he Dabbs house sat out on Nine Mile Road. The brick manor painted white was a Henrico County museum and visitor center. In June 1862, the home served as Robert E. Lee's first headquarters as the new commander of the Army of Northern Virginia. Lee got the job on June 1 when General Joseph E. Johnston was wounded at Seven Pines.

On June 23, armed with the intelligence Stuart had gathered on his ride, Lee convened a council of war at the house with an all-star Confederate lineup. He unveiled his plan on how they were going to roll away the Federal Army from Richmond to Stonewall Jackson, James Longstreet, and the unrelated A. P. Hill and D. H. Hill.

From Stuart's reconnaissance, Lee knew McClellan's right flank was separated from the bulk of the rest of his army, hanging out to dry on the north side of the flooded Chickahominy River. Lee decided at the conference to go on the offensive and attack the vulnerable flank, hoping to force a retreat of the Army of the Potomac. Two days later, the Seven Days Battles began.

Hiram was busy planning his own offensive at the same spot. In front of the Dabbs house, a long folding table was set up in a patch of grass under a red maple, surrounded by a circular driveway. Behind them stood three flagpoles, normally flying the American, the Virginia, and the Henrico County flags. Hiram had temporarily taken down the American flag and ran up General Lee's headquarters flag. The HQ flag flickered thirteen stars in the shape of a rounded A, symbolizing the Ark of the Covenant on a canton of blue.

Hiram took off his coat and tie and put on his worn, wide-brimmed officer's hat to get down to business. He rolled out a large map of the Richmond area on the table, while Pat and members of various reenacting units, both North and South who had sprung to the call, gathered round. As the men studied the map, Gordon and Hezekiah chugged up slowly in the Falcon into the circular drive. Hiram spotted them, broke away from the group, and waved them down. Gordon stopped and Hiram, with his face flushed, looked down at Gordon in disappointment.

Hiram raised one of his arms in exasperation. "Gordon, where have you been? I haven't heard a word from you since yesterday. You're not exactly the 'eyes and ears of my army,' are you?"

Sinking from another of Hiram's reprimands and hoping to get back into his good graces, Gordon blurted out, "General, I have brought you intelligence on the enemies' positions."

Hiram shook his head. "Sometimes, Gordon, you're an impediment." Hiram couldn't stay mad at Gordon, and his manner mellowed. "We won't discuss this any longer. Help me find Raleigh and Jimmy."

Hiram walked back to the table, looked over the men he needed to aggregate, and pointed at the map. "Let's cover the four roads east of town the same way Lee did during the Seven Days. We can meet at Glendale and sweep up to Cold Harbor. I want the Pennsylvania Bucktails, the Bible Company, and the 15th Virginia Infantry covering Williamsburg Road. The Louisiana Tigers, the Bethel Regiment, and the New York Straw Hats can push down Charles City Road. The Crazy Delawares, the Hampton Legion, and the 44th Virginia Infantry can comb Darbytown Road. Who'd I leave out? Oh yeah, the Lousy 33rd, you can help cover Darbytown Road too."

Gordon and Hezekiah joined the circle, and Hiram pointed to Gordon, "And I want the 14th Virginia Infantry to cover New Market, Long Bridge, and Carters Mill Roads." Then Hiram looked at Pat. "It's probably better if you drive Gordon and Hezekiah, since some of the enemy knows Gordon is driving that Falcon.

"I have some other units coming in soon, so I'll deploy them as they arrive. According to our scouts, everybody needs to be on the lookout for the occupants of a gray utility truck with Confederate battle flags on the sides, a red Lexus, and a black Mercedes. If you run into any of these enemy groups, don't approach them because they're armed and dangerous. Report their location to me, and stay clear of them. Remember, our objective is to find Raleigh and Jimmy, not to get anyone killed."

CHAPTER 41

J immy scratched his multiple mosquito bites received the night before and moaned, "Are we just going to sit here all day, Dad?"

"For the hundredth time, we'll sit here as long as it takes. I'm sure Gordon and Pat are out looking for us, but so is the enemy. If we try to walk out of here, there's a good chance those people will find us first."

Jimmy put his hand on his stomach. "I'm hungry." The bologna sandwiches Lester Littlefeather had given them yesterday had worn off long ago.

Raleigh put his head in his hands, wishing he had broken his own "no cell phones while reenacting" rule, because this wasn't a drill. He wasn't sure how much more bonding time he could take with his son. He hadn't slept much and was in an especially foul mood without his morning coffee.

They had bivouacked on the Malvern Hill battlefield among the sweetgums, where two slave cabins stood in 1862. In the middle of the night, the sky erupted into a violent thunderstorm, lighting up the battlefield for about an hour. Terrified of lightning strikes, they stayed on the ground during the pouring rain, the equivalent of lying in a creek.

Starting to dry out in the midmorning sun, Raleigh and Jimmy were becoming damp again from their own perspiration as the heat came on and the bobwhites called. Dirty, exhausted, out of food and water, and worried someone might pounce on them at any moment, they were learning firsthand how a campaigning Civil War soldier felt.

The father and son passed the time by staying out of sight of patrolling park rangers but could see the occasional civilian vehicle coming and going along the highway that split the battlefield. The Battle of Malvern Hill had a much different outcome than the reenactment they had helped perform the Sunday before.

Swatting mayflies still out in June, Raleigh and Jimmy watched a few tourists drive in to see the place where the Confederates had suffered suicidal results by charging uphill in an open field. The Federal cannons blew holes into the Confederate infantry line with exploding canisters, dispersing deadly shrapnel. The Confederates called it "canned hellfire." The cannons had the effect of giant shotguns, taking out fifty to one hundred Rebels at a time, blowing men to indistinguishable bits and making accurate casualty counts difficult. The butcher's bill came to over five thousand Confederates killed or wounded. But the Confederates got their licks in with around three thousand Federals hit, even though the Confederate infantry never came close to penetrating the Federal line.

Malvern Hill was one of the many examples in the American Civil War of using the obsolete Napoleonic tactic of massing men to overwhelm the enemy. It worked for the French emperor over a half century before, but the tactic was seldom successful during the Civil War. If success was achieved, it came at a high cost. By the 1860s, rifled weapons had improved, and spinning shot launched out of a spiral-grooved barrel, like a football out of a quarterback's hand, propelled the projectile farther with more accuracy. This newfound precision made charging and piercing an enemy's line much more difficult than in previous wars. But the boys at West Point had trained to fight Napoleon's way and were slow on the uptake of the full consequences of the change in technology, yielding disastrous results.

Jimmy rubbernecked the field. The tranquil setting had few reminders of the "majestic murder" that had taken place. He sprawled where the closest Confederate advanced during the battle, 130 yards down from the six twelve-pounder Napoleons placed hub-to-hub by the park service, marking the Federal artillery position.

Jimmy remembered Gordon telling the story of his ancestor Second Lieutenant James Barrett of the 37th Virginia, part of Jackson's Division, that wasn't in on this fight but was on burial detail the next day. After living through the Seven Days Battles and seeing the carnage at Malvern Hill, Barrett wrote, "I think that the Richmond fight within itself, would gratify the ambition of the most blood thirsty warrior."

Two and a half months later, on September 17, 1862, like so many men from Appalachia, James Barrett lay dead on the battlefield at Antietam on America's deadliest day.

Raleigh spotted a VW Beetle pulling up to the interpretive shelter. As the passengers pulled themselves out of the clown car, Raleigh named them off, "Pat, Gordon, Hezekiah."

Jimmy bounced across the open battlefield like a cottontail, trampling the young soybeans that had replaced the wheat cut from the field two weeks earlier. He hollered and waved his kepi in jubilation. Raleigh walked peacefully behind him.

Gordon got on his phone to Hiram. "We found them. You can call everybody off."

"What are you going to do now?" Hiram asked.

"We need to be at Cold Harbor by five, but we'll probably just stay here until then."

"I'm sending you some horses."

"Some horses?"

"Just in case you need them, and in a few minutes, you're going to get a call about a truck. Don't ditch this one." Hiram hung up without saying good-bye.

Gordon joined the reunion. After some slaps on the shoulders and handshakes, Jimmy's hunger kicked back in. "Have you got anything to eat?"

"Sure," Pat said. "Ann packed a cooler full of food for us."

"You'd better hold on to her," Raleigh advised quietly.

CHAPTER 42

The pards picnicked underneath the shade of the small flat-roofed interpretive shelter, positioned behind where the bulk of the Union artillery parked in 1862 during the Battle of Malvern Hill. They gazed a thousand yards away to the other end of the field of fire, barely able to make out the three cannons marking the inferior Confederate right battery.

Malvern Hill was the seventh day of the Seven Days Battles. The battles had occurred between June 25 and July 1, 1862. This climax of blood baths of the Peninsula Campaign was second only to Gettysburg in casualties. General McClellan was derided as the Virginia Creeper for taking most of the spring of 1862 to move his army up the seventy-five-mile-long peninsula between the James and York Rivers in hopes of capturing Richmond and ending the war.

On the first day of the Seven Days Battles, McClellan's men had gotten close enough to Richmond to see the city's church steeples. They attacked at Oak Grove, where the airport is now. McClellan was trying to move even closer to set up siege guns against the city but failed.

On the second day of the Seven Days, Lee went on the offensive and attacked the isolated Federal right flank, north of the Chickahominy River near Mechanicsville at Beaver Dam Creek, causing McClellan to withdraw. This set up the next five days of Lee fighting a retreating Northern army.

Even though Lee was outnumbered, took heavier casualties, and was the clear victor in only one of the Seven Days Battles, these disadvantages were no match for McClellan's paranoia. The Northern general's delusion that a larger Confederate force would overwhelm him caused McClellan to run from the face of victory. With McClellan fleeing, Lee had a chance to destroy the Union Army, meaning a chance to end the war in the South's favor. But in the disarray, it never happened, and the slaughter bled on for almost three more years.

As the reenactors studied the battlefield, Gordon's phone rang. He clicked the receive key. Before he had a chance to spill his standard greeting he heard, "It's Bet. Where are you?"

"I'm at Malvern Hill."

"I heard Mary Beth helped you out of a jam."

"Yeah, how did you know?"

"I sent her, and I have word the Greeks and the Compatriots are also out in the East End looking for you."

"We've already run into the Compatriots and gave them the slip."

"I'm sure they're still looking for you. You're going to be at Cold Harbor at five, aren't you?"

"We'll be there."

"Good, I just got off the phone with the FBI to confirm they will be too. I'm procuring you a backup truck. I'll have it for you at the White Oak Swamp Bridge. Be careful. I love you."

"You what?"

"Nothing. I'll talk to you later."

Three trucks pulling horse trailers drove up. On the sides of the trailers were the words "3rd New Jersey Cavalry" painted over a picture of a tan butterfly. Pat walked up to the passenger side of the lead truck. Julius sat by the window, and Ann was in the driver's seat.

"What are you doing here?" Pat asked, surprised, almost annoyed.

Julius pushed his glasses up on his nose and lightly wagged his open fingers toward Ann. "I received a call from Miss Calico, who was very concerned about your welfare. So I called Hiram and he told me what was going on, and he called in the cavalry for you."

Ann leaned over. "You gave me a ride. I thought I would return the favor."

Pat turned a little red. "This is nice of you, but I don't think it's going to be necessary."

Julius pulled at his shirt collar and held on to it. He looked Pat straight in the eye. "You know, Mr. McCandlish, I will never be you, but if I were, and I had a special friend as delightful as Miss Calico here, and she offered me a ride, I would accept." Julius nodded his head back, still holding on to his collar. "And the Flying Butterflies, portraying perhaps the best-dressed soldiers of the entire Civil War, have graciously agreed to lend you their horses. I think it would be the polite thing to do if we went ahead and unloaded these large land mammals in case you change your mind."

Pat wasn't going to argue with Julius.

The cavalrymen, decked out like Civil War superheroes, stepped out of the other two trucks, wearing visorless caps, blue jackets adorned in a profusion of gold braids and burnished bell buttons, and blue pantaloons with yellow stripes down the side tucked into their black leather riding boots. Cloaks, with an orange lining and a tasseled hood, wrapped over their torsos, created a butterfly effect when these riders galloped on their horses.

By the time the Butterflies had their animals out of the trailers, a black Mercedes pulled into the parking lot entrance and stopped, blocking the way out. The pards recognized the German machine that chased them from the farm yesterday.

Pat looked at Raleigh, then whispered to Julius, "I guess we'll go ahead and take those horses now."

Raleigh called a huddle. "Let's calmly get on the horses and trot down the battlefield. No gallops. They haven't spotted us yet. No need to draw attention."

Raleigh, happy at the chance to be back on a horse, was first to mount. He climbed onto an iron gray American Saddlebred, the same as Traveller. Feeling like a freshly appointed god of war, he pointed down at his pards. "Saddle up."

One of the Butterflies handed Gordon the reins of a chestnut Morgan, the same as Stonewall Jackson's horse. The breed could go longer with less food and had the ability to stay steady under fire. Even though the horse was a compact, Gordon still needed a boost from the cavalryman.

There were three Canadian ponies left. The hearty, good-natured, Appaloosa-colored ponies were the size of small horses, and Pat made sure Hezekiah and Jimmy were properly in the saddle before he mounted. They all took off across the battlefield while Julius and Ann stalled the mobsters with charm. The Papadopoulos brothers didn't realize their marks were getting away.

When the reenactors made it to the Confederate side of the battlefield, they picked up the pace and cut over to Willis Church Road. They needed to get to Cold Harbor, and the quickest way was to follow the steps of the Seven Days Battles backward. Leaving the site of the seventh day, the reenactors were well on their way to the site of the sixth, Glendale.

Once they were out of view, their trot turned into a canter, and they followed the tree-lined country road, crossing the small and slow-moving Western Run. Raleigh, with the scare in him, urged his pards to put it into a gallop, going another mile until they made it to the Glendale National Cemetery. The cemetery was located in the Federal rear of the Glendale battlefield. Glendale was a particularly nasty affair, plunging into extensive hand-to-hand combat where the main weapons were bayonets and rifle butts, a rare occurrence of close-range killing during the Civil War.

The reenactors paused at the cemetery gates connected to a chest-high stone wall and looked back. No sign of the Greeks, but they knew the Papadopouloses were bound to catch up with them. For refuge, they entered the two-acre cemetery that interred soldiers from the Civil War to the Vietnam War. Riding their horses down the driveway past the POW/MIA flag, they went behind the caretaker's lodge. The lodge now served as the NPS Glendale/Malvern Hill Visitor Center.

After dismounting, Raleigh motioned to Jimmy to go over to the sidewall beside an outbuilding where he could see the road. Jimmy ran across the lawn, hoping not to be detected, and peered down to the main road. In a couple of minutes, he ran back. "The Mercedes just went by."

Betting the Greeks wouldn't double back, the reenactors rode out of the gate, continuing north, following the high corn along the highway to the Riddell's shop intersection. This junction of country roads was the major objective for General Lee during the Battle of Glendale. Lee displayed his military genius, planning to have his divisions meet at this crossroads to cut McClellan's retreating army in half. Like so many Civil War battles, when the general's plan was executed, it lacked communication, coordination, and movement. Instead of striking a decisive blow, it turned into a bloody mess.

The reenactors stopped at the intersection and looked all three ways, with no sign of the black Mercedes. They turned east onto Charles City Road, leading to the truck waiting for them at the White Oak Swamp Bridge. They hadn't traveled far when they pulled up in their tracks. On the right side of the road was a Citgo station with a convenience store, and parked in front was the Compatriots' gray utility truck.

"Let's just go behind the store," Raleigh hissed. The troopers slinked behind the store, then got back on the road. They broke into a full gallop, racing past ranch houses with orange day-lilies in front and hay fields in the back. When they turned north onto Elko Road, they looked back and saw no one behind them. The reenactors slowed down to descend the hill to the White Oak Swamp.

The half-mile hill and the marshy creek at the bottom proved to be formidable physical barriers for Stonewall Jackson, pursuing the Federal Army on day six of the Seven Days, trying to provide reinforcements at Glendale. Jackson's men took heavy artillery fire as they tried to repair the White Oak Swamp Bridge. Jackson withdrew his men, then fell asleep, most likely exhausted from his stellar Shenandoah Valley Campaign and the march back to Richmond. He was faulted for not crossing the swamp and ascending the hill in a timely fashion, allowing McClellan's army to escape.

When the reenactors reached the bottom of the hill, Raleigh and Jimmy recognized Lester Littlefeather's tow truck, and there was Lester wielding a chainsaw and waving them on. They trotted onto the modern highway bridge laid over the black water of White Oak Swamp Creek. With a crack and a thud, a tupelo tree Lester felled came down behind them, closing off the road. Parked in front of them was an old Yankee blue International Harvester truck.

"That must be our ride," Gordon said.

Bet stood on the bridge and waved them forward, dressed in her nineteenth-century half-mourning lavender garb.

"Who is that?" Pat asked.

"That's Bet," Gordon said.

"Oh, so that's Bet." Pat took the opportunity to tease Gordon back. "Hubba-hubba."

"Shut up."

They got off their horses, and Gordon tried to embrace Bet, but she only gave him marching orders. "Tie your horses to the historical markers, the keys are in the truck, and there are Springfields and cartridge boxes behind the seat. Go on and get out of here." Another falling tree crashed behind them.

They took their standard seating positions in the truck with the adults in the cab and the teenagers in the bed. As Gordon pulled out, he looked back to wave at Bet and saw the gray utility truck blocked by the trees. They hurried up to Highway 60.

Down from the intersection stood another old fire tower. As they traversed the four-lane highway, a red Lexus pulled out from beside the tower. Gordon made it across the highway but was forced to halt at a stop sign a short way down Meadow Road.

Hezekiah shouted through the window, "Do you see them?"

Gordon shouted back, "Yeah, you two get down." Seeing the Lexus coming up on them, Gordon sped down the road to the Richmond and York River Railroad crossing. A train engine idled up from the crossing, but the gate wasn't down. Puzzled and cautious, Gordon noticed the arm of the engineer motioning for him to go on. The reenactors couldn't see what the engine was pulling until they were right at the crossing.

Pat cried out in awe as they banged over the tracks, "I'll be damned. It's the 'Land Merrimack.'"

After the reenactors passed, the locomotive slowly pulled a flat car out to block the road. Mounted on the car was a thirty-two-pound Brooke naval rifle, the weight related to the amount of solid shot the gun could hurl. Wrapped in iron rails for protection, the cannon's barrel protruded out of its shield. It was a replica of the first armored railroad battery, used by General Lee at Savage's Station, and the Gabrielites were on the wrong end of it.

At first glance, Fattah screamed in frustration, "Not another train blocking our way." Then he was gobsmacked, looking into the open barrel as Leela speedily backed up the Lexus, and the reenactors escaped up the hill to the Savage's Station battlefield overlook.

"Stop the truck," Raleigh clamored. "I need some air."

They piled out of the truck among the historical markers, lining the dirt pull off, telling the story of day five of the Seven Days Battles. The reenactors looked past a farmer's field down into the gently sloping valley where they could see and hear the constant vroom of Interstate 64.

In the valley, a muddled-on-morphine Magruder failed to stop the withdrawal of the Yankee army. Not because of his drug impairment, but mainly because Jackson was too engaged observing the Sabbath to come to his aid. Although Magruder couldn't stop the Yankee retreat, he did expedite it. In the Federals' haste to leave, they abandoned 2,500 men at a field hospital, including members of the 16th New York Volunteer Infantry wearing their famous white straw hats.

Taking in the view, the air wasn't soothing Raleigh. He started to hyperventilate. Raleigh steadied himself by leaning forward and grasping a "Freeman Marker," named after Douglas Southhall Freeman, the Pulitzer Prize–winning author of *Lee's Lieutenants*. The marker was a four-foot square of concrete block, capped with a cast-iron plate inscribed with Civil War site information. Freeman had worked with the Richmond Rotary Club to erect fifty-nine of these historical markers in the Richmond area in 1925. Raleigh abruptly barfed on the description of Savage's Station and convulsed even more when Gordon's phone rang.

Gordon, repulsed and amused by Raleigh's regurgitation, still managed to say, "Your humble and obedient servant, Gordon Barrett."

"Gordon, it's Jeff Dansey. Are you okay?"

"Yeah, thanks to the 'Land Merrimack.'"

"Whoever was chasing you backed off once I pulled out my big gun." Jeff laughed. "The thing wasn't even loaded."

"How did you know to be here?"

"Kim talked to Hezekiah a couple of days ago and thought you were in trouble. So I telegraphed Hiram and he called my boss's boss, who arranged for me to take Hiram's "Land Merrimack" out for a ride."

You could hear the relief in Gordon's voice. "It's nice to know somebody who has the right toy for the right job."

Jeff laughed again. "Hey, can you put Hezekiah on? Kim wanted to talk to him."

Gordon handed it to Hezekiah. "It's your girlfriend."

"Shut up." Hezekiah took the phone.

"Hezekiah, are you safe?" the soft, sweet voice spoke over the noise in the engineer's cab.

"Yeah, I'm fine."

"Oh, wait a minute. Daddy is telling me to tell your uncle Gordon that Hiram is waiting for him at Cold Harbor."

"I'll let him know. Uh, hey, maybe we can go to the movies sometime this week?"

"That would be fun."

Gordon grinned without displaying his teeth. "All right, Hezekiah, this isn't the time to be making dates. Go ahead and get off the phone."

Hezekiah looked back at Gordon, perturbed. "I got to go."

"Take care of yourself. Good-bye."

"Bye." Hezekiah hung up and handed the phone back to Gordon. "Kim's father said Hiram is waiting for you at Cold Harbor."

Raleigh revived, wiping spittle from his mouth. "Let's stop wasting time and get over there."

The reenactors packed back into the truck and headed down Grapevine Road. Trumpet creeper bloomed along the roadside as the men covered the ground of day four of the Seven Days. The fourth day brought a lull in the fighting with the minor actions at the Battle of Garnett's and Golding's Farms, wrapping up in the morning from the night before. McClellan busied himself mismanaging his retreat while Lee sat tight at Gaines's Mill, waiting for Stuart to provide him intelligence on McClellan's movements.

The reenactors passed the beige, red-tin roofed Trent house that had served as McClellan's headquarters. In the field surrounding the house, Thaddeus Lowe had launched his balloons for Union aerial reconnaissance. The only thing launching today in the field were purple martins from their round house, reconning for mosquitoes.

Gordon drove over the Chickahominy River at the site of the corduroy Grapevine Bridge built by the 5th New Hampshire Infantry, where so many Civil War soldiers of both sides had passed. The reenactors raced up another ranch house road with subdivisions creeping in. It was three and a half more miles on the rising highway to the overlapping battlefields of Gaines's Mill and Cold Harbor.

CHAPTER 43

Two major battles of the Civil War were fought on the same ground nine miles northeast of Richmond, Gaines's Mill and Cold Harbor. These battles were the first and last great victories for Lee as the commander of the Army of Northern Virginia.

The Battle of Gaines's Mill took place in 1862 when the war was young and the South still had plenty of men to waste, and they did. The Battle of Cold Harbor took place in 1864 when the war had grown old and the North still had plenty of men to waste, and they did.

The reenactors arrived at a five-way intersection of rural roads at five o'clock in the afternoon. Scruffy in appearance, the intersection was the strategic junction of Cold Harbor. No waterfront or cooling effect was discernible. The name meant a place where you could get a bed for the night but nothing hot to eat.

They puttered on down the road in the Harvester, past the Garthright house. In this house, Union surgeons had worked for ten days straight in 1864, as Mrs. Garthright sheltered in the basement with screams of agony from the patients reverberating throughout the house and blood dripping down on her from the floorboards above. Across the road was the Cold Harbor National Cemetery, holding Union soldiers who had written their names and addresses on pieces of paper and pinned them inside their coats, so their bodies could be identified. Before the day of dog tags, soldiers longed not to become unknown and for their remains to be returned to their loved ones.

A half-mile farther, Gordon turned into the Cold Harbor portion of the Richmond National Battlefield. The parking lot was full of cars and trucks. Some of the trucks hauled horse trailers or flat trailers loaded with artillery pieces.

At the edge of the lot was a meadow, part of a three-mile front where, with the first light of June 3, 1864, at four thirty in the morning, Eastern Standard Time, Federal troops surged through a thick ground fog toward almost impenetrable Confederate earthworks. The Confederate response was a volcanic eruption of firepower, resulting in thousands of Federal casualties. The failed attack turned into Grant's biggest blunder of the war.

This evening, there was a party in the killing field. All of the units that had met earlier at the Dabbs house, and then some, were there. A regimental brass band pumped period music into the air.

Gordon found Hiram holding a ladle and standing over a cooking pot exuding delicious vapors. "No hog and hominy tonight, my friend. Everybody will eat like Union officers. The mess is being prepared by the Les Garde des Fourchettes, the guards of the forks, and we'll be having frogs."

"What are you doing here, Hiram?" Gordon asked, irked and anxious about his presence and everyone else's.

Hiram set down his ladle. "No, 'thank you, Hiram, for saving my butt by sending horses, a truck, and a train'?"

"Hiram, I appreciate everything," Gordon said with genuine gratitude in his voice. "And not just what you did for us this afternoon, but for everything you have done for me in the past."

"Then you should appreciate that I thought the best thing to do was to have everybody meet here so you would have backup when the elephant arrives."

Gordon's phone rang, and he answered in his usual manner, insulting Hiram again with the interruption.

"This is Howard. What is going on over there? The targets are supposed to show up at six. They're not coming anywhere near the place with that crowd. You've got to get those people out of there."

Gordon hung up. "That was the FBI. They want everybody to leave."

"You've got to be kidding? Just leave you here to be killed?"

"The FBI will give us the protection we need. We've got to do this on our own, Hiram. If we don't, we're going to lose the gold."

Hiram wavered. "Fine. We'll move this social down the road to Beaver Dam Creek, but if you need us, let me know." Hiram retrieved his ladle, raised it above his head, and started herding everyone out of the park.

The caravan slowly moved five miles west to Beaver Dam Creek, reestablishing the cookout. Once the parking lot emptied, the FBI sedans slipped in, dropped off agents, and left quietly. The G-men took their places, hiding behind the visitor center, the trees, and the trenches. Gordon and his pards remained in the open.

The rendezvous hour of six o'clock came and went. At six thirty, there was still no sign of the gray utility truck, the red Lexus, or the black Mercedes. Seven o'clock arrived, then eight o'clock. At eight thirty, a black sedan pulled into the parking lot, and Howard got out to talk to the reenactors.

"Looks like they're no-shows. The deal was for you to deliver these groups to me today and the gold would go to your charity. You missed your chance, so you can deliver the gold to my office tomorrow morning or I'll be issuing arrest warrants for all of you."

More sedans pulled in to pick up the agents dispersed around the battlefield. Then all of the Feds left as the sun was going down.

"What are we going to do now?" Raleigh asked.

"I don't know," Gordon said as he gazed over the battleground.

Raleigh looked at Gordon, but Gordon continued to look out over the frontline. Raleigh came around and got directly in

Gordon's line of sight. "Where are we supposed to stay tonight? Those locos are still out there looking for us, and I can't spend another night on a battlefield. What are we going to do?"

"I don't know, Raleigh," Gordon repeated in a whisper and turned away to walk to their borrowed truck. The rest followed, and they got in.

Gordon pulled out slowly to head west to the Beaver Dam Creek cookout. He glanced in his rearview mirror, and there in the distance the gray utility truck appeared. His heart jumped, and he stomped on the gas, making the heads of his pards fly backward.

Raleigh scorned, "What are you doing now?"

"Look who's behind us."

Raleigh looked back. "Boys, get down!" Raleigh screamed with his head out the window.

Hezekiah and Jimmy threw themselves down in the truck bed, and Hezekiah turned to Jimmy. "Here we go again."

"Turn here." Raleigh pointed madly at the Watt House Road. They followed the curvy road down to Boatswain Creek and back up the hill to the national park's portion of the Gaines's Mill battlefield.

The reenactors leapt out. They grabbed the Springfields and cartridge boxes from behind the seat and ran a one-hundred-yard dash from the parking area to the woods. Jimmy instinctively stood on the edge of the forest as a picket, while the others bolted down the dark trail, slipping on pea pebbles and tripping on exposed tree roots. At the bottom of the trail, they reached Boatswain Creek, a trickle in a shallow, sandy ditch. In 2003, Hurricane Isabel opened the forest here, ripping up trees along the creek, allowing the day's last light of rosy hues to shine through.

Raleigh turned around with fear on his face. "Where's Jimmy?"

The utility truck pulled into the parking area. Garnett, Carter, and Wendell got out, carrying AR-15s and sporting extra magazines on belt pouches. Garnett had come along to ensure the reenactors didn't get away this time.

"There's one of them," Wendell said, seeing Jimmy across the way. He raised his weapon, but before he had a chance to shoot, Jimmy jumped back behind the screen of trees and ran down the trail.

Raleigh greeted him with a hug. "Boy, you've got to stay with us."

"They're right behind us, Dad."

Pat pointed. "Let's hide across the creek."

With not much time to think, the reenactors crossed the water where there was no trail and waded through the ferns on the other side. They reentered the protection of the dark forest, whacking their way through briars and hollies. They stopped about thirty yards from the creek, finding cover behind some trees halfway up a hillock to load their Springfields.

When the Compatriots made it to the bottom of the trail, there was no sight of the sentry. They peered across the creek with suspicion but couldn't see anything through the new undergrowth sprouting up. Nothing moved in the almost unbreathable humid air. A mile away, they could hear the cars buzzing on Interstate 295, crossing the Chickahominy. Overhead coming out of Richmond International, a plane rumbled through the clouds. But inside the Gaines's Mill woods, dappled by the soft radiance of twilight, there was silence except for the sweet singing of a Louisiana waterthrush, synchronized to the dancing of lightning bugs.

Carter broke the tranquility. "We know you're down here. Just come on out and we can talk."

Jimmy sneezed from the mold. Wendell shot as a reflex, and the reenactors hit the ground.

Garnett glowered at Wendell, then apologized across the creek. "Sorry, that was an accident. Come on out now and see us. Don't make us come in there and get you."

In the parking lot above the woods, the red Lexus glided in beside the utility truck and the Gabrielites heard Wendell's gunshot. Not wanting to meet the gunfire, the Gabrielites walked around the woods by passing the restored 1835 Watt house, taking a farm road enclosed by high split-rail fencing. At the first break in the fence, they cut across a field to pick up the other end of the loop trail through the forest.

Another "Freeman Marker" guarded the trail entrance. The monument commemorated the spot at Gaines's Mill, day three of the Seven Days Battles, where Confederate General John Bell Hood led his Texas Brigade in a frontal assault, breaking the Union line in the last of the daylight on June 27, 1862. The legend of the Gallant Hood was born on this spot as a daring and fierce, some would say crazed, combat leader without peer.

Fattah, Leela, and Hark all looked at the sign, noting the achievement with contempt. They entered the woods and walked halfway down the hill, stopping among the skeletal remains of giant oaks from the nineteenth century lying on the ground, and waited.

Stealthily, the Papadopoulos brothers pulled into the parking lot. Lichas got out with a pistol in one hand and an Italian sub in the other. Bob was unsandwiched. They took the route of the Gabrielites, but stopped at the edge of the forest, unable to see the parties below them.

Jimmy sneezed again and Wendell shot again.

"Damn it, Wendell." Garnett commanded, "Would you stop doing that?"

The Gabrielites froze on the second shot, and the mobsters clung to their position.

Carter gave notice. "Boys, if you ain't coming out, we're coming in."

The reenactors sprang up and fired down on them with their Springfields, completely missing their marks. The Compatriots let off full clips, and the reenactors hit the ground again.

Pat grunted. "I think we're a little outgunned."

Raleigh hugged the earth. "Jesus Christ, those were real bullets they shot at us."

Gordon pushed leaf litter away from his eyes and mouth. "Well, we did shoot real Minié balls at them."

Raleigh panicked. "I don't want to die like a dog in a ditch."

"You're finally getting your chance to be a real soldier," Gordon chafed. "You always said you wanted to know what it was like."

Raleigh confronted the magnitude of the moment. "I don't want to die."

Hezekiah pointed upward. "Whoa." In the sky, a multicolored hot-air balloon, made from dress silk, floated above them.

Bugles screeched out and drums sounded. A cannon fired close by, and they heard its solid iron projectile booming toward them like a freight train. The bolt hit directly behind them, throwing dirt on their backs.

They looked at each other. "That's got to be our guys," Pat said.

Raleigh clenched his teeth. "Great, now we get to be killed by friendly fire."

The Compatriots looked around in confusion as they feverishly switched out their magazines. The Gabrielites grew nervous, but the Greek brothers held steady.

Pat shivered. "Feel that cold air?"

"It's late June in central Virginia," Gordon said. "There is no cold air."

The tops of the trees started to sway back and forth until they were violently bowing to their breaking points, but there was no wind. A hideous, fiendish roar rose up from the creek bed, as if emitted by an entire brigade of raging, rampaging men.

"Let's get out of here," Garnett shouted as the ground started to tremble. The Compatriots sprinted up the quaking hill, meeting the Gabrielites face-to-face.

The Gabrielites raised their weapons but looked behind the militiamen and saw what the Compatriots had seen, a thundering horde of howling Confederate soldiers flashing bayonets and stampeding up the wooded hillside in the dusk. Soldiers, wrapped in an unstoppable madness, seeing a landscape shaded in red, rabidly screaming and laughing. The terrifying torrent of human aggression exploded through the woods, hell-bent on destroying all life forms in its path. The Gabrielites turned around and scrambled in self-preservation.

The Papadopoulos brothers saw the ebony and the ivory retreating toward them, and beyond, a sea of men in gray and butternut. They fired at the soldiers, but the wave of apocalyptic fury rolled unwaveringly up the hill. The brothers smelled and tasted the fear, and fled to escape certain death from the overwhelming murdering mass.

The gangsters and the wannabe revolutionaries flushed out of the woods and rushed headlong across the field and down the farm road to the parking lot.

Pulling in late for the soiree were the dark sedans. The FBI agents jumped out, employed their weapons, and told the enemies of the state to drop theirs. The enemies obliged, but Lichas was slow to drop the remains of his sub. Bob surrendered his weapon but fell into hysterics when he saw a cannonball buried in the hood of his Mercedes. He shrieked, "They hurt my car. They hurt my car," and had to be subdued by the agents.

Carter looked over his shoulder and barked with fear, "Don't shoot us. Shoot them."

Agent Howard looked past Carter and saw no one behind them. He snapped back, "Lay down on the ground with your hands behind you."

Everyone complied, frightened and disoriented and momentarily relieved the FBI was there.

Wendell wailed as he was being cuffed, "They're going to kill us. We've got to get away from them."

"Shut up and die like a man," Garnett ordered, his beret lost in the flight and his bald head reflecting in the gloam.

"Nobody's going to die," Howard reassured his prisoners.

"Tell that to the hundreds of Confederates coming up the hill right now, you idiot," Fattah protested with his face in the grass and his kofia on the ground in front of him, exposing his head of gray hair.

Beside a rising crescent moon, the reenactors emerged from the forest and joined the federal agents.

Howard took a good look around. "There's no Confederate army after you. There's just these five guys and they're harmless."

"Thanks," Gordon said, feeling slighted.

"No, no. There's an army in there," Leela implored from her position on the ground. "Didn't you hear the white devils screaming?"

"Don't worry. We're taking you in as fast as we can." Howard pulled up a cuffed, silent, and disillusioned Hark, handing him over to another agent, and turned to speak to Gordon. "What did you do to them?"

Gordon shrugged. "We didn't do anything to them."

"They're convinced they saw an army of Confederate soldiers in the woods racing after them."

"We heard a lot of commotion, but we thought it was Hiram with all of the units coming back to rescue us."

"Most of Hiram's party is still over at Beaver Dam."

"We didn't really see anything. We were hiding on the other side of the creek."

"Well, they all saw something that scared the hell out of them."

Gordon moved in to change the subject and close the deal. "You got your men. We get the gold to buy battlefields, right?"

Howard nodded.

The huge, colorful balloon descended in the misty night air and landed in the grass beside the parking area. Bet popped out of the basket and ran to meet Gordon. She took her brave, Southern man into her arms and didn't let go.

Bet spoke with her chin tucked over Gordon's shoulder, out of breath and her heart pounding, "I was doing recon and saw you were in trouble. I called the FBI back, then called Hiram, who called the Richmond Howitzers. Sorry, the Howitzers' first shot was a little off. I think I gave them the wrong coordinates."

Gordon pulled away from her warm embrace, noticing she was completely out of mourning dress and her hair unconfined. "But who was making all that noise with the bugles and drums and the rebel yells?"

Bet looked puzzled. "I didn't hear anything. I must have been in an acoustic shadow."

"What about the weird weather front that came through with the blast of cold air? Did you have a hard time staying aloft?"

"Cold air? What are you talking about?"

"You didn't see the trees bowing till they almost broke?" Gordon remembered and a chill cut to his marrow on the hot summer night. "It's June 27, the anniversary of Gaines's Mill."

They turned in unison to look back at the lightless forest, and he whispered, "Maybe it was the massive cannon fire of 1862 making the trees bow?" Gordon contemplated the battlefield and shuddered. "Maybe it was the ghosts of General Hood's Texas Brigade charging up the hill?"

CHAPTER 44

G ordon couldn't stop smiling as he walked out of the Richmond FBI office with his pards on Monday morning. They had just finished meeting with Howard. The FBI would issue a press release on the recovery of the gold, and the capture of the domestic terrorist groups and the mobsters.

The prisoners would be charged with multiple crimes including extortion, attempted murder, and kidnapping. No charges would be brought against Sy Meyer.

The reenactors would receive reward money equal to the value of the gold, placed in escrow to purchase Civil War battlefields minus 5 percent to restore and maintain Shockoe Hill Cemetery. Howard said it would take years for the claims on the gold to be worked out in court and what was left would revert to the government. In the meantime, because of the gold's historical value and for public relations, the Feds would allow a traveling exhibit.

Gordon beamed. "We'll be touring with the gold. We'll be the rock stars of reenacting. Hey, I'm feeling so good I'm thinking about driving up to the Gettysburg reenactment in a couple of days. Who's with me?"

Raleigh put on his hat to shade his face from the sun. "I don't like going up there. They never let you win." Then he put his arm around Jimmy. "Besides, I don't think we're going to be reenacting for a while. Gayle's getting out of the hospital today, and we're taking her home. I've got some fences to mend."

Jimmy looked happy for the first time in a long time.

Pat flipped his kepi onto his head. "I don't think I'm in for Gettysburg. I've had enough reenacting for a while, and I think I've found a woman I'd like to get to know better. I'm probably going to be spending most of my time with her."

Gordon was about to say something smart but thought maybe it was time for him to start exercising a little restraint. "That reminds me. I have to call Bet, and Hezekiah, aren't you taking Kim to the movies? Maybe we can double date."

Hezekiah rolled his eyes into the back of his head as if he were dying. Gordon reached out and smacked the bill of the kepi Hezekiah hadn't bothered to take off while he was inside the office. Gordon adjusted his slouch hat onto his head. "What a week of Civil War campaigning, huh, gentlemen?"

"I'm just glad it's over," Pat said.

Raleigh gazed up to the sky and squinted. His forehead furrowed and he hung his head, but then raised his chin in reconciliation and smiled his unnatural smile. "Oh, it's never going to be over."

The End

The wise should adapt themselves to the present, even when the past seems more attractive, both in the clothes of the soul and in those of the body.

—Baltasar Gracián
1601–1658
The Art of Worldly Wisdom

BOOK GROUP
DISCUSSION QUESTIONS

1. Each of the main characters in *Confederate Gold* is taking refuge in reenacting. Is it a blessing or an impediment for each of them? Do you find Civil War reenacting silly and offensive or an enriching hobby that educates others and pays tribute to our ancestors?

2. There is a complicated and evolving relationship between the male characters. Which men were your favorites and why? How does each of the men or boys take a leadership role at different times and in different ways?

3. Which women characters were your favorites and why? How did the women change as the story progressed? How do the women and men affect and change each other? Is the novel a love story as well as a thriller?

4. There are many side characters in the novel. Which one was your favorite and why: Sy Meyer, Hiram George, Julius Bohannon, Aunt April, or someone else? How did each of these characters contribute to the plot?

5. The two extremist groups are drawn large in the book but represent factions in our present-day society, people who feel alienated, used up, and forgotten by our economic system. Do you feel these characterizations are

accurate? Do you know anyone who feels outraged at our society or economic system?

6. Did you see the portrayal of the Greek mobsters as steeped in stereotypes? Do you think there is organized crime in the South?

7. Racial tensions are portrayed in the novel both in an extreme manner of the Compatriots and Gabrielites willing to start race wars and in the nuanced, playful banter of Powhatan. Do you see racial tensions in your own life? If so, do you feel they are the result of the legacy of slavery? Will there always be racism and classism?

8. The novel takes many twists and turns. Did you find the plot in the realm of possibility? Does the plot carry the characters through Richmond and its history in a plausible manner?

9. Civil War history is woven throughout the story. Was this a good way to bring the history to life or a distraction from the action? Do you agree or disagree with the way the author presented and analyzed the historical facts?

10. The setting of the novel is Richmond, Virginia. The author often refers to Richmond as the main character of the book. Did you feel the setting was effectively created? Did reading the book make you want to visit Richmond? Which historic sites and locations would you like to visit?

11. Charles Dickens thought Richmond was a vile place in 1842 because slavery was a sanctioned trade. Is there anything humans do today that might be considered vile

in the course of history? How might someone visiting from another culture describe your community?

12. Bet Van Lew was a hero to some and a traitor to others. How does time affect people's opinions of historical figures? Who is respected or disrespected today who may be viewed later in a different way?

13. The Civil War generals fought with Napoleonic tactics. How has war changed over the last 150 years? What do you think the author thinks about war? Is this an antiwar novel?

14. How do you feel about preserving Civil War battlefield land? Should we develop the land as a way to put the war behind us, or should we save it as a way to jog our national memory of the United States's defining event? Is saving Civil War battlefield land equivalent to saving Civil War monuments?

15. At the end of the book, Raleigh says, "It's never going to be over." Do you believe that is true? Will the Civil War continue to be relevant to our lives and our society?

ACKNOWLEDGMENTS

I wish to thank the people of the following businesses, agencies, museums, parks, historic sites, and organizations of the Richmond–Petersburg, Virginia, metropolitan area:

Aldridge Metal Detector Sales & Service
Alexander's
American Civil War Museum
Berkeley Plantation
Black History Museum & Cultural Center of Virginia
Blandford Church and Cemetery
Bob Moates Sports Shop
Buddy's Place
Charles City County Parks & Recreation
Confederate Memorial Chapel
Country Style Donuts
Edgar Allan Poe Museum
Enon United Methodist Church
Evelynton Plantation
Half Way House Restaurant
Hanover County Parks & Recreation
Hebrew Cemetery – Congregation Beth Ahabah
Henrico County Recreation & Parks
Henricus Historical Park
Hollywood Cemetery
Jefferson Hotel
King's Barbecue

Library of Virginia
Maggie L. Walker National Historic Site
Mama J's
Marlbourne
Mariners' Museum (Newport News, Virginia)
Mediterranean Bakery & Deli
Pamplin Historical Park & National Museum of the Civil
    War Soldier
Petersburg Department of Tourism
Petersburg National Battlefield Park
Pocahontas Chapel
Regency Square Mall
Richmond City Council Slave Trail Commission
Richmond Department of Parks, Recreation & Community
    Facilities
Richmond Metropolitan Convention & Visitors Bureau
Richmond National Battlefield Park
Richmond Public Library
Richmond Railroad Museum
Richmond Yacht Basin
Sons of Confederate Veterans
St. John's Episcopal Church
St. Paul's Episcopal Church
St. Peter's Episcopal Church
Studley General Store
Theatre VCU
The Valentine
United Daughters of the Confederacy
Veterans Affairs National Cemetery Administration
Virginia Civil War Trails
Virginia Department of Historic Resources
Virginia Museum of Fine Arts
Virginia Museum of History & Culture

Virginia State Capitol
Visions Dance Club
Westover Plantation

Thanks to Mari and Keith Minton for website development.

A special thank you to Emily Gulati for the cover photograph and
many of the website photos.

And with deep gratitude, I wish to thank my dear wife, Dianne,
for her endless edits and encouragement, and for providing our
family with the care and support that allowed me to write.

—Penn Miller

SELECTED BIBLIOGRAPHY

Alden, Peter, et al. *National Audubon Society Field Guide to the Mid-Atlantic States*. New York: Alfred A. Knopf, 1999.

Barrett, James H. to L.D. Fletcher. July 23, 1862. In the author's possession.

Beth Ahabah Museum & Archives. "Hebrew Cemetery." September 3, 2016. https://bethahabah.org/bama/ hebrew-cemetery/#.

Billings, John D. *Hardtack and Coffee, or The Unwritten Story of Army Life*. Boston: G. M. Smith & Co., 1887. Reprinted with introduction by William L. Shea. Lincoln: University of Nebraska Press, 1993.

Boatner, Mark Mayo, III. *The Civil War Dictionary*. New York: Vintage Civil War Library, 1991.

Bowers, Q. David. *Lost and Found Coin Hoards and Treasures: Illustrated Stories of the Greatest American Troves and Their Discoveries*. Atlanta: Whitman Publishing, LLC, 2015.

Brewer, James H. *The Confederate Negro: Virginia's Craftsman and Military Laborers, 1861–1865*. Durham, NC: Duke University Press, 1969.

Brody, Seymour "Sy." "The Only Jewish Military Cemetery Outside of Israel is in Richmond, Virginia." SeymourBrody. com. September 4, 2016. http://seymourbrody.com/ceme-tery/home.htm.

Buckley, Gail Lumet. *American Patriots: The Story of Blacks in the Military from the Revolution to Desert Storm*. New York: Random House, 2001.

Burke, Louise L., and Keith F. Ready. *Parks, Preserves, and Rivers: A Guide to Outdoor Adventures in Virginia's Capital Region*. Richmond, VA: The Metropolitan Foundation, 1985.

Burnham, Phillip. "Hollywood: A Changing Legend." *Richmond Surroundings*, April/May 1993.

Burns, Brian. *Lewis Ginter: Richmond's Gilded Age Icon*. Charleston, SC: History Press, 2011.

Burton, Brian K. *Extraordinary Circumstances: The Seven Days Battles*. Bloomington: Indiana University Press, 2001.

Calos, Katherine. "Journey into slavery passed through Richmond." *Richmond Times-Dispatch*. November 11, 2013.

Campbell, Joseph and Bill Moyers. *The Power of Myth*. Edited by Betty Sue Flowers. New York: Doubleday, 1988.

Carneal, Drew St. J. *Richmond's Fan District*. Richmond, VA: Council of Historic Richmond Foundation, 1996.

Cigliano, Jan, and Sarah Bradford Landau, eds. *The Grand American Avenue, 1850–1920*. San Francisco: Pomegranate Artbooks / The Octagon, the Museum of the American Architectural Foundation, 1994.

Coggins, Jack. *Arms and Equipment of the Civil War*. Garden City, NY: Doubleday, 1962. Reprint, Wilmington, NC: Broadfoot Publishing Company, 1990.

Collier, Malinda W., et al. *White House of the Confederacy: An Illustrated History*. Richmond, VA: Cadmus, 1993.

Cosel, Janice H, and Laura Jo Leffel. "A Case Study of Pocahontas Island: Resistance to Post-Impact Evacuation in a Historic Black Community Virginia." *Electronic Journal of Emergency Management*, Number 1, 1999. August 20, 2005. http://members.tripod.com/~Richmond_ESM/ej0103.html.

Coski, Ruth Ann. *The White House of the Confederacy: A Pictorial Tour*. Richmond, VA: Carter Printing Company, 2001.

Davis, William C. *The Civil War Reenactors' Encyclopedia*. Guilford, CT: The Lyons Press, 2002.

Dees, Morris, and James Corcoran. *Gathering Storm: America's Militia Threat*. New York: HarperCollins Publishers, 1996.

Dennison, Will. *Springing to the Call! How to Get Started in Civil War Reenacting*. Marietta, OH: Camp Chase Publishing Company, 1994.

Dickens, Charles. *American Notes for General Circulation*. London: Chapman and Hall, 1842.

Dovi, Chris. "Look Away, Look Away." *Style Weekly*, May 7, 2008. June 6, 2008 http://www.styleweekly.com/richmond/look-away-look-away/Content?oid=1370255.

Driggs, Sarah Shields, Richard Guy Wilson, and Robert P. Winthrop. *Richmond's Monument Avenue*. Chapel Hill: University of North Carolina Press, 2001.

DuPriest, James E., Jr. *Hollywood Cemetery: A Tour*, 3rd ed. Richmond, VA: Richmond Discoveries Publications, 1989.

DuPriest, James E., Jr., and Douglas O. Tice, Jr. *Monument & Boulevard: Richmond's Grand Avenues*. Richmond, VA: Richmond Discoveries Publications, 1996.

Dyer, Gwynne. *War*. New York: Crown Publishers, Inc., 1985.

Egerton, Douglas R. *Gabriel's Rebellion: The Virginia Slave Conspiracies of 1800 and 1802*. Chapel Hill: University of North Carolina Press, 1993.

Faust, Drew Gilpin. *This Republic of Suffering: Death and the American Civil War*. New York: Alfred A. Knopf, 2008.

Foote, Shelby. *The Civil War: A Narrative*. 3 vols. New York: Random House, 1958–74.

Frassanito, William A. *Grant and Lee: The Virginia Campaigns 1864–1865*. Gettysburg, PA: Thomas Publications, 1983.

Furgurson, Ernest B. *Ashes of Glory: Richmond at War*. New York: Alfred A. Knopf, 1996.

— — — . *Not War But Murder: Cold Harbor 1864*. New York: Alfred A. Knopf, 2000.

Gardner, Alexander. *Gardner's Photographic Sketch Book of the Civil War*. New York: Dover Publications, Inc., 1959.

Garrison, Webb. *Brady's Civil War*. Guilford, CT: The Lyons Press, 2000.

Garrison, Webb, and Cheryl Garrison. *The Encyclopedia of Civil War Usage: An Illustrated Compendium of the Everyday Language of Soldiers and Civilians*. Nashville: Cumberland House, 2001.

Gorman, Mike. "Hospitals." Civil War Richmond. January 22, 2017. http://mdgorman.com/Hospitals/hospitals.htm.

Gracián, Baltasar. *The Art of Worldly Wisdom*. Trans. Christopher Maurer. New York: Doubleday, 1992.

Hacker, J. David. "A Census-Based Count of the Civil War Dead." *Civil War History*, December 2011.

Hadden, R. Lee. *Reliving the Civil War: A Reenactor's Handbook*, 2nd ed. Mechanicsburg, PA: Stackpole Books, 1996.

Hall, Raymond L. *Black Separatism in the United States*. Hanover, NH: University Press of New England, 1978.

Harter, Eugene C. *The Lost Colony of the Confederacy*. Jackson: University Press of Mississippi, 1985. Reprint, College Station: Texas A&M University Press, 2000.

Heidler, David S., et al., eds. *Encyclopedia of the American Civil War: A Political, Social, and Military History*. Santa Barbara, CA: ABC-CLIO, 2000.

Horwitz, Tony. *Confederates in the Attic: Dispatches from the Unfinished Civil War*. New York: Pantheon Books, 1998.

James River Park. "James River Park Conservation Easement: Belle Isle (AREA 1-H)." September 5, 2016. http://www.jamesriverpark.org/documents/james-BL-easement/BelleIsle/index.html.

Johnston, J. Ambler. *Echoes of 1861–1961*, 2nd ed. N.p.: Priv. print, 2000.

Kimball, Gregg D. *American City, Southern Place: A Cultural History of Antebellum Richmond.* Athens: University of Georgia Press, 2000.

Kloos, James E. *Hollywood Cemetery C.S.A. Generals.* Cleveland, OH: Classic Printing Corp., 1996.

Kollatz, Harry, Jr. "Lincoln in Richmond." *Richmond Magazine,* October 7, 2009.

Langenscheidt Publishing Group. *Greater Richmond Virginia Street Map Book,* 2nd ed. Alexandria, VA: Langenscheidt Publishing Group, 2000.

Lankford, Nelson. *Richmond Burning: The Last Days of the Confederate Capital.* New York: Viking, 2002.

Lee, Heath Hardage. *Winnie Davis: Daughter of the Lost Cause.* Lincoln: Potomac Books, University of Nebraska Press, 2014.

Leisch, Juanita. *Who Wore What? Women's Wear 1861–1865.* Gettysburg, PA: Thomas Publications, 1995.

Lohmann, Bill. "A tribute to soldiers' lives lost on Belle Isle." *Richmond Times-Dispatch,* May 28, 2015.

Loth, Calder, ed. *The Virginia Landmarks Register,* 4th ed. Charlottesville: The University Press of Virginia, 1999.

Lowry, Thomas P. *The Story the Soldiers Wouldn't Tell: Sex in the Civil War.* Mechanicsburg, PA: Stackpole Books, 1994.

Madden, David, ed. *Beyond the Battlefield: The Ordinary Life and Extraordinary Times of the Civil War Soldier.* New York: Touchstone, 2000.

Madison, Nathan Vernon. *Tredegar Iron Works: Richmond's Foundry on the James.* Charleston, SC: The History Press, 2015.

Marx, Robert F. *Buried Treasures You Can Find: Over 7,500 Locations in all 50 States.* Dallas: Ram Books, 1993.

Mathew, William M. *Edmund Ruffin and the Crisis of Slavery in the Old South: The Failure of Agricultural Reform*. Athens: University of Georgia Press, 1988.

McCrum, Robert, William Cran, and Robert MacNeil. *The Story of English*. New York: Viking, 1986.

McPherson, James M. *Battle Cry of Freedom: The Civil War Era*. New York: Oxford University Press, 1988.

Melton, Jack. "Cannon Identification: Guns & Howitzers." *Camp Chase Gazette*, September 2008.

Mewborn, Horace. "A Wonderful Exploit: Jeb Stuart's Ride Around the Army of the Potomac, June 12–15, 1862." *Blue & Gray Magazine*, August 1998.

Mitchell, Betty L. *Edmund Ruffin: A Biography*. Bloomington: Indiana University Press, 1981.

Mitchell, Mary H. *Hollywood Cemetery: The History of a Southern Shrine*. Richmond: Library of Virginia, 1985.

Moore, Samuel J. T., Jr. *Moore's Complete Civil War Guide to Richmond*, rev. ed. Richmond, VA: Samuel J. T. Moore, Jr., 1978.

Morgan, James F. *Graybacks and Gold: Confederate Monetary Policy*. Pensacola, FL: Perdido Bay Press, 1985.

Mullins, L. Cleo. "The Four Seasons of the Confederacy: Interim Report of Examination and Treatment." Virginia Historical Society, May 21, 2012. July 30, 2016. http://www.vahistorical.org/hoffbauer/assets/files/June-2012-report.pdf

New York Times. "$10,000,000 Is Reported Buried in Virginia; Said to Be a British Loan to Confederacy." October 31, 1947.

Novak, Claire E. "Getting Started in the Cavalry, Historic Horsemen: 21st Century Cavalry Riders." *Camp Chase Gazette*, March 2007.

Patrick, Rembert W. *The Fall of Richmond*. Baton Rouge: Louisiana State University Press, 1960.

Peters, John O. *Richmond's Hollywood Cemetery*. Petersburg, VA: The Dietz Press, 2010.

Rhea, Gordon C. *Cold Harbor: Grant and Lee May 26–June 3, 1864*. Baton Rouge: Louisiana State University Press, 2002.

Robertson, James I., Jr. *Stonewall Jackson: The Man, The Soldier, The Legend*. New York: Macmillan, 1997.

Roth, Dave, and Horace Mewborn. "The General's Tour: Stuart's Ride Around the Army of the Potomac, June 1862." *Blue & Gray Magazine*, August 1998.

Ryan, David D. *Four Days in 1865: The Fall of Richmond*. Richmond, VA: Cadmus Marketing, 1993.

— — —. *A Yankee Spy in Richmond: The Civil War Diary of "Crazy Bet" Van Lew*. Mechanicsburg, PA: Stackpole Books, 1996.

Salmon, John S., comp. *A Guidebook to Virginia's Historical Markers*, rev. ed. Charlottesville: University of Virginia Press, 1994.

— — —. *The Official Virginia Civil War Battle Guide*. Mechanicsburg, PA: Stackpole Books, 2001.

Scott, James, and Edward Wyatt. *Petersburg's Story: A History*. Petersburg, VA: Titmus Optical Co., 1960.

Sears, Stephen W. *To the Gates of Richmond: The Peninsula Campaign*. New York: Ticknor & Fields, 1992.

Speer, Lonnie R. *Portals to Hell: Military Prisons of the Civil War*. Mechanicsburg, PA: Stackpole Books, 1997.

Taylor, L. B., Jr. *Civil War Ghosts of Virginia*. Williamsburg, VA: L. B. Taylor, 1995.

Tyler-McGraw, Marie. *At the Falls: Richmond, Virginia, and Its People*. Chapel Hill: University of North Carolina Press, 1994.

Tzu, Sun. *The Art of War*. Trans. Samuel B. Griffith. Oxford: Oxford University Press, 1963.

USA Civil War Web Site. "Union Casualties at Cold Harbor." February 27, 2016. http://www.usa-civil-war.com/Opinions/c_h_casualties.html.

USA Civil War Web Site. "U.S. Civil War Photographs: Jeb Stuart's Ride Around McClellan." January 20, 2014. http://www.usa-civil-war.com/Stuarts_Ride/jeb_stuarts_ride.html.

Virginia Department of Historic Resources. "National Register of Historic Places Registration Form: Robert E. Lee Monument," August 2002. September 5, 2016. http://www.dhr.virginia.gov/registers/Cities/Richmond/127-0181_LeeMonument_2006_NRdraft.pdf.

Ward, Geoffrey C., Ric Burns, and Ken Burns. *The Civil War: An Illustrated History*. New York: Alfred A. Knopf, 1990.

White, Ralph R., and Philip J. Schwarz. *Seeing the Scars of Slavery in the Natural Environment*. Richmond, VA: James River Park System, 2002.

Williamson, Samuel H., and Louis P. Cain. "Measuring Slavery in 2011 Dollars.*" MeasuringWorth.com. August 24, 2014. http://www.measuringworth.com/slavery.php.

Wirt, William. *Sketches of the life and character of Patrick Henry*. Philadelphia: Published by James Webster, 1817.

VISIT CHECKLIST OF SITES FEATURED OR MENTIONED

Chapter 1
_ Westover Plantation
  Berkeley Plantation (see Chapters 7, 8, and 9)

Chapter 2
  Evelynton Plantation (private)

Chapter 3
_ Monument Avenue
  _ Arthur Ashe Statue
  _ Matthew Fontaine Maury Statue
  _ Stonewall Jackson Statue
  _ Jefferson Davis Statue
  _ Robert E. Lee Statue
  _ Jeb Stuart Statue
_ Byrd Park
_ Virginia Commonwealth University
_ Monroe Park
_ Second Presbyterian Church
_ Union Presbyterian Seminary

Chapter 4
_ Haxall Flour Mill Canal
_ Tredegar Iron Works Gun Foundry
_ American Civil War Museum at Historic Tredegar (formerly
  the American Civil War Center at Historic Tredegar)

_ Richmond National Battlefield Park Visitor Center at Tredegar
  Iron Works
  _ Abraham and Tad Lincoln Statue
  _ Tredegar Iron Works Company Store
_ James River and Kanawha Canal (dry bed)

Chapter 5
_ Manchester Docks

Chapter 6
_ Church Hill
  _ St. John's Episcopal Church and Cemetery
    _ George Wythe Grave, Virginia's first signer of the
      Declaration of Independence
    _ Elizabeth Arnold Poe Grave, Edgar Allan Poe's mother
      (mentioned in Chapter 37)
  _ Libby Hill Park & Overlook
    _ View that gave Richmond its name, from here the curve
      in the James River reminded William Byrd II of the River
      Thames from Richmond Hill in England
    _ Confederate Soldiers and Sailors Monument (mentioned
      in Chapter 5)
    _ Lucky Strike Smokestack

Chapters 7, 8, and 9
_ Berkeley Plantation
  _ House
  _ Gardens
  _ Taps Monument
  _ Riverfront
_ Windsor Farms
_ University of Richmond

Chapter 10
_ Visions Dance Club
_ Young's Spring in Bryan Park

Chapter 11
_ Belle Isle, James River Park System
  _ Belle Isle Pedestrian Bridge
  _ Belle Isle Civil War Prison Camp Site
  _ Hollywood Rapid
_ National Museum of the Civil War Soldier (part of Pamplin
  Historical Park)

Chapter 12
  Varina Farms (private)
  Tree Hill Farm (private)
_ Richmond Evacuation Fire Historical Marker (East Main &
  Ninth Streets)
_ The Fan
  _ West Avenue
  _ St. James's Episcopal Church
  _ Meadow Park
    _ First Virginia Regiment Statue
    Fox Elementary School (public school)
    Buddy's Place (relocated to 600 N. Sheppard St. in 2015)
_ Boulevard
  United Daughters of the Confederacy Headquarters (private)
_ Virginia Museum of History & Culture (formerly Virginia
  Historical Society)
  _ War Horse Statue
  _ Mural Gallery: Four Seasons of the Confederacy

Chapter 14
_ The Valentine (formerly Valentine Richmond History Center)
  _ Café and Boxwood Garden

_ Edward Valentine Sculpture Studio
_ Wickham-Valentine House

Chapter 15
_ Jackson Ward
    _ Richmond Dairy
    _ Maggie L. Walker National Historic Site
    _ Maggie L. Walker Statue
    _ Hippodrome Theater
    _ Mama J's
    _ Bill "Bojangles" Robinson Statue
    _ Black History Museum and Cultural Center of Virginia
_ Richmond Convention Center (Richmond Visitors Center)
_ Virginia Union University

Chapter 16
  Marlbourne (private)

Chapter 17
_ Confederate Memorial Chapel
_ Virginia Museum of Fine Arts
_ Richmond Howitzers Monument
_ Oregon Hill
_ Hollywood Cemetery
    _ Chapel (cemetery's office)
    _ Jefferson Davis Grave
    _ James Monroe Grave
    _ John Tyler Grave
    _ Jeb Stuart Grave
    _ Confederate Memorial Pyramid
    _ George Pickett Grave
    _ Gettysburg Dead
_ Five Forks, Petersburg National Battlefield Park

Chapter 18
_ Jefferson Hotel
  _ Rotunda
  _ Grand Staircase
  _ Thomas Jefferson Statue, Palm Court Lobby

Chapter 21
_ Mediterranean Bakery & Deli

Chapter 22
_ Chimborazo Visitor Center & Medical Museum, Richmond
  National Battlefield Park
_ Chimborazo Park Overlook
_ Powhatan Hill Park (site of Parahunt's village)
_ Jewish Confederate Soldiers' Section, Hebrew Cemetery
  Almshouse (private)
_ Shockoe Hill Cemetery
  _ John Marshall Grave
  _ Elizabeth Van Lew Grave

Chapter 23
_ Oakwood-Chimborazo Historic District
_ Confederate Section, Oakwood Cemetery

Chapter 24
_ Petersburg Skyline
_ Colonel George W. Gowen Statue,
  48th Regiment of the Pennsylvania Volunteers
_ King's Famous Barbecue, Petersburg, VA
_ Main Unit, Petersburg National Battlefield Park
  _ Visitor Center
  _ The Dictator
  _ Battlefield Park Tour Drive
  _ Fort Stedman

Chapter 31
_ Interstate 95 James River Bridge
_ Richmond Wastewater Treatment Facility's Eternal Methane Flame
_ Philip Morris Cigarette Brands Pop-art Pylon
_ Half Way House Restaurant
_ Drewry's Bluff (Fort Darling), Richmond National Battlefield Park

Chapter 32
_ VCU Medical Center
_ Museum of the Confederacy (now part of the American Civil War Museum or ACWM, in 2019 exhibits will move to the Historic Tredegar site)
_ White House of the Confederacy (also now part of ACWM)
_ Seventeenth and Dock Streets (Lincoln came ashore south of this intersection)

Chapter 33
_ Eastern Fortifications, Richmond National Battlefield Park
  _ Battlefield Park Road
  _ Fort Gilmer
  _ Fort Johnson
  _ Fort Harrison
  _ Fort Hoke
  _ Fort Brady
_ Richmond Yacht Basin (private)
_ Jordan Point
_ Dutch Gap Cutoff (Dutch Gap Conservation Area)
_ Battery Dantzler Park (northern end of the Howlett Line)
_ Citie of Henricus (Henricus Historical Park)
_ Deep Bottom Park

Chapter 34
_ New Market Heights
_ Rocketts Landing
_ James River and Kanawha Canal (restored)
_ Mayo's Bridge
    Southern States Cooperative Feed Mill (private)
_ Richmond Railroad Museum
_ Floodwall Walk
_ Richmond and Petersburg Railroad Bridge Abutments including the Manchester Wall
_ T-Pot Pedestrian Bridge connecting the Manchester Wall and Brown's Island (T. Tyler Potterfield Memorial Bridge)

Chapter 35
_ Long Bridge Road

Chapter 36
_ Hanover Town

Chapter 37
_ Shockoe Bottom
    _ Lumpkin's Jail Site
    _ Main Street Train Station
    _ 17th Street Farmers Market (mentioned in Chapter 36)
    _ Edgar Allan Poe Museum (Old Stone House)
    _ Virginia Holocaust Museum
    _ Libby Prison Site
    _ Virginia Capital Trail beside Dock Street

Chapter 38
_ Ginter Park
_ A. P. Hill Monument
_ Mordecai Farm Site at Brook Road and Azalea Avenue (southwest corner)

- Stuart's Mortal Wound Site (Telegraph Road, south of Virginia Center Parkway)
- Richmond's Outer Defenses at Brook Run Shopping Center
- Brook Bridge over Upham Brook
- TransAmerica Bike Trail
- Kilby's Station
- Virginia Central Railroad Underpass

  Winston Farm Site (private)

  Hickory Hill (private)
- Hanover County Courthouse
- Clay's Birthplace Historical Marker (US 301, 4.5 miles south of Hanover County Courthouse)

  Henry Clay Birthplace Site (private)
- 36th Wisconsin Volunteer Infantry Monument
- Enon United Methodist Church
- Haw's Shop (Studley)
- Patrick Henry Birthplace Site
- Studley General Store

  Captain William Latané Grave, Grainfield Farm (private)
- Totopotomoy Creek
- Latané's Mortal Wound Site (Studley and New Bethesda Roads Intersection)
- Old Church
- Garlick's Landing
- Tunstall's Station

  White House Landing (private)
- St. Peter's Episcopal Church, New Kent
- Talleysville Intersection
- Chickahominy River Bridges, Providence Forge
- Charles City
- Lawrence Lewis Jr. Park (Wilcox's Landing)

  Weyanoke Point (private)
- Westover Church

Chapter 39
_ Capitol Square
  _ Governor's Mansion
  _ Virginia State Capitol
  _ Washington Equestrian Monument
  _ Bell Tower
_ St. Paul's Episcopal Church

Chapter 40
_ Dabbs House Museum & Henrico County Tourist
  Information Center
_ Seven Pines National Cemetery

Chapter 41
_ Malvern Hill, Richmond National Battlefield Park

Chapter 42
_ Oak Grove Battlefield Site (Richmond International Airport)
_ Beaver Dam Creek, Richmond National Battlefield Park
_ Glendale National Cemetery
  _ Glendale/Malvern Hill Battlefields Visitor Center,
    Richmond National Battlefield Park
_ Riddell's Shop Intersection
_ White Oak Swamp Bridge
_ Richmond and York River Railroad Crossing
_ Savage's Station Battlefield Overlook
  _ Savage Station "Freeman Marker"
_ Golding's Farm Historical Marker (N Airport Dr, west of I-295
  exit 31 interchange)
  Trent House (private)
_ Grapevine Bridge Site

Chapter 43
- _ Cold Harbor Intersection
- _ Cold Harbor National Cemetery
- _ Cold Harbor, Richmond National Battlefield Park
  - _ Garthright House
  - _ Cold Harbor Visitor Center
- _ Gaines's Mill, Richmond National Battlefield Park
  - _ Watt House
  - _ Boatswain Creek Trail
  - _ Whiting's Advance "Freeman Marker"